Burying Daddy:
A Small-Town Tragedy

Jeff Wiles

Published by Kindle Direct Publishing

TABLE OF CONTENTS

PROLOGUE

The story you are about to read is based upon actual events that occurred in a small South Carolina town following the days after my father's death. I have told this story to at least a hundred people in the past couple of years. Most of them do not believe me, including a few county detectives. But this story, whether incredible or not, is the honest-to-God truth. I would like to thank my uncle, who teaches English at a small community college, for assisting me with grammar and introducing me to a thesaurus, where I learned a lot of big words. And I would also like to thank him and my wife for their encouragement during the writing of this novel. The names of people and places have been changed to protect the privacy and anonymity of the characters mentioned in this story. I hope you enjoy it and believe it. Thanks.

INTRODUCTION

In the small town of Turkey Creek, South Carolina, Luke Stiles' daddy is known as the Legend. Although Luke never thinks much about his father's reputation, when his dad dies from a stroke, Luke begins a quest to find out the reason behind his daddy's nickname. Along the way, a mysterious woman and a friend of his dads give him clues that will help answer his questions. In the process, Luke questions his beliefs about family, life, death, eternity, and . . . yes . . . even God. In the end, he loses the most important thing to him.

THE DEATH

I watched my father die on a hot July day in the summer of 2015.

He died in a hospital in Atlanta, Georgia. July 20th was the date, a Monday.

About ten o'clock that morning, a redheaded nurse with a kind smile and a freckled face disconnected my father from the machine that had been keeping him alive for almost a week. She said he would pass quickly once removed from the machine. But, for three hours, I listened to him grunt and gurgle and fight for every bit of air he could inhale until finally, the last breath came, the last bit of life departing from his never-to-breathe-again lungs.

He was only fifty years old, too young to die. But there he was, lying lifeless on that hospital cot, with no heartbeat, no pulse, nothing. I would never hear his voice again, hear him laugh, see him smile, see him sitting in the stands at one of my ballgames, or spend another Christmas morning with him. His life was over. And yet there seemed to be so much I didn't know about him, so many unresolved mysteries about this man who was my father.

In Turkey Creek, South Carolina, my father, John Wilson Stiles, was a legend. People told me that all the time. "Are you John Stiles' boy," they asked, and, when I told them that I was, they would just chuckle a bit and shake their heads. "So, you're the son of the Legend," some would say. "I guess so," I always answered. But what had earned him this honorable nomenclature, what had propelled him to the status of legend – I had no idea. It could not have been his athletic ability.

Stiff Jenkins, one of his best friends, told me my father had been fast when he played high school baseball and could run down any ball hit to centerfield, but, according to Stiff, his arm wasn't worth a shit and neither was his bat. I never remember seeing any trophies sitting on his shelves or even tucked away in the back of some closet. I am almost certain that being a fast outfielder was not the reason for his legendary status. So, what was it?

Fudge Pickens, another of Daddy's close friends, told me that my father was the smartest man he had ever met. And I could believe that. Daddy could fill out an entire crossword puzzle during a commercial break. And he read a lot, at least one book a month. Even though he dropped out of college the first time he attempted to get a degree, he went back later and graduated second in his class with a major in economics and a minor in mathematics—all while working full-time and helping Momma raise us children.

But I don't think that made him a legend. Hell, most people didn't even know he had a degree. He never even used his degree to advance in the company where he worked. They put him in sales for a year. But Daddy hated it. He claimed there were too many counterfeit people working in sales and marketing and human resources—people always wanting to be promoted, always wanting to make more money. After a year, he requested a return to his former position as a warehouse clerk on the night shift. He stayed there until his sickness forced him to cease working altogether. So, I don't believe his education or deceptive intelligence made him a legend.

Then, I thought about his creativity. Daddy was always writing. He even had a few articles published in local journals. In fact, he had written two novels and self-published them. He always kept some in the basement, so if anybody wanted one, he would give them one. Yet few people knew about those books. Then there were the songs he had written while playing the guitar. I rarely heard him play. Momma said he gave it up when he got saved since he always liked to drink when he was playing.

I never knew he had written any songs until a couple of days ago when I walked into the basement and found his guitar. I opened the case, and, sure enough, beneath that guitar, in a manilla folder, were about twenty songs on laminated sheets of paper. I thumbed through them for a few minutes, imagining Daddy writing those words on a piece of notebook paper while strumming a guitar and perhaps sipping a beer.

I wondered why he never tried any harder than he did to have his songs or novels published by a literary agency. Maybe he was afraid of rejection or failure or maybe he never thought his songs or books were worthy of publication. Maybe he just didn't want any notoriety. Still, those books in the basement and those songs in that guitar case were not what made Daddy a legend. Not enough people knew about them.

There had to be something else, something that was not so furtive or ambiguous, something Daddy did that impressed many people, not just his family and closest friends. There had to be a more substantial reason. But the few close friends Daddy had never talked much about the past. I suspected that whatever made Daddy a legend had happened a long time ago, perhaps before I was born. And I supposed discovering exactly what incident or incidents validated his infamous status as the legend of Turkey Creek, South Carolina, would likely be an onerous quest. But I wanted to know. Standing there looking at his lifeless body, knowing he would never breathe again, I almost felt like I needed to know.

I looked around the room, the suddenly silent room. Four people were in the room when Daddy died. Of course, I was one of them. Then, there was my sister, Katie. She was nearly two years older than I was and had just graduated from college with a degree in elementary education. She sat in a chair beside Daddy's bed, and my younger brother, Carter, who had just turned fifteen, sat on the arm of the chair. They were both crying, not loudly but loud enough that their sobs helped quell the still palpable sounds I had been listening to for the last three hours, the macabre final breaths of my father.

Me, I was trying not to cry, some part of me believing that the withholding of tears would prove I had evolved into manhood and was ready to be the patriarch of my suddenly fatherless family. I looked over into the far corner, where the fourth person in the room was sitting, Stiff Jenkins, the most feared man in Turkey Creek, South Carolina, and one of my father's closest friends. His oldest son, Cody, was the same age as I was. We had grown up playing ball, fishing, hunting, and taking the same classes together in high school. Cody was probably my best friend – well, hell, there ain't no probably to it – he was my best friend. And, in my mind, Cody's father, Stiff, was the one who should have been called the legend.

At Turkey Creek High School, Stiff Jenkins still held the record for most home runs and RBIs. He was drafted right out of high school by the White Sox, drafted early, maybe in the third or fourth round. They even gave him a big signing bonus. But, after playing only a year in the minors, for some reason, Stiff joined the Army, became an Army Ranger, and did a couple of tours of duty during the first Gulf War. He returned to Turkey Creek in the fall of 1993, learning, in the military, how to kill a man with his bare hands, or, at least, that is what people believed.

I guess every small town in America has its own badass. Well, Stiff Jenkins was Turkey Creek's badass. Nobody would mess with Stiff, and everybody wanted to be his friend. When he attended a ball game, people flocked around him. He didn't even have to move. Wherever he stood, people just gathered around him. I guess everybody wanted to believe that Stiff Jenkins was their friend. So, according to my way of thinking, Stiff should have been the legend, not my father.

But why was Stiff even there? Not that I was going to ask him to leave. Nobody would have done that. Besides, Stiff and my father had been friends for many years. And I am certain that Stiff knew the reason everybody in Turkey Creek called my father a legend. Some folks even said Stiff and Daddy had secrets that could never be shared with others. Some folks even claimed the reason Stiff had been such a frequent visitor to my father was not that their friendship was that great, but that Stiff wanted to be certain no deathbed confessions were made. I didn't want to believe that, but just like all the stories I had heard about my father, I could not conclusively dismiss the idea.

I tried to watch Stiff without him noticing my stare. He had been there since before daylight, not saying a word, just sitting in that chair, sipping on a bottle of pop every now and then, and looking at Daddy. Seems like the whole time we were there, his gaze never altered. His eyes were always on Daddy. Finally, I walked over to him and placed a hand on his shoulder.

"Thanks for coming," I said.

He looked up at me, the most feared man in Turkey Creek, and I saw a tear trickling down his cheek. And I knew then that Stiff knew. He knew what I wanted to know. But would he tell me, or would I just have to decipher all the hodgepodge stories about my father in a solitary quest to discover why, of all the people that had passed through Turkey Creek, my daddy was the one they called the Legend?

TURKEY CREEK, SOUTH CAROLINA

Before I tell you anymore, I guess I should tell you about my hometown of Turkey Creek, South Carolina. It is a small town that straddles the creek for which it is named, tucked into the far western corner of the state, only fifteen minutes away from the Georgia border. People say that Turkey Creek was once a beautiful town, a thriving town, a town where you could get just about anything you wanted. There was a movie theater, a hotel, a bowling alley, a grocery store, a steak house, and even a JCPenney store on the downtown square.

Then the cotton mill closed, and people began moving away—some to Greenville, some to Anderson, some even as far away as Columbia or Athens, Georgia. There were a few towns closer than those, but a person was lucky to find a job in one of those towns. Even if you did, that still meant a thirty- to forty-minute commute to work each day. From Turkey Creek, nothing was close. So, people just began to move away.

And then there came the flood of 2000. I was only five years old, but I remember what I saw sitting on the porch with Daddy, the waters of a creek that almost went dry during the hot months of summer raging down the low-lying streets of the town. It buckled the foundations of houses and moving cars, an aquatic monster bearing its entrails as its overwhelming currents forged its path of destruction. Street signs and downed timber and railroad tines floated on the tumbling waves. Even the caskets, corpses, and bones from graves were unearthed. The ferocious currents barreled through town pompously, like the display of destruction was some sort of trophy that the usual placid stream wanted everyone to notice. I don't think I will ever be able to forget that day. I don't see how anyone could.

By the following spring, the state had reinforced the flood zones with concrete walls. But nobody wanted to rebuild in Turkey Creek. Most of the business owners didn't want to spend a bunch of money on restoring businesses that were barely profitable before the flood, even though the governor had declared Turkey Creek a disaster area and offered business owners and homeowners low-interest loans. All the flood of 2000 did was initiate another exodus from Turkey Creek. The town that had once a population of almost five thousand people deteriorated into a town of empty buildings and vacant lots and forsaken houses.

By the time of the government census in 2010, there were less than a thousand people residing in Turkey Creek. There was no movie theater, no bowling alleys, no grocery stores, and no places for women to go shopping on a Saturday afternoon. There was only a gas station, a bar, a barber shop, a courthouse that seemed too ornate and large for a town with such a small population, a post office, four churches, one Mom-and-Pop restaurant, the high school, and probably the most distinguishing relic of the town's bygone days: the pair of baseball fields where boys played during the spring and summer.

The one thing that survived the closing of the cotton mill and the destruction of the flood of 2000 and the diminishing population was the town's love of baseball. Turkey Creek had won the state championship in baseball more than any other high school in South Carolina, twenty-five times since 1960. The banners were draped across the outfield walls. Twenty-five state championships and forty-one regional championships.

In other places, parents read their children bedtime stories from the Bible or some fairy tale book about people living happily ever after. But, in Turkey Creek, fathers told their sons bedtime stories about Ty Cobb and Babe Ruth or maybe the state championship team that they played on when they were young. We entered school knowing more about Mickey Mantle,

Hank Aaron, and Satchel Paige than we did any other historical figures. We could name the starters for the All-Star Game, the American League, and the National League. We could tell you who won the Cy Young award last year, who won the batting title, and what team won the World Series.

At night, we would sit by our fathers and watch the Braves play on television. Our fathers would talk to us about pitch location and bat speed and how to hit your cutoff man and when to bunt and when to try a hit and run. In Turkey Creek, if your son could not play baseball, then you were ostracized and so was he. Really, in Turkey Creek, you had no choice. You had to teach your son to play baseball because baseball was all we had. People might say there were no jobs in Turkey Creek, or that the only people that remained in Turkey Creek were rednecks and white trash, but nobody could deny that we knew how to play baseball.

Me? I guess I did my part to continue the tradition. In fact, I even had the school record for strikeouts. I was left-handed (Daddy said that was the only good trait I inherited from my mother), so they began teaching me to pitch at an early age. By the time I entered my senior year of high school, I was touching the low 90s with my fastball. The small schools that we played couldn't catch up with it. I was offered a full scholarship to Clemson University.

But, during my freshman year, I tore the ligaments in my elbow and haven't thrown a ball since then. I haven't even wanted to. That was two years ago, but it seems like forever sometimes. Anyway, that was the end of my baseball career. I dropped out of college and came home, started working with a friend of mine who owned his own landscaping business, and accepted my fate as one of the many great ball players who had passed through Turkey Creek High School.

People told stories about me for a little while, just like they did Stiff Jenkins and Roger Dawson and Mac Simmons, and, if I was really lucky, they might even retire my number sometime in the future and pin it up on the wooden scoreboard. I imagined myself at forty, sitting in some restaurant or bar, meeting someone I once played ball with, and eavesdropping as he told his wife and children about Luke Stiles, how he could throw the piss out of the ball, and how he once struck out twenty batters in a single game. Stuff like that mattered in Turkey Creek, South Carolina.

But watching my daddy die that morning in an Atlanta hospital, baseball didn't seem that damn important anymore. Oh, I was still proud of my accomplishments and even prouder that my accomplishments made my father proud of me. But the way Turkey Creek applied merit to a boy based solely on his ability to play a sport, I never could entirely accept that way of thinking. There were too many boys walking through the halls of the high school, weighted down with the burden that they had disappointed their fathers because they did not make the high school baseball team, too many kids feeling worthless because they never learned to play baseball or didn't even want to play baseball.

And I suddenly felt a bit guilty for my younger brother, Carter, and how hard I had been on him for the last couple of years, ever since Daddy had taken sick. He was the starting catcher on the varsity team last year, batted .375, and made 2nd team All-Region, but I would still chastise him after some of his games, identify every mistake he made – you didn't back up the throw to first, you were too flat-footed behind the plate, you were dropping your shoulders on every swing.

Now, he was sitting there by my sister, crying harder than I had ever seen him cry. What did baseball matter? All he wanted was what I wanted: a little more time with Daddy, a little more time with the legend of Turkey Creek, a few more stories, a few more laughs, a few more opening-day deer hunts. That was all I wanted; that was all Carter wanted. I guess watching someone you love die sort of changes your perspective on life, at least for a little while. I recognized life would continue even though Daddy had passed, that there would still be baseball played in Turkey Creek, and that there would be fathers ridiculing their sons for striking out or making an error.

I walked over to Carter and placed my hand on his shoulder. Being a big brother wasn't easy, or, at least, I had not allowed it to be for me. After Daddy took sick and Momma asked him to leave because she was tired of dealing with his mood shifts, I sort of felt as if I was responsible for the development of Carter as a baseball player and a man. That was probably the real reason I didn't put much effort into recovering from my injuries. I was tired of sitting up there in those dorm rooms, missing home, Turkey Creek, Momma and Daddy, and Carter. I didn't want to play baseball anymore. I just wanted to go home.

After a few more minutes of consoling my siblings, I walked to the waiting room, where other family members and friends were waiting. I didn't have to say anything; I guess they sensed that Daddy was gone just by my return. I sat by the vending machine. Aunt Marilyn and her daughter, Chelsea, were crying. Daddy's older brother, my Uncle Randolph, was trying to console them, hugging them and telling them everything would be okay, that Daddy was in a better place, all the usual bullshit you hear after somebody dies.

I wondered sometimes how my Uncle Randolph ever made it out of Turkey Creek with any sort of sanity. He never played baseball, never played any kind of sport. All he did was read books, so I suspected he was teased a good bit when he was younger. He had managed to forge a good life for himself, I guess. He graduated valedictorian from Turkey Creek, attended Furman University in Greenville on a full academic scholarship, and then continued from there to the University of South Carolina, where he received a doctorate degree in literature. Now, he was a professor at a small college in the North Carolina mountains, married, and with two grown children. Chelsea was thirty years old and close to Daddy. Alex wandered away from the house about five years ago, and nobody ever knew his whereabouts. He just showed up from time to time, then disappeared again.

As far as Uncle Randolph, he seemed like a good man. He and Daddy had gone on some backpacking trips when they were younger. Daddy had a photograph album of all their trips pushed underneath his bed. He would pull it out occasionally and reminisce about their hiking trips.

Daddy seemed to always enjoy being in the woods. I think the loss of mobility was the primary reason he spiraled into depression. Daddy had always been active and strong. I don't think he knew how to live any other way.

Across the room from Uncle Randolph, Daddy's pastor was sitting, reading a magazine. He stood up and moved to the chair next to me when I sat down. He put his arm around me, like he wanted to console me but did not know whether to say anything or remain silent. Along the back wall were three of Daddy's closest friends: Huck Strawhotne, Blake Barnes, and Fudge Pickens. They had all played ball together, them and Stiff and Daddy. But that wasn't why those four men had asked off work and drove all the way to Atlanta and sat in the waiting room for four hours while my father was taking his final breaths.

The bond between these three men and Stiff and Daddy was too powerful to have been inaugurated in a few years of playing ball together. Some other components had to be responsible for the bond. Hell, I had only been out of school for four years and already lost touch with most of the boys that had been on my team. What was it? What happened that cemented these four men and my father into an impenetrable yoke? Maybe if I could expose that secret, I would know why my daddy died the legend of Turkey Creek.

THE WAITING ROOM

A few minutes later, Stiff Jenkins walked into the waiting room, trailing my brother and sister. He pressed a hundred-dollar bill into my palm as he shook my hand, reminding me that he would meet me in the morning at the funeral home, then nodded to the three men sitting against the rear wall of the waiting room. They all rose at once, following Stiff into the hallway, each of them patting me on the shoulder as they exited the room.

I could sense that my pastor and Uncle Randolph were relieved that they were gone. For men like them, men who had never seen violence and never played competitive sports, they were always uneasy around people like Stiff and Fudge and other friends of my father, their behavior and conversations always manipulated, either self-consciously or consciously, by the omnipotent aura that Stiff and his disciples seem to cast into the spaces they inhabited.

Even though Daddy's friends would always speak to Pastor Tim and Uncle Randolph, words, by both parties, seemed to be reserved and carefully chosen, like there existed this invisible border between them that neither party wanted to breech, a border that divided the just from the unjust, the holy from the unholy, the men who did what they wanted to do from the men who did what they were supposed to do. I wondered how Daddy seemed to fit so easily into both worlds when nobody else did. How could his circle of friends include the pastor of his church and a man as notorious as Stiff Jenkins?

With Stiff and his disciples gone, I guess Pastor Tim became comfortable enough to ask if he could pray for the family. We stood in a circle, Pastor Tim and Katie and Carter and me, holding hands and closing our eyes while the pastor pleaded for God to show us mercy and grant us comfort in these hours of hardship. At the conclusion of the prayer, Uncle Randolph bellowed an Amen, while he fitted his professor-looking fedora back onto his head. Then, he stood, shook Tim's hand, tugged at his bowtie, and told me where they would be spending the night, just in case I needed him. And, after a few more exchanges of pleasantries between him and Tim, Uncle Randolph helped his wife and daughter, who were still crying, to their feet. And they left, with Pastor Tim following close behind.

Now, it was just us three—the offspring of a legend—sitting not a hundred feet from the room where my father's lifeless body lay. I imagined them zipping the body bag and carrying him to the morgue where the body would lie until a hearse came to transport it back to South Carolina. I imagined all of that while listening to two nurses giggling in the hallway, talking about their nails and who was their favorite on American Idol. Katie was still trying to console Carter, who was still sobbing and sniffling and wiping his nose with tissue from the box on the corner table. I didn't want to believe that Daddy was dead. I guess none of us did. I guess I just wanted to believe he was invincible. Maybe all children think of their fathers that way. I know I did.

After we left the hospital, we stopped to eat at a restaurant next to the interstate. None of us knew what to say. We ate our meal in silence, while the people around us talked and laughed in loud and irreverent voices, nobody knowing we had watched our father die that morning, nobody even caring that we had. The world just continued as if Daddy had never been here at all. The waitresses asked if we needed more tea, Sportscenter was airing on the television, and people were discussing plans for the weekend. The world seemed too happy for me; the world seemed too alive.

I gave Katie the hundred-dollar bill Stiff had given to me and told her I would be waiting for them outside. I didn't want anything more to eat. I didn't want anything except to be alone, to be in my house in Turkey Creek, South Carolina, where, at least, the world seemed to make a little sense. I turned on the radio and fingered a pinch of Copenhagen into the corner of my mouth. Then, I just stood there, leaning against the hood of Katie's car, watching people walk in and out of the restaurant—old couples, families, teenagers on a date—the world still moving, and me not wanting to take another step.

"You know Mrs. Lydia wanted to come," I remarked to Katie on our way home.

"I know," she replied grumpily. "I just didn't want her there. She is not family."

"Stiff ain't family, either," I answered.

"I know, but that is different, and you know that."

Katie and I had never agreed on the subject of Lydia Cornell. She entered my father's life a few months after the divorce of our parents was final. But for some reason, Katie had never been fond of her. Maybe she just didn't like the thought of another female in her father's life, but, hell, Momma had dated several men since the divorce. And Katie didn't seem to be bothered by that a bit.

I never could understand why she seemed to resent her so much. I appreciated the way she had taken care of Daddy—cooking for him, taking him to church on Sundays, and helping him get to a ballgame if he felt like going. I texted her as soon as Daddy passed, just as I promised. She responded with a simple thank you and the mundane promise to pray. I was tired of hearing the banal responses of people: "We'll be praying for you"; "Let us know if we can do anything for you"; "He is in a better place now." How in the hell did they know Daddy was in a better place? I wasn't even sure myself of his eternal destiny, or if there even existed a place where there was eternal peace and bliss.

I glanced out the window at the twilight sky, the way the

colors all merged into an iridescent pallor, the brightness of the day's blue sky perishing in ineluctable hues of purple, orange, and yellow. I remembered when Daddy first began taking me deer hunting with him, and we sat in deer stands before dawn. I remember the way light would trickle so furtively into the woods, slicing the shadows until all that was hidden before became identifiable and clear. I remember the sound of squirrels scampering through fallen leaves and the way a deer could appear so suddenly, as if they had been there since the first light and you had just overlooked them.

Things like that—watching the colors of the sky at sunset and watching morning develop in corpses of oaks and hickories—things like that were once reassuring confirmations of a higher deity, of the existence of God. Driving back to Turkey Creek, South Carolina, that evening, however, I wasn't sure of anything anymore, only that Daddy was dead and we would never go hunting or fishing together again. As beautiful as the sky was, I just couldn't seem to find God in any of the colors. I twisted the top off my can of Copenhagen and shoveled another pinch behind my lips.

"Do you ever wonder why they called Daddy a legend," I asked, hoping to atone for bringing up the subject of Lydia.

"What?" Katie asked.

"You know how everybody in town says he is a legend. Well, don't you ever wonder why they call him that? I mean, it seems to me that you would have to do something special to be called a legend. And I don't know of anything Daddy ever did that was that spectacular."

"Wasn't he a good athlete?" Carter asked from the backseat.

"Average," I answered. "Nothing spectacular."

"Well, wasn't he a good hunter and fisherman?" asked Carter.

"He killed a few good deer, but only two worth mounting. And I have seen pictures of him with some nice-sized bass. But lots of fellows around here have killed big deer and caught nice bass."

"Maybe it was because of how strong he was," Carter responded, wanting desperately to believe there was some noble act in his father's life that warranted his infamous moniker.

And he was strong, there was no denying that. In fact, the only trophy I ever knew Daddy to possess was one he won in a weightlifting contest in Anderson in 1990. He benched the most for his weight class—315 pounds—and he only weighed 160. He kept the trophy in a box of knickknacks stored on the shelf of the bedroom closet. I doubt even that would have propelled him to become a legend. Most people didn't even know about that accomplishment. Just to suffice the suspicions of my younger brother, I agreed with him that Daddy's strength may have indeed been the reason they called him a legend, even though I gave no substance at all to that conjecture.

"Why does it matter?" asked Katie in a voice that indicated our conversation was annoying her.

Momma always said that Katie used anger to camouflage sadness. And I guess that is what was happening then because she certainly didn't seem to be in the mood for conversation.

"At least he didn't have some stupid nickname like Stiff or Fudge," Katie continued.

"That's true, I suppose," I said, electing to terminate the conversation I had started for the sake of my sister.

I reached over and turned up the volume on the radio, and we drove the rest of the way without conversation. Each of us, in our own way, attempted to cope with an emotional anguish that eclipsed any other pain we had ever endured, physical or emotional. We drove back to Turkey Creek as the day turned into night, and the blackness enveloped us, each of us trying to imagine life without Daddy.

THE STROKE

The first stroke happened in August of 2011. I don't remember the exact date, just that we had only been in school a few days when the principal summoned me to his office and told me that something bad had happened to my father. He didn't say how bad or even what had happened. He just said he was still alive but in the hospital and that Momma wanted me to go get Carter from school and meet her at the hospital. I picked up Carter, and we drove to the Anderson hospital with dozens of scenarios inaugurating in my mind: a car wreck, an accident at work, a heart attack.

When we arrived and walked into the room where Daddy was, he looked like a man I had never met. He was hooked up to several machines, barely conscious, and the color of his skin had faded. Momma was sitting in a chair crying but stood and hugged both of us when we entered the room. Pastor Tim was also there. He was leaning against the corner closet, stuffing a breath mint into his mouth. I wanted to say something to Daddy, but I didn't know what to say. I didn't even know if he would have heard me had I spoken.

Carter was less bewildered. He scrambled from Momma's embrace and walked straight to the bed, lifted Daddy's hands, and began talking to him. I just stood there silent, not knowing how to react, not even able to believe what I was seeing. I thought this kind of stuff only happened to elderly people, not people forty-six years of age and especially not people as strong and fit as my father. Seeing him in that hospital bed in such an enervated condition did not seem to fit into reality.

That day was only the beginning of Daddy's troubles. In fact, that day was the beginning of trouble for all of us, even Katie, who didn't arrive until that evening. She had to drive from Rock Hill, where she was attending college. From that day forth, our family would never be the same. I think about that day often when I am alone or lying in bed with my eyes open, unable to sleep. Who could have predicted that what happened to Daddy on that late summer day in 2011 would not only lead to his eventual death but to the demise of our family, a family that once seemed unbreakable, a family I guess I wanted to believe was invincible?

The doctors were never able to diagnose with absolute certainty the cause of Daddy's stroke or whatever medical phenomenon that happened to him that day. They did MRIs, CAT scans, heart catheterizations, and all sorts of other tests on him, but none showed anything out of the ordinary.

Within a week, Daddy was back home, feeling good again. He went back to work, exercised in the afternoons, and jogged on Saturday mornings. Everything seemed to be normal again. We just assumed that whatever happened to him that day was some sort of fluke.

Around Thanksgiving, however, he had another incident. Nothing was normal after that one. The right side of his body was paralyzed. With rehabilitation, he regained strength in his arm, but his right leg was permanently damaged. When he walked, he had to use a cane. If he had to walk a long distance, someone had to push him in a wheelchair. All he could do was drag that right leg. He never could get it to bend.

Of course, he was unable to work any longer, he couldn't exercise as he wanted, and he couldn't go hunting or fishing without assistance. And the doctors still seemed dumbfounded by his condition. They offered him no prognosis. The strokes continued to happen repeatedly. They sent him to a specialist in Greenville, a specialist in Charleston, and a specialist in Augusta, Georgia. None of them could determine the cause of the strokes, and, all the while, Daddy was spiraling into an abysmal depression. All he wanted to do was sit at the house, watch television, or maybe read a book. He never wanted to go anywhere. I guess he was embarrassed or ashamed of his condition.

His depression, while understandably present, placed an intolerable encumbrance on my mother. She was only forty-three years old when the strokes began, and I guess the thought of taking care of someone for the rest of her life was more than she could bear. She asked him to leave in January of 2014. And he did.

With the money he received from the government, he rented a small trailer about five miles outside the town limits of Turkey Creek. And that is where he lived until he went to Atlanta for an operation and died. As far as Momma, well, she just went wild for a little while, hanging out in bars, drinking all the time, staying gone all night sometimes, nobody knowing where she was. She became, quite possibly, the most hated woman in Turkey Creek. And, although no one ever criticized her in my presence, I heard the rumors that floated around town about her.

During all this commotion in my life, I had to have surgery on my elbow. Then, they wanted me to go to rehabilitation so I could be pitching again by next season. But too much had changed in my life. And I couldn't discover the motivation to attend rehabilitation or even the desire to play baseball anymore.

I moved back home to live with Momma and Carter and went to work with a friend of mine named Judd Southerland. Sometimes, in the evening, I would ride over to Daddy's house and watch a Braves game with him and take him some wings or pizza. I would try to remember the way life used to be. Those nights when I was a little boy, coming home from Little League practice, tired and sore, falling asleep in Daddy's lap while watching the Braves play. Those nights that seemed so long ago now, perpetually lost like some forgotten dream. Life seemed so perfect back then. Momma and Daddy seemed so happy with one another. We seemed so happy as a family, going to church together on Sundays, going to the beach during summer vacation, and playing kickball in the backyard.

Then, everything changed suddenly and so drastically. And now it was hard for me to believe we were ever that family. Daddy was dead, Momma was spending most of her time with a man from some hick town in Georgia and hardly ever coming home, and I hadn't thrown a baseball in almost two years. What in the hell had happened? And why had it happened? I wanted things to be the way they used to be. I wanted Momma and Daddy to still be married, to still be living in the same house. I wanted Carter to be seven years old again, the bat boy for our little league all-star team, running back and forth through the dugout. And I wanted to be that twelve-year-old kid again, warming up in the bullpen, number 8, Luke Stiles, a boy who still believed in dreams, a boy who still believed he was going to be the best pitcher to ever come out of Turkey Creek, South Carolina.

I imagined myself sometimes making it to the majors, running out to the pitcher's mound, looking up into the stands, and seeing Momma and Daddy and Katie and Carter, everybody cheering for me, everybody shouting my name, my family still together. So much for those dreams. They were as dead as Daddy was in that hospital room in Atlanta, Georgia, zipped up in a bag and waiting to be moved to the morgue.

Ms. Lydia

I am not exactly certain when or why Ms. Lydia Cornell entered my father's life, but for the past year or thereabout, she had been with him almost every day and even some nights. She cooked for him, cleaned his house, helped him with his laundry, took him to his doctor appointments, took him to church on Sunday mornings, and even helped him to an occasional ball game when Daddy felt like attending.

I appreciated all she had done for him, and I know Daddy's moods were uplifted by her presence. Carter liked her also. Hell, they even went to the movies together sometimes on Saturday afternoons. But Katie, for some reason, was never fond of her. She didn't like her being over at Daddy's place all the time and suspected that there was some ulterior motive for her kindnesses.

I don't know what ulterior motive there could have been. Certainly, her motive couldn't have been the expectation of a large inheritance. All Daddy owned could have been tossed into the bed of a small bed pickup truck. I guess all she did for Daddy stemmed from her love for him. At least, that is what she told me, and I had no reason to believe otherwise.

Ms. Lydia was a bit older than my father, maybe by six or seven years. She had lived in Turkey Creek all her life, so information about her was not difficult to obtain. She had once been a nurse at the hospital in Greenville, but, about five years ago, she developed Parkinson's Disease and, subsequently, had to quit working. About a year after that, she left her husband of twenty-five years and moved in with her daughter, who was single and renting a trailer in a trailer park just outside of town.

I don't know why she left her husband. He seemed like a good man to me—not that I knew him well, just maybe enough to give him a nod when our paths crossed. I had never heard anyone speak ill of him. Some people said he was reserved and private, but, hell, there were several people like that in Turkey Creek. I didn't know the reason for their divorce. They both seemed nice to me. They didn't seem like the type that would get divorced, but I guess you just never know.

Anyway, when we got back home from Atlanta, I wasn't ready to go to sleep. Too much was on my mind. I drove over to the trailer Daddy had been renting since he and Mom had split. It was about five miles outside of town at the end of a private dirt road, on about a half-acre lot, Turkey Creek directly behind it. Daddy had built a huge deck on the back of the trailer, and, at night, when the waters were high, if you could stand the mosquitoes, you could sit out there and listen to the currents of Turkey Creek meandering through the woods.

Daddy had always wanted to convert the deck into a screened porch, but that never happened. I suppose there were many things he wanted to do but never did. I wondered what his biggest regrets were, what he wished he would have done more, what he wished he would have done less, and what he wished he would have tried but never did. Then I contemplated my life, what regrets would accompany me on my death bed, what guilt, and what sins.

It was nearly eleven o'clock when I pulled into the driveway. I noticed Ms. Lydia's car parked beneath the steel carport and the lights on in the trailer. I tapped on the door. She hollered for me to come on in, so I pushed open the door and stepped into the trailer.

"How are you doing?" she asked politely, glancing up from the ironing board she had stretched across the kitchen bar.

She was pressing one of Daddy's dress shirts—the shirt in which he would be buried, I supposed, since I had asked her to select an outfit to take to the funeral home.

"I'm okay," I answered, scanning the familiar room, the recliner where Daddy always sat, the sofa where I slept sometimes when

I stayed overnight, the book he was reading before they took him to Atlanta—still bookmarked about halfway through, a book that he would never finish.

How could he have known when he read the final words of that bookmarked page that those would be the last words he would ever read? I picked up the book and held it in my hand, imagining it being in my father's hands, his fingers flipping the pages, reading glasses sloped across his nose—the *Ox-Bow Incident*. I remembered having to read that novel for a book report in high school, I guess Daddy was just reading it for fun. I set the book back on the round glass table and settled into the recliner.

"I wish I could have seen him one last time," she remarked, holding up the shirt she had been ironing as she scanned for any overlooked wrinkles.

"I wish you could have too," I answered. "I don't know why Katie —"

"Shhh," she interjected, not allowing me to finish my sentence. "What you children have been through has been difficult. And each of us reacts differently to the trials we have in life. I am not mad at Katie for not wanting me to be there. I just thank the Lord for this last year, for giving me the opportunity to take care of your father, for the many conversations we have had, for the secrets that we have shared, for the times we laughed, for the times we cried. Being able to spend this last year with your father has been one of the greatest blessings of my life."

She placed the shirt on a hanger and hung it on the knob of the back door, giving it a few swipes with her hand. Then, she walked over to the sofa and sat on the side closest to me and placed her hand on me.

"Your father was a beautiful man, Luke," she said, as if I needed that reassurance. "I would have married him had he asked me."

"Did you ever tell him that?"

"Oh, yes," she said, chuckling a bit. "Several times. But he just didn't want me to feel obligated to take care of him or 'share in his suffering,' as he used to say. Of course, I always felt that caring for him helped me to forget about my own suffering."

Her hand began to tremble a bit as she talked, a symptom of her Parkinson's. Recognizing that I had noticed the tremor, she removed her hand from my knee and placed it under her leg.

"I guess living with Parkinson's Disease is hard, isn't it," I asked.

"Well, it's not fun," she replied, shaking her head. "But at least I can still care for myself. At least, I am not sitting in a nursing home somewhere."

She pulled a tissue from the box on the end table and wiped her eyes. She had been beautiful when she was younger; anyone could have known that from looking at her. She had even been Miss Turkey Creek in her senior year of high school. I guess that was a big deal back then when the cotton mill was still running, and folks were making a good living. Now, nothing seemed to matter much in Turkey Creek, nothing except baseball.

"Would you like a cup of coffee?" she asked.

"No, ma'am," I answered, rapping my fingers anxiously on the arm of the recliner and scanning the pictures of us when we were young on the mantle above the fireplace.

Ms. Lydia once told me that Daddy would sit up at night sometimes, unable to sleep, place the pictures in his lap, and just stare at them. I wondered what thoughts must have been passing through his mind on nights like those. I wondered how many times he had sat in this lonely trailer and thought about me, and me not even knowing.

"He loved you children," she remarked, noticing, I suppose, my intense inspection of the photographs. "Don't think he ever got over having to leave y'all."

"I know," I answered, rising from the chair and picking up a few of the photographs myself—old in dollar-store frames, some of us, some of his parents, some of his nieces and nephews, all spread across the mantle, like some kind of story, some kind of photographic autobiography.

"Did you say Daddy and you shared secrets?" I asked, startling her a bit, I surmised.

"We did," she replied, stuffing a pillow behind her back.

"Why do you think everybody called him a legend?"

She chuckled again, perhaps relieved the question was not as formidable as she supposed. "I don't have any idea," she said. "But I have heard many people call him that. I just figured it must have been something that happened in the past, before he married your mother, probably something he did with Stiff."

"That's what I don't understand. Everybody knows Stiff. Everybody knows what he does, and everybody is afraid of Stiff. You can visit any little town in this county, and people will know who Stiff Jenkins is. Why isn't he the legend? Why is my father the legend?"

"I wish I could answer that question, Luke," she replied remorsefully.

I picked up one of the photographs and held it in my hand. The 2007 Little League State Runner-Ups was encrypted into the frame. There I was, number 8, standing on the back row—tall, lanky, smiling, believing still in the magic of home runs and no-hitters and walk-off hits and the way it felt when you touched home plate, and all your teammates swarmed around you and patted you on the helmet.

Life was magical back then, swaddled in the fragrance of summer evenings and the swirls of infield dirt that pirouetted in a slide to second base, the clamor of parents in the metal bleachers, your teammates chanting your name when you were standing at the plate, the dust of the pitcher's mound, the humming of the floodlights, the smell of concession stand hot dogs. I wanted life to be that simple again. I wanted to stand at home plate again and glance over to my coach for a sign. I wanted to hear my teammates chanting my name, and I wanted to hear the crowd erupt into a roar when I hit a home run. I wanted happiness to be that easy to obtain again. I wanted life to be that easy again.

I studied the faces of the others in the photograph. Some of them were still in Turkey Creek, but most had left. Chuck Simon, leadoff hitter, in the Air Force, stationed in Hawaii. Logan Barnes, shortstop, going to college somewhere in Florida. Cody Jenkins, Stiff's oldest son and my best friend, living in Greenville, working as a welder in some metal shop. Bates Bridges, catcher, could throw out any damn body that tried to steal a base in Little League but never played another game of baseball. After the year we finished second in the state, he started smoking pot and doing meth and was serving time now in the state penitentiary for manslaughter.

Who could have ever predicted his life would be so tragic, looking at that photograph, him smiling so big, his hands clutching the trophy? I remembered his voice, the way he would walk to the mound sometimes and tell me to change the signs or to just relax if I was struggling with location. I would never be able to remember him any other way, and I would never be able to imagine him as an inmate with a number on his back, sleeping on a cot behind a locked door every night. I wanted him to be twelve years old forever, standing in the dugout and stuffing his mouth with sunflower seeds. Hell, I wanted us all to be twelve years old forever, to live in some place like that place where Peter Pan lived, where you never had to grow up because all growing up seemed to do was erase dreams and fantasies and grind you down with disappointments, sorrows, and heartaches.

I felt as if I would spend the rest of my life trying futilely to discover the happiness I knew when I was twelve years old, the happiness that had made me smile in that photograph I was now holding in my hand—a young man, twenty years old, shattered elbow, shattered dreams, divorced parents, dead father. Being twelve years old seemed so long ago, like ancient history you studied in some high school history class.

I placed the photograph back on the mantle. I didn't want to be in my father's trailer anymore. Too many memories and too much sadness. I turned and looked at Ms. Lydia. She was staring at me and smiling—smiling as I had been smiling in that photograph, smiling like Bates Bridges had been smiling in that photograph. I wondered what sorrows scintillated behind her facetious grin and what tragedies she thought her smile could camouflage because I knew damn well her life had not been easy. There had been a divorce, affairs, disappointments, and Parkinson's Disease. Did she believe her smile could conceal all of that? Did she believe that her smile could make me believe I could be happy again—that I could be as happy as I was when I was twelve years old and everybody in Turkey Creek patted me on the back when I walked into a store just because I could throw a baseball harder than any other boy my age? I could not be deceived that easily anymore. I had watched my father die that morning, and happiness seemed, at that time, an emotion I would never experience again.

"Well, thank you for taking care of my father, Ms. Lydia," I said, sidling towards the door. "We would have probably had to put him in some sort of assisted living program had it not been for you."

"It was my pleasure, Luke," she answered, still trying to smile, even though I could see the tears forming in her eyes. "How is Carter doing?"

"Seems to be taking it pretty hard," I replied, opening the front door.

"Well, I will be praying for all of you," she said, wiping her eyes again with the tissue.

I nodded my head and began to walk out the door.

"Hey, Luke," she called, just as the door was about to close. "There was one question your father asked me once that sort of puzzled me."

I walked back into the trailer. Ms. Lydia rose to her feet and entered the kitchen. She poured herself a cup of coffee and leaned against the marbled counter.

"What was it?" I asked.

"Well," she began, slurping at her coffee. "We had just come back from church one night and were sitting on the couch eating some ice cream. You remember how your Daddy loved his ice cream, don't you," she inserted, casting a smile toward me like there was still a chance she could lift my spirits.

I just nodded my head nonchalantly, hoping she could sense that I just wanted her to continue with the story.

"I remember we had enjoyed a particularly wonderful service that evening and that your Daddy had been to the altar for prayer. Well, while we were eating our ice cream, we were discussing the service as we often did. Then, your daddy asked me this question I did not know how to answer. He asked, 'If you confess your sins before God and some of those sins were crimes, do you think God expects us to then admit to the authorities our commission of those crimes, or is he just satisfied with our confession to him?'"

"I didn't know how to respond to that question, Luke. I still don't. But I just had a feeling that, in his past, there was some sort of illegal act he had committed that he had never revealed to anyone, something that really bothered him. I don't know if that's the truth, but that was just the feeling I had."

"But he never did tell you what it was?"

"He never did, honey," she answered, shaking her head slowly as if she was so disappointed that she could not offer me any further information.

I stood there in the doorway, silent and still, the draft of a summer evening fanning me through the netted screen. Was this why people identified my father as a legend—because of some unsolved crime that people suspected he had committed and gotten away with? Was that enough to become a legend in Turkey Creek? Maybe, I suppose.

What I didn't know at the time was that the question Ms. Lydia had told me about would direct me into the secret world of a group of small-town men who were fiercely loyal to one another and where secrets were well preserved. Looking back, I probably should have been satisfied just not knowing. I should have gone home, buried my father, and gone on with my life. But I just couldn't shake the feeling of wanting to know why he was the legend.

THE BAR

There was only one bar in Turkey Creek—a dilapidated square of cinder blocks and panel-framed walls with dark windows you couldn't see through and a Bud Light neon sign flashing above the one door leading into the place. I don't even think the bar had an official name. People called it Floyd's because Floyd Owens owned it, but there were no signs saying Floyd's—just a piece of cardboard paper hanging from a hook on the front door. On one side, Floyd had written Open, and on the other side, Closed.

Floyd lived right behind the bar in a squalid single-wide trailer submerged so succinctly in a sea of crabgrass and wild onion and ragweed that you would have sworn the place was abandoned. The only place where there was no grass was to the left side of the trailer, where Floyd had his mangy dog chained to a sweet gum tree. Over the years, the mongrel had worn a circle in the yard where no grass would grow. For some reason, Floyd only cut his grass three or four times each year, not nearly enough to keep the grass low in Turkey Creek, where the summers were hot and afternoon thunderstorms were common. Most people began mowing their lawns around the first of April and didn't stop until Thanksgiving.

Some people said Floyd purposely kept his grass high to ward off visitors. Since there were a bunch of snakes in Turkey Creek, most people were wary of wading through high grass unless it was winter. And since winters were short in Turkey Creek, that meant people would be wary of walking through his yard most of the year. If people were right about him not wanting any visitors, I guess keeping his grass high was a reliable method of deterring company.

As far as I know, Floyd had never been married. But he did have a daughter. She never did live in Turkey Creek, though, so I didn't know much about her, didn't even know her name, only that she sometimes came to the bar and helped Floyd out on weekend nights. Most of the time, Floyd tended the place by himself, sitting behind the bar and talking to what few customers might be there. Sometimes, he would have the television on if there was a ballgame he or somebody else wanted to watch. Floyd seemed to prefer a quiet bar where people could carry on a conversation without having to yell. He even seemed to get a bit frustrated when someone would drop a few quarters into the jukebox and select some songs to play.

Me, I never went there often, just on occasion to shoot a game of pool. Not that Floyd minded me being there because I was under drinking age. He knew everybody in town and who was old enough to drink and who was not. In fact, he seemed to enjoy my visits. We would talk about baseball a bit, he would talk about fishing, and, sometimes, he would even ask me to give one of his intoxicated patrons a ride home.

Fudge Pickens, on the other hand, was in there almost every night. I remember how often Daddy would get a call from Floyd, asking Daddy to come pick up Fudge or to come down there and settle Fudge down when he became agitated. Quickly, Fudge was earning the reputation of the town drunk.

For as long as I can remember, the infamous title of town drunk had belonged to Squirrel Camby. But he died a few years back, and Fudge seemed the heir to the vacated position. Sometimes, when there was nobody to take him home and Floyd wouldn't let him drive, you could see Fudge staggering down the sidewalks at night, trying to get to his house or his mother's house or somebody's house where he could sleep for a while.

I don't know exactly what led Fudge to become an alcoholic. Whenever I asked Daddy, he just said we all have our demons and left it at that. All I knew about Fudge was what everybody else knew about him. He played college football for two years at a small college in Georgia, then got homesick and returned to Turkey Creek, where he made a living working on cars in small-town garages. He had never married, and he did not have any children. He had, however, lived with several women; some were from Turkey Creek, and some were from other nearby towns. His relationships never lasted long. Eventually, whoever he was living with would get tired of his drinking and mood changes and ask him to leave. And you would see him again staggering down the sidewalks of Turkey Creek.

About five years ago, Fudge was helping a friend put shingles on his mother's house. Somehow, Fudge slipped and fell off the roof, breaking several vertebrae in his back. The injuries required several surgeries and many hours of rehabilitation, but Fudge was never able to return to work. I remember how long he had to stay in the hospital and how Daddy would go and visit him almost every day. Even when he returned to his mother's house, Daddy would often stop by on his way home from work. Sometimes, he would bring Fudge a biscuit, and they would sit on the porch for a while, eating biscuits and reminiscing about whatever it was they wanted to remember about their lives in Turkey Creek—the sorrows, regrets, and, of course, the good times when they played baseball.

Sometimes, it seemed that, in Turkey Creek, life ended when you stopped playing baseball, like that last time you ran off the field and into the dugout and stuffed your bats and glove into your pack, you took your last breath, you inhaled your last bit of oxygen. Although you would not die, life would never be the same as it was on that baseball field. In that dugout were more than aluminum bats and batting gloves and empty packs of sunflower seeds and bubble gum wrappers. In that dugout were dreams and hopes and laughter and jokes and boys still so naïve that they believed in fairy tales and falling in love and dreams coming true. I tried to imagine Fudge sitting in that dugout, his catcher's gear on (because Fudge always caught), talking with Daddy and Stiff and Baker and all the other boys on the team.

I imagined their conversations were not so different than the ones I had with my teammates when I played. We talked about hunting and fishing and four-wheel drive trucks and which girls would let you go all the way and which girls would not. That was all that mattered in the dugout. That was all we thought would ever matter. Then time passed. Some of us got jobs, some of us went to college, and some of us got married, but life was never as simple or as beautiful as it was in that Turkey Creek High School dugout.

That night, the night I left Ms. Lydia at Daddy's trailer, I noticed Fudge's truck at Floyd's. I decided to stop, still not ready to go to sleep, even though I had only slept a couple of hours the night before. There were only three people in the bar when I entered, not counting Floyd, Fudge sitting on a barstool, and the Kendall twins playing a game of pool. I walked over and sat beside Fudge, who had not noticed my approach.

"Hey there boy," he said cheerfully, wrapping his arm around my shoulder. "How have you been holding up?"

"Okay, I guess."

"Do you want a can of soda, Luke?" Floyd asked.

"Sure," I answered.

"What will it be? Got Dr. Pepper, Sprite, and Coke," he announced.

"Dr. Pepper will be fine," I answered as Floyd lumbered toward the freezer, his gait hindered by age and several knee operations.

"How is Carter doing?" Fudge asked.

"Taking it pretty hard."

"How about Katie?"

"Hard to say," I answered, pushing in the tab of my Dr. Pepper can. "She just seems angry. Hard to talk to her."

"Losing your Daddy ain't no easy thing," said Floyd, dumping a cigarette from the pack he kept in his sleeve pocket. "Ain't easy at no age, but losing him while you are still young makes it even tougher."

"I guess so," I replied, taking the first sip of my pop.

I studied the pictures on the wall behind the bar. I had never really noticed them before, but there was one of Floyd and his daughter. They were younger in the picture. She was sitting on top of a race car, and Floyd was standing beside her, dressed in a racing uniform, his hands making sure his daughter didn't fall.

"Did you race cars at one time?" I asked Floyd, pointing at the photograph.

"Hell yeah," Fudge blurted before Floyd had a chance to reply. "You never knew that? Hell, Floyd even won a few championships up there at the Greenville Speedway, didn't you, Floyd." Floyd just nodded his head, wiping at a wet spot on the bar.

"How long ago was that?" I inquired.

"Oh hell, I can't remember exactly," he answered. "I quit sometime during the eighties. Had too many wrecks. And parts of my body started hurting more and more," he chuckled. "You will know about that one day."

"Damn right," Fudge agreed. "Hell, I can't even take a step now without something hurting."

One of the Kendall twins approached the bar and asked Floyd for two more beers.

"Sorry about your daddy, Luke," he said, nodding his head at me.

"Thanks," I answered.

Floyd brought two beers to the Kendall twin and opened them for him. The twin reached into his pocket and placed a few crumpled dollar bills on the counter.

"You ain't getting no damn more," Floyd warned. "You need to take your asses home, or you ain't gonna get up for work in the morning."

"We ain't as old as you, Floyd," the twin said, laughing as he walked back to the pool table. "Don't need twelve hours of sleep a day."

Floyd flipped the twin off with his middle finger, then walked back to where Fudge and I were sitting.

"Smart asses," he grumbled, grinning at me as he spoke.

But there was no chance of cheering me up that day. My father was dead. And the acceptance of that truth was becoming an increasingly difficult encumbrance. I listened to the clamor of the balls on the pool table, the twins laughing, and the soft tones of country music emanating from the radio Floyd kept on a shelf above the freezer. The world seemed so sad, so melancholic, the way dreams twisted and disseminated and fell apart, the way things you thought would endure forever perished in the mundane passage of moments, the way people died and nothing changed.

I had woken up that morning with a father, a friend, and a mentor. Now, his lifeless body was wrapped in a blanket and stuffed into some vault in a morgue in Atlanta, Georgia, as if his life never mattered at all. And here in Turkey Creek, South Carolina, everything was the same, everything would always be the same.

"Hard to believe," Fudge commented. "First, Gomez. Now, your daddy."

He took another swallow of beer and shook his head.

"Why did they call my daddy a legend, Fudge," I asked, startling him a bit.

He looked at Floyd for a moment, looking at him with a gaze that seemed to furtively convey some sequestered message. Then, Floyd lifted the door that separated the back of the bar from the

41

main floor. He walked over to the pool tables and began talking with the Kendall twins.

"Did your daddy ever tell you about Ricky Swanson?" Fudge asked.

I just shook my head and didn't say a word, anxious for Fudge to continue talking, believing that I would finally learn the reason why everybody in Turkey Creek considered my father to be a legend.

"Well, your daddy never was much of a fighter when he was young. Not like me anyway. I always wanted to battle with somebody and thought I was the toughest guy in Turkey Creek. But your daddy—he always seemed to try and avoid trouble. He had been in a few scraps in high school, but most of them were broken up before anyone got hurt.

"All that changed when he had enough of Ricky Swanson. That son of a bitch was a smart ass that hardly nobody could stand. Of course, most everybody was scared of him, though, because he drove a motorcycle. His daddy had been in jail, and Ricky went around telling everybody that his daddy was in Hell's Angels, even though nobody I knew even knew where his daddy lived.

"Anyway, one day, he and your daddy got into some kind of argument at lunch, and Ricky wanted to fight after school, down there in the field behind what used to be the hardware store. Well, your daddy couldn't be a pussy and just not go, so they met down there in that field after school. Of course, everybody had heard about it by then, and there was a crowd of people waiting down there to see the fight. And guess what happened?"

"What?"

"Ricky Swanson beat the hell out of your daddy," Fudge said chuckling.

"Then how did that make my daddy a legend?"

"That ain't the end of the story," Fudge continued. "A few weeks later, your daddy ambushed Ricky Swanson on this trail he used to walk home, beat him with a two-by-four or something and crushed his knee so bad that Ricky Swanson never walked right again. Then, about three or four years after that, Ricky Swanson shot himself on that same trail.

"Even though I know your daddy had nothing to do with that, lots of folks around here began spreading the rumor that your daddy murdered Ricky Swanson and just made it look like a suicide. And I guess that is where the legend comes from, that story being told so much that lots of folks started believing it."

"But you know my daddy didn't do it?"

"Hell no," Fudge asserted. "Ricky Swanson shot himself for the same reason most young men kill themselves: a damn woman."

"How come I ain't never heard that story?"

"Well," Fudge began after gulping down another few swallows of beer. "For one reason, it don't get told as much as it once did. Half the folks in this town ain't ever even heard of Ricky Swanson. Another reason is that even the folks who do know the story, wouldn't feel comfortable telling you, Carter, or Katie about the story. Just wouldn't be the decent thing to do, tell a man's kid some hodgepodge tale about their father shooting a man twenty-five years ago, a tale that most of them know ain't got a bit of truth in it."

I finished my Dr. Pepper in silence, not knowing how to absorb the story I had just been told or whether to believe Fudge or not. Maybe he was just telling me the story wasn't true to preserve the integrity of a man who had been one of his best friends. Maybe Daddy had murdered Ricky Swanson.

I twisted the tab of my empty soda can until it fell off, then shoved it down the drinking hole. By then, the Kendall twins had stopped playing billiards. They were leaning against the jukebox, swapping stories and laughing with Floyd. The world was still the same for them; Turkey Creek was still the same.

As for me, everything seemed different—the town, the bar, the music playing on the radio, the pictures on the television. I wondered if life would ever be normal again. I wondered how it could be.

Fudge pulled a can of Copenhagen from the back pocket of his faded blue jeans.

"Here," he said, offering me a pinch. "Your daddy was one of the best men I ever knew," he continued, perhaps sensing the story had disturbed me a bit. "I promise you he didn't have anything to do with Ricky Swanson dying on that trail."

"How can you be sure?" I asked, stuffing Fudge's offertory pinch into my mouth.

"I am sure," he said, packing a pinch of his tobacco between his fingers. "So, don't go worrying about that, okay? If I had any doubt about it, I would tell you. But I have no doubts."

"What about when he beat him with that two-by-four? Did he get in trouble for that?"

Fudge shook his head, spit a bit of tobacco juice into an empty Mountain Dew bottle sitting on the bar, and then pushed the bottle in front of me.

"Like I told you before, your daddy was probably the smartest man I ever met. He made sure when he ambushed Ricky Swanson on that trail that there were no witnesses, so there was no way they could prosecute him. Would have been just Ricky's word against your daddy's word." Fudge crushed his beer can and tossed it into the trash bin behind the bar. "But there was one witness," he began again. "Your daddy didn't know it at the time, but there was one person down there in the woods that saw what he did."

"Who?"

"Stiff," he answered. "Stiff Jenkins saw everything."

"What was Stiff doing down there?"

"I don't know. Probably trying to sneak into Judge Bishop's pond. I just know he was there. He probably wasn't but about fifteen or sixteen years old at the time, just a kid. Hard to imagine Stiff as a kid now. Hell, it is hard to imagine any of us as kids. But we were at one time, just a bunch of kids running around this mill town, raising hell and chasing pussy—just as you are now."

"So that's what earned my daddy the nickname Legend? What happened to Ricky Swanson?"

"As far as I know," Fudge answered, spitting into the empty Mountain Dew bottle. "If there is some other reason, I don't know about it." He stuffed the can of Copenhagen into his back pocket. "Why do you want to know all of this anyway?" he asked.

"I don't know," I answered humbly. "Just curious, I guess."

"Well, I ain't trying to tell you what to do," he began, in a more serious voice. "But there might be things your father did when he was young that you would be better off not knowing about."

"What do you mean?" I asked.

He shrugged his shoulders and glanced around the room once or twice as if he wanted to be certain nobody else had come into the bar.

"I'm just saying," he replied, his voice almost like a whisper. "You know how things are between Stiff and your daddy. People say they have some secrets between them. Now, I don't know if that is true or not, but I wouldn't suggest poking around too much in Stiff's business." He spit another pellet of tobacco juice into his plastic bottle spittoon. "I know Stiff loved your daddy, and I know he loves you. But there are some things Stiff don't want anybody to know about, so I wouldn't pry too much. Do you understand what I am saying?'

"I guess so," I replied, rising from the barstool.

But I didn't understand. How could any of this be possible? Was Stiff Jenkins that much of a badass? And what kind of secrets did he and Daddy have? At first, I thought when people told me that Daddy and Stiff had secrets, that meant he might know where Stiff's still was. Everybody in the damn county knew that Stiff made moonshine. Maybe Daddy knew who Stiff beat up for owing him some money. Maybe the secrets were darker than what I imagined and graver than what I wanted to believe. And maybe what Fudge was telling me was right. Maybe there were some things about my father I would be better off not knowing.

I didn't know what to think anymore. I glanced up at the television. The Braves were playing out West against the Diamondbacks, losing two to nothing in the fifth inning. If Daddy was still alive, he would have been watching the game. Maybe I would have been watching it with him, eating some hot wings from Little Perry's, the only restaurant in Turkey Creek.

Suddenly, I realized how much I was going to miss him. I became so angry at God for letting him die, for letting him suffer for five years, for allowing my family to fall apart. Nothing seemed fair anymore; nothing seemed right. I wanted to bang my fists into the wall, to grab a pool stick and beat it against the wall until it splintered into pieces. I wanted to see my daddy again. I wanted to be twelve years old again, standing in the batter's box, glancing over my shoulder, and seeing Daddy in the stands sitting beside Momma. Why couldn't life be that way anymore? Why did everything have to change? I tossed my empty soda can into the trash bin and started toward the door, lifting a hand in the air.

"I'll see you fellas later," I shouted to Floyd and the Kendall twins. "How much do I owe you for the soda, Floyd?"

Floyd grabbed a pool stick from one of the Kendall twins. "I oughta come over there and beat the hell out of you with this damn pool stick for even asking me that question." The Kendall twins and Fudge laughed at Floyd's response. "You just let me know if you need anything. And tell Katie and Carter that I asked about them."

"I will," I said as I opened the front door.

"Listen," Fudge said. "Your daddy was one of the greatest men I ever knew, one of the best friends I ever had. I could never tell you what all he has done for me and a lot of other people in this town. Remember him that way, okay?"

I nodded my head towards Fudge, then closed the heavy wooden door. It was thundering in the distance. I could see flashes of lightning speckling the western horizon. I didn't want to believe that Daddy was dead. I didn't want to believe that we would never watch a Braves game again. I sat in my car for a moment and dialed the radio to a station that broadcast the Braves game. I sat there for a while, listening to the game and remembering all I could about my father. I remembered the first home run I hit and how proud I felt placing that ball in his hand. I remembered the day he taught me to ride a bike, the first fish I caught, and the first deer I killed. All these memories wrapped around me and cuddled me in a way I could find solace.

I looked around at the town of Turkey Creek, what I could see of it from the parking lot of Floyd's bar anyway—the empty buildings, the remnants of the textile mill, the abandoned houses, the baseball fields. A town defined by tragedy, scarred and derelict, taking its final breaths. I didn't know how much longer Turkey Creek would last or how many more people the town could bear to lose. There was already talk about tearing the high school down and building a new one on Highway 28. This would merge Turkey Creek with Twin Falls, another dying town.

Despite my hometown's grim future and derelict appearance, I was glad to be a resident of Turkey Creek. It was where I belonged, where I wanted to spend the rest of my days, and where I wanted to die—Luke Stiles, the son of the Legend.

JUSTIN GOMEZ

Justin Gomez. I had almost forgotten about him until Fudge mentioned his name. According to Daddy, Justin Gomez had been his best friend since he could remember. When they were young, their families lived on the same road—Blanchard Road, a dead-end road that angled southward on a precipitous slope from where the cotton mill stood. Daddy said he could hardly remember a day in his childhood when he didn't see Justin. Of course, I never heard many people refer to him as Justin or even Justin Gomez. Most people just called him Gomez.

Gomez himself was sort of a legend in Turkey Creek, I suppose, or a tragedy, whichever way you chose to look at things. To me, there didn't seem to be much that separated the two. Legends, tragedies. Heroes, losers. The two opposites seemed near to me as if a person could spend his or her adolescence believing they were destined for greatness, created by an omnipotent God to be a hero or legend, only to have fate, for whatever reason, shove you off the trail that you thought you were supposed to be walking—the trail you were certain would lead to your life purpose and hurl you down into a deep abyss where there was only despondency, disappointment, disillusionment, and people who once thought their life mattered. Then, they had to accept the brutal fact that it never had or would.

Anyway, according to Daddy and just about everyone else that was Daddy's age, Justin Gomez may have been the best athlete to ever pass through Turkey Creek. He could run faster than anyone, throw the ball harder, and hit the ball farther. In 1981, the year Turkey Creek won the Little League State Championship, Gomez was the one pitching that game. By the time he was in the tenth grade, he was throwing harder than anyone on the varsity team, some of his fastballs reaching the low 90s. He pitched the whole season without giving up a run.

In his sophomore season, he led the team in home runs and RBIs. He was the only sophomore in the history of Turkey Creek High School to make the All-State team. And baseball was not the only sport in which he excelled. In football, he ran for 2700 yards in his sophomore season, a Turkey Creek High school record that has never been broken. He made All-State in football, too, and even had his name in the *Street and Smith* magazine, which listed the top prospects in each state.

After his sophomore season, Gomez began smoking pot and drinking liquor whenever he could find some. About halfway through the football season in his junior year, he was dismissed from the team. By December, he had dropped out of school completely. The following year, he got some girl from Georgia pregnant. He married her and got a job at the cotton mill. Eighteen years old, the best athlete in Turkey Creek was working the graveyard shift at a cotton mill, already a daddy and a high school dropout. Maybe the drugs and alcohol contributed to his fall from glory, or maybe it was because his parents divorced when he was only seven, and his mom remarried some asshole that beat the hell out of Gomez whenever he got drunk. Or maybe it was just another inequity of life, some divine example that even the most gifted of us are susceptible to living a wasted life.

Whatever the cause, the marriage only lasted a couple of years. That girl moved back to Georgia to live with her parents and took the kid with her. Daddy told me that Gomez tried at first to keep in touch with his son, but, eventually, he just quit trying—don't know why. After that, Gomez just sort of drifted from town to town, living in one town for a little while, then another town. Sometimes, he would come back to Turkey Creek for a while. He married again, I think, for just a brief spell, but he never had any more children.

Last spring, around the time the dogwoods were beginning to bloom, Gomez came to visit Daddy one evening. They grilled some burgers, drank a few beers, and swapped some stories— the stuff they usually did when they got together. I remember stopping by there for a while, just long enough to eat a burger and listen to a story or two. Gomez seemed the same while I was there. But I guess he really wasn't.

Later that night, Gomez told Daddy he had cancer and that the cancer had spread throughout his body. Said he probably only had a few months to live. And he was right. He died that August. I remember when they moved him for the last time from the hospital to his mother's house. He only had a few more days left to live, and he wanted to spend them in the house where he had been reared. Besides, there was nothing else the doctors could do for him except give him morphine to ease the pain.

Daddy visited him every night. I went with him once, sat in a corner chair, and listened to them talk. Daddy always sat in the chair next to the bed, so he could be close to Gomez, who could not talk very loud anymore.

"Here you go," Daddy said, offering Gomez a can of tobacco, as he settled into his seat. "Picked this up for you today at the store. It's your favorite brand, that old cheap shit."

Gomez struggled to get a pinch into his mouth, his fingers weakened by the cancer.

"I don't know if I should be doing this or not," he remarked, motioning for Daddy to give him the spit cup on the nightstand. "They say it'll give you cancer."

"Well," Daddy said, handing Gomez the spit cup. "You're just shit out of luck then. I spent three dollars on that can. I ain't gonna watch it go to waste. And I sure as hell ain't putting that crap in my mouth."

Gomez laughed as he handed the can back to Daddy. When he leaned forward, the bed sheets fell from his shoulders, and I

50

could see how the disease had emaciated his body. He was always so muscular and fit, even though he never exercised that much, according to Daddy. He was just one of those people who was lucky like that. He looked the same whether he exercised or not.

That evening, he didn't look lucky at all. In three months, he had lost more than thirty pounds. Sitting there on the bed that night, he seemed weak and scrawny. Believing he had once been a stellar athlete and the kind of man who could get almost any woman he wanted was difficult to do.

"Who's that sitting in the corner over there? Your boy," he asked, spitting his first plume of juice into the plastic cup.

"Yep," Daddy answered. "Every now and then, he still hangs around the old man."

"I know you're proud of him," Gomez commented in his weak voice. "I would be."

"Yeah, he ain't too bad of a kid."

"I think about him sometimes, Stiles," Gomez admitted sadly.

"Who?" Daddy asked.

"My son," Gomez confessed, sadness swallowing his emaciated countenance. "I wonder what he looks like, what he is doing, whether he did good in school or not, what his Momma tells him about me, or if she even does."

The last of the afternoon light faded from the room. Shadows fell across my father's chair, the bedsheets, the nightstand. Death lingered in the air ominously, a persistent and palpable presence.

"I know you do," Daddy answered.

"I wish there was some way I could see him again, to tell him that I love him," Gomez said, beginning to whimper. "You know I went looking for him a few years back. Drove over to Georgia where his momma's parents lived. But they didn't live there anymore. I couldn't find out any information on where they might be. Just gave up. Came back home." He spit into the bottle again and wiped his eyes with the back of his knuckles. "Do you still have the key to my storage building?" Gomez asked.

"Yeah," Dad answered.

"Remember what I asked you to do for me?"

"I remember."

Daddy rose from his seat and shook Gomez' trembling hand.

"I love you, Stiles," Gomez said softly. I didn't even know men talked like that, but I guess, when death is so near, you say a lot of things you wouldn't ordinarily say.

"I love you too, brother," Daddy answered. "I'll be back tomorrow to check on you."

"We sure as hell had a lot of fun, didn't we," Gomez said, not wanting to let go of Daddy's hand.

"We sure did," Daddy agreed.

Later that evening, Daddy took me to see Gomez' storage building. Inside, the storage shed looked like the wall of a Bass Pro Shop. There must have been ten deer head mounts in there and at least a half dozen largemouth bass. There was even a set of elk antlers and a bear-skin rug.

"Where did all this stuff come from?" I asked.

"Gomez killed all these deer and caught all these fish."

"Did he kill that elk?" I asked. Daddy just nodded. "How about that bear?" Again, Daddy nodded.

"He went out West for a little while and worked as a hunting guide. Two things Gomez liked—hunting and smoking pot."

I chuckled a bit at Daddy's comment, still admiring the impressive display of deer heads in the building.

"That is where he got the elk and bear," Daddy said.

"Well, what did he mean, Daddy, when he asked if you remembered what to do with his storage building when he died?"

"Well, I hope I can find his son. I am going to try. Then, maybe I can give him all this stuff or at least offer it to him. Gomez wants him to have it."

"What if you can't find him?"

"I'll find him," Daddy assured me.

Daddy flipped the light off on the storage building, pulled the roll door down, and locked it. Seemed kind of sad to me. All that Gomez had accomplished in life was tucked into a twelve-by-twelve storage shed that he paid forty dollars a month to rent.

Sometime later that night, Gomez took his final breath. His mother walked into the room that morning and found him dead. There had been nobody with him—no wife, no children, no siblings. I wondered if he was awake when he took his final breath—if he was aware of what was happening. If he was, I wondered how lonely he must have felt, knowing he was about to die, looking around the room and seeing nobody there.

People once filled the stands of Turkey High School Stadium just to watch him play football. Kids would ask for his autograph after the game, certain that he would be famous one day. But the fame never came, and the autographs were worthless. Justin Gomez died alone in a bedroom at his mother's house at the age of forty-nine—just another tragic ending to a once heralded Turkey Creek athlete. How many yards he had rushed didn't matter anymore. How fast he could throw a ball didn't matter. His life ended in insignificance. Hell, there weren't even that many people at the funeral.

Six weeks later, I drove Daddy to a military base in Georgia and watched him give a soldier the key to that storage building. I don't know how Daddy found Gomez' son so quickly. I never asked. On the way back home, we only talked about baseball. We talked about the Braves and the game they had played the night before. We talked about Turkey Creek's high school team, how they had fared last year, who would be returning next season, who would be graduating, and if they would have enough pitching to make it through the playoffs. We talked about stuff like that because that was what we had been trained to do—camouflage our sorrows and encumbrances beneath stories of baseball, like baseball was all that mattered, like, as long as there was baseball being played in Turkey Creek, South Carolina, everything else would be okay.

THE PORCH

Turkey Creek was sort of eccentric in its appearance. It almost resembled a funnel, with the main part of the town settled on a flat plot of land and the roads that veered from Main Street ascending and wrapping concentrically around the main part of town. From our porch, you could see most of the town. You could see the churches, the baseball fields, the grocery store —even the people walking down the sidewalks. Sitting on the porch sometimes made me feel as if were in heaven, the way I could see what people were doing and them not even aware of my observation.

I had lived in the house since I was three years old. I don't remember ever living anywhere else, though I knew we had. My parents bought the house at a reasonable price from my mother's uncle, who left Turkey Creek after the mill closed. I am not certain of the exact purchase price, but I know it must have been pretty low because the mortgage had been paid for a while.

The house was not in the greatest shape. The roof leaked after a hard rain, and the kitchen floor was in dire need of replacement. Some spots in the floor sagged so much that I was scared to walk across them. But it was home, the only home I had ever known, and that reason alone made it a special place to me.

Anyway, Katie was sitting on the front porch when I finally got home, even though it was nearly midnight. She was sitting on the porch, smoking a cigarette.

"Thought you quit," I said, as I passed by her and settled into the porch swing, the chains creaking a bit at the pull of my weight.

"I did," she responded. "Just needed one tonight."

"Where is Carter?" I asked.

"Sitting in his room," she answered, taking a drag off her cigarette. "Listening to Johnny Cash."

"Well, Daddy sure did like Johnny Cash."

"Yep," Katie replied, rising from her chair and smothering her cigarette against the porch banister, then flipping the butt into the yard.

"Have you heard from Momma?" I asked.

"Talked to her a little while this morning."

"What did she have to say?"

"Not much," Katie answered, returning to her rocking chair. "Just said to let her know if we needed anything. That was about it."

"Ashley is supposed to be coming down tomorrow afternoon. She might spend the night," I informed Katie.

Katie shook her head and fired up another cigarette. Ashley Astings and I had been dating for over a year. She was a student at the University of Georgia, studying to be a pharmacist. I met her through Judd, my partner in the landscaping business. Judd's girlfriend and Ashley were cousins. Five months ago, on Valentine's Day, I had asked her to marry me, and she said she would. She was so sweet and kind and pretty. I loved spending time with her. I felt so comfortable in her presence. She had been trying her best to counsel me through these difficult days.

Ashley's father had died young, also, so I guess she thought she could empathize with me more than others. Ashley was barely a year old when her daddy died. Her mother remarried a couple of years later, so the only father Ashley ever knew was her stepfather. She couldn't even remember her real father—she had never had a relationship with him—so I didn't grant her well-meaning condolences any more merit than I did the condolences of others. But I was glad she was coming. She was easy to talk to, and I enjoyed her company. I knew I would feel better once she was here.

"Well," Katie said, after a few moments of uneasy silence. "Have you found out why they called Daddy a legend yet?"

"Not really," I answered, chuckling. "Stopped down at Floyd's and talked to Fudge. He told me a story about Ricky Swanson. Have you ever heard that story?"

"Yeah, I have heard it a few times," Katie admitted. "Think it is just a bunch of bullshit."

"Probably is," I agreed. "But that was the first time I ever heard it. Still don't think that is why they called him a legend, though."

"Why are you all of a sudden so interested in how he got his nickname?"

"I don't know," I mumbled, shrugging my shoulders. "Guess I just never thought about it much until these last few days."

"Do you really think you want to know?"

"I don't know the answer to that question, either," I confessed. "In a way, I want to know. But there is another part of me that is afraid of learning something about Daddy I may not want to know."

"I have to show you something," she said, rising from her seat. She balanced her half-finished cigarette precariously upon the porch railing, then walked inside. When she returned, she was carrying a cedar box. "I found this in the back of the hall closet not too long ago. Been keeping it under my bed ever since."

"What is it?" I asked curiously.

"Just a box of stuff Daddy wanted to keep, I suppose." She began emptying the contents of the box. "Your first home run ball, Carter's first home run ball, some dance trophy I won when I was like seven. Got a few pictures in here, too. One of you and him with a deer, one of him and Carter with a stringer of fish, one of me dressed in camouflage. Think that was the day he talked me into going turkey hunting with him. And a few other knickknacks: old report cards, pictures we colored for him, a letter Mom wrote him, a copy of his brother's obituary."

She closed the lid and set the box back down on the porch.

"All that stuff seems pretty normal, doesn't it?" she asked, not caring if I replied or not.

"I guess so," I answered.

"But that wasn't all that was in the box, Luke."

She opened the box again and pulled out a handful of newspaper clippings. As she began to read one, she started to cry.

"What's the matter?" I asked.

"These newspaper stories are disturbing," she confessed between sobs. "I don't know why they would be in this box."

She wiped her eyes, then unfolded one of the yellow and fragile clippings. Katie's fingers opened it carefully.

"Two men from Cook County, Georgia, reported missing," she began.

Then, she opened another one.

"Micheal Cross, a resident of Turkey Creek, South Carolina, dies in a single-car accident on Highway 28. Howard Williams presumed drowned after his boat was found empty on Lake Russell."

She set the papers in her lap, folding them carefully into their original forms.

"What does all this mean, Luke?" she asked. "Why would Daddy have these newspaper clippings in his box? Do you think he had something to do with these disappearances and deaths? I mean I have always heard you don't cross Stiff Jenkins, that when people mess with Stiff, they go missing. But I always thought that was just talk. And then I find this shit in Daddy's chest box. I don't know what to think. Was Daddy a murderer? Did he kill people?"

"Let me see them," I said.

I opened each one carefully, reading every word and studying the dates. I didn't want to believe my father had ever killed anyone. But there was sure as hell some reason he had saved these newspaper clippings.

"I don't want Carter to see these," Katie whispered, still crying a little. "I don't want him to think anything bad about Daddy."

"That's a good idea," I agreed, handing the papers back to her. "And you need to go inside and get some rest. We are supposed to meet Stiff at the funeral home tomorrow morning at nine."

"I guess you are right," she murmured, carefully placing the contents she had removed from the box back into it.

Katie walked back into the house. I pulled a can of Copenhagen from my back pocket and inserted a pinch. That box had been my confirmation. There was more to Daddy becoming a legend than that Ricky Swanson story. There were secrets more profound, more illicit, mysteries that would take more than just a conversation with Fudge Pickens at Floyd's bar to decipher. These secrets had been honored for years by men with a fierce loyalty to each other. How in the hell was I going to convince them to break their silence?

I stood and leaned against the banister and spit into the yard. How could all this be true, all these stories about Stiff and Daddy and the other members of their clan? This was Turkey Creek, South Carolina, for crying out loud, not New York City. If I had not been born and raised here, I would have probably just thought of it as a shithole town. How could there be men living here dangerous enough to kill?

From where I stood, I watched Fudge back his truck out of Floyd's parking lot and drive slowly down the pole-light-illuminated streets. He was right. I knew he was. I didn't need to go any further with my investigation into the origin of my father's nickname. The Ricky Swanson story should have been enough to satisfy my curiosity. But seeing those newspaper clippings just invigorated my fervent desire to delve into my father's past. I was no longer afraid of what I might discover. I wanted to know the truth, especially about those two men who had disappeared in Georgia. One of them was named Anderson Dill. The other one was named Cleve Astings—the father of the girl I had just asked to marry me.

TURKEY CREEK CEMETERY

Turkey Creek Cemetery was located at the end of a winding, deceptively precipitous, and narrow road aptly named Cemetery Road. There were no houses on Cemetery Road, just woods on both sides and a few meadows overgrown with kudzu and crabgrass. It was a lonely road, especially at night. Even in the day, the road seemed sort of creepy to me. The way the shadows of the trees dominated the surface, sunlight was only allowed to dapple in a few sporadic spaces.

I remember following the hearse up the road when Grandpa died (my paternal grandfather). I also remember how long it seemed to take to get to the cemetery. I was only ten years old then, but I remember that drive to the cemetery more than anything else about the funeral—don't know why, but I just do. Actually, the road was only a little more than two miles in length, but, for some reason, following that hearse made it seem a lot longer.

Ashley had texted me while I was at the restaurant with Blake and informed me that she would be a little late. When Blake dropped me off at the house, I decided to ride up to the cemetery. I wanted to see the plot Stiff had bought for Daddy and where it was located. I didn't even tell Katie or Carter that I was going. I just left. Guess I wanted to be alone for a while and try to absorb everything that had been happening: Daddy dying, the newspaper clippings, the conversation I had with Fudge at the bar, the conversation I had with Blake at the restaurant.

Everything was so confusing. All I wanted to do was mourn the loss of my father, but all these other things were making that hard to do. I guess it was my fault, though, for wanting to investigate why they called my daddy the legend. Guess I should have just let that be what it had always been: a mystery, a small-town fairy tale. But my thoughts just would not let me forget about it, especially since Katie had shown me those newspaper clippings.

I always knew my Daddy as kind, gentle, and loving. I couldn't imagine him ever hurting anyone. The way he treated us, the way he treated his friends, the way he treated people he didn't even know. I remember this one time, we were eating breakfast at Little Perry's. For some reason, it was just me and Daddy. I couldn't have been more than eight at the time. I remember seeing this woman walk in with her three children. I don't remember what her name was, but I remember seeing her in church occasionally. I also knew her husband had abandoned them, and she was having a lot of financial trouble. They even took up a love offering for her at church one Sunday. Anyway, when Daddy and I finished eating, Daddy walked up to the register to pay for our meal. After he paid for our meal, he told the woman behind the register that he wanted to pay for the meal of that woman and her children.

I remember Daddy doing things like that, things that made me want to grow up to be like him, to have a heart as generous as his heart. Todd Rosman, the youth pastor at the church we attended, told me one time not too long ago—while we were sitting in the waiting room of the hospital and they were running some tests on Daddy—that my father always gave him the yearly bonus they gave him at work each Christmas. He said that Daddy would put that money in his hand and tell him to use it on the youth. That was the kind of man I knew my Daddy to be. That was the kind of man I wanted my daddy to be. Now, because of my incessant desire to pry into his past, that image of him had become blurred and incoherent. I didn't know if I could ever think of him that way again.

The sun was high in the sky by the time I reached Turkey Creek Cemetery, another hot summer day in South Carolina. I parked my truck against the side of the road and began walking the main path that led through the scattering of tombstones, sweating after only a few steps.

Turkey Creek Cemetery was a beautiful place, an unusually flat three to four-acre plot of land surrounded by hardwood forests. In the winter, when the leaves were off the trees, you could stand at the back of the cemetery and see Turkey Creek and the town. It looked like a postcard almost or a picture you would see in a magazine. I don't think many people knew how beautiful the cemetery was, especially during the months of winter.

But one person did—Stiff Jenkins. He was probably the last person I would have thought appreciated the subtle beauty of Turkey Creek Cemetery. But there he was that day, sitting on one of the benches beneath the shade of two sprawling dogwood trees. I hadn't noticed that he was there when I parked my truck because he had parked at the back of the cemetery in the shade.

I couldn't just walk past him and pretend I did not see him, even though I really wanted to be alone for a while, so I walked over and sat on the bench beside him. He was holding the same Coke bottle he had been holding that morning at the funeral home, only now he was wearing his Turkey Creek High School baseball cap—I guess to shade his eyes from the sweltering summer sun.

"What are you doing here, Stiff?" I asked, settling onto the bench.

"I like to come up here and sit sometimes," he said. "Think about things, think about life." He spit into his Coke bottle and tugged at his ball cap. "Seems peaceful up here," he continued lethargically, like maybe he had just wanted to be alone also, unbothered by the world for a while.

"Sometimes, I walk around and look at these tombstones and wonder about what that person's life was like. There is a couple buried over on the far right that lost four children. None of the children even lived a year. I can't imagine what it would be like to even lose one child, much less four." He paused for a minute, scratched at a scab on his forearm. "And over there," he began again, nodding his head toward the left side of the cemetery. "Over there where the oldest graves are, there are two brothers buried side by side. Both died in the Civil War, on the same day, in the same battle. Fredricksburg, Virginia."

He shook his head and looked around at the tombstones. "Just think about how many stories could be told from the people that are buried here."

"Carter likes to do that."

"What's that?"

"Visit old cemeteries," I answered. "Especially historical cemeteries. He liked anything to do with history, old battlefields, and old churches. He and Daddy were always visiting places like that."

"He is a smart kid," Stiff commented.

"Yeah, he is," I agreed.

"So is his sister," Stiff added. "What in the hell happened to you?"

"I don't know," I answered, chuckling. "Guess I just got the looks."

Stiff laughed at my response, then opened a can of Copenhagen and offered me a dip. I fingered a pinch of tobacco between my lips and gum and gave him back his can.

"You know," he said. "Losing your daddy is going to be tough on all of you, but I think it may be hardest on Carter. Hell, he is just fifteen years old, and his daddy is already dead."

"I know," I agreed. "He and Dad had become really close."

"I know," Stiff said. "We talked about that a lot. That was one of the things your daddy was worried about after he and your mom got divorced, that he and Carter would never be close. He was really happy that he was able to spend so much time with him. I guess, if there is a silver lining in your daddy getting sick, it would be that your daddy and Carter got to spend a lot of time together. They may have never become that close had your daddy still been working." He placed the can of Copenhagen into the back pocket of his jeans. "Of course, he spent a lot of time with you also, even when he was working. He did a good job of spending time with his children—a lot better job than I have done."

"Hell, Cody thinks the world of you, Stiff."

"I know he does. And I am glad he does. But a man is always going to think he could have spent more time with his children." He placed his arm around my shoulder. "If the Lord ever blesses you with children, make sure you spend as much time as you can with them. And not just playing baseball. Find out what they like to do and do that with them as much as you can. Baseball ain't nearly as damn important as people in this town make it out to be."

He stood and stretched—as if he had been sitting for quite a spell, and his legs were sore. "Do you want me to show you where your daddy's plot is?" he asked.

"Sure," I answered, following him into the sea of tombstones.

"I tried to get it as close to his father's and his brother's graves as I could," he spoke while he walked. "And there it is," he announced, pointing to a plat of grass with borders marked by two strands of carpenter's string.

It seemed so small—like it wasn't even big enough for a coffin. But I knew it had cost Stiff thousands of dollars. I stepped over the strings and stood on the plot of grass that would be dug up the next day by bulldozers, the plot of land where my father's remains would disseminate back into the dust of the earth. And I thought about how sad it would be that nobody would ever be buried beside him. I imagined people visiting the cemetery years from now and walking by his grave, wondering why there was no wife buried beside him.

"Your grandpa's grave is right there," Stiff announced, pointing to my grandfather's headstone. "And Wade is right there beside him."

I stepped back over the strings and trudged slowly toward my grandfather's grave, trying to remember things about him as I walked—the sound of his voice, the way he laughed while watching reruns of the Andy Griffith Show, seeing him in the bleachers at my ball games, eating ice cream sandwiches with him on the front porch of his house.

Grandpa was a good man—a great man really. He was a carpenter. That was how he made his living—framing houses, making furniture, building decks. He could do about anything with wood that could be done. People were always stopping by his shop and wanting him to make something for them. I guess he had earned the reputation of being the best in that line of work, at least in this county.

One morning, Grandma found him dead in his shop. He had suffered a massive heart attack and was just lying there dead, slumped against a heap of scrap wood. Took Daddy a while to get over losing his father. Took Katie and me a while, too. Even took Momma a while. We used to visit his grave every few months, but, standing there that day with Stiff, I could not remember the last time I had visited his grave. It had to have been at least a couple of years.

"Your Daddy spent a lot of time up here," Stiff remarked, reminding me of his presence. "Put a lot of flowers on this grave," he continued. "Shed a lot of tears in this spot."

"Yeah," I answered. "Guess I know how he feels now."

I turned and looked at the tombstone beside Grandpa's grave. It was the tombstone of Daddy's younger brother who died when he was only twelve—struck by a car while riding his bicycle.

Daddy never talked much about Wade. Momma said he just didn't like to talk about the incident because Daddy was there when it happened. He saw the car hit his brother's bicycle and watched his brother die. I couldn't imagine how that must have affected him.

"What was Wade like?" I asked Stiff.

"Well," he began slowly. "He was a damn good ball player, that was for sure. He was the one that pitched the game that year that got us in the Little League state championship game."

He spit another pellet of tobacco juice into his empty plastic bottle and screwed the cap back on.

"That was a hard day for a lot of people, the day Wade died. We were just a bunch of kids, and none of us wanted to believe that we could die. At that age, you think only old people die. You don't think somebody that you just got through playing little league baseball with could die. But death comes whenever the good Lord gets ready for us, I guess. Just take a walk around this cemetery. It ain't just old folks buried in here."

"Did Daddy ever talk about Wade?" I asked.

"Not much," replied Stiff. "Not much at all." He took off his ball cap and swatted at a horsefly that had been pestering him. "And I ain't ever been the kind of man who tried to get someone to talk about something they didn't want to talk about."

He took another swipe at the horsefly. This time, he knocked it to the ground, then crunched it beneath the sole of his cowboy boots.

"How is your grandma?" he asked, changing the subject. "Have you been to see her lately?"

My paternal grandmother had been in a nursing home in Anderson for almost two years. She had Alzheimer's Disease. The last time I visited her, Daddy was with me, and she didn't even recognize him, her own son. She just talked crazy stuff about seeing somebody on a tractor and why some lady did not pick her up on Sundays anymore to take her to church. None of what she said made any sense.

"Probably been a couple of months," I replied. "Don't really see the point of visiting her to tell you the truth. She doesn't know who I am; she doesn't know who anybody is."

I could feel the sun blistering my face as I stood there, me and the most dangerous man in Turkey Creek. I wondered why life had to be so cruel, why some people had to die so young, and why Grandma would have to live the final years of her life not even knowing who she was—not able to remember who she had been, not able to remember the happy moments of her life.

"Do you think we ought to bring her to the funeral?" I asked.

"Do you think she would know why she was there?"

"Probably not," I sighed. "Probably just worry the hell out of us."

"Then I wouldn't bring her," said Stiff. "Not if she is that bad."

He fashioned his fly-swatting ball cap back onto his head, then turned and took a few steps toward his truck.

"Cody is coming down tonight," he announced. "He is going to be off the rest of the week. Maybe this weekend, y'all can do a little fishing in the pond."

"That sounds like fun," I answered. "I talked to him this morning and told him to give me a call when he got here."

Stiff nodded his head, then continued toward his truck. The world didn't seem right anymore, not my world anyway. I didn't want to live in a world with dead fathers, buried secrets, shattered dreams, and people wasting away in nursing homes— not even knowing who in the hell they were. I wanted to live in a world where there was happiness and peace, where I could visit my grandparents on a Saturday afternoon, where I could sit on the couch after a day's work and watch the Braves game with my father.

This growing-up shit wasn't as fun as I thought it would be. I guess that is a lesson we all learn eventually. You spend your whole adolescence wanting to be a grownup and the rest of your life wanting to be young again. I watched Stiff get into his truck and drive away, and then I walked back to the plot of grass where my father would be buried. I knelt and pulled up a handful of grass and dirt and held it in my hand for a little while. I don't know why. Guess I just wanted to feel the earth that, in two days, would be dumped upon my daddy's coffin.

THE KITCHEN

Momma was the only one home when I got back to the house. She was unloading a bag of groceries when I walked into the kitchen.

"Bought you some groceries," she said, as she stuffed some canned vegetables into a cabinet. "Some things you like," she added, waving a box of macaroni and cheese.

"Thanks," I replied, helping her empty the bags. "Where are Katie and Carter?" I asked.

"They drove over to the trailer. Katie wanted to start packing up a few of your daddy's things." We put the last of the groceries into the cabinets, then tossed the bags into the trash can. "Are you okay?"

"I don't know," I mumbled. "I just don't know."

"Is it because of your Daddy passing?" she asked, moving closer to me. "Or is something else bothering you?"

"Well," I began, "why did they call Daddy the legend?"

"What?" she asked, surprised by my question.

"You know how everybody around here calls him the legend. Why do they call him that?"

She pulled a chair from the kitchen table and sat down. Light coming in from the kitchen window skirted across her face.

"I really don't know," she replied. "I just thought all his friends had nicknames, and that was his."

"I think there is more to it than that," I suggested, staring out the kitchen window into the yard where Daddy once planted his garden.

I remembered how Momma would help him in the garden sometimes. I also remembered how young they seemed back then and how in love they seemed to be. I remember them sitting in the backyard swing together—sometimes at the end of the day as the pallid tints of dusk fell around them. Life seemed so different then. Everything did. In the evening, we would occasionally play kickball or badminton. We laughed so much back then, like life would always be fun, like we would always be happy. I couldn't believe how much life had changed since then, how much we had changed.

"Come here," she said, pulling out a chair for me. "Sit with me for a minute."

I grabbed a bottle of water and obliged her request. Everything seemed different now; everything seemed like a memory. Even the kitchen table. I remember sitting around the table with Momma and Daddy at suppertime, Carter still sitting in his highchair. I thought about how, even back then, even when we seemed like the perfect American family, the man sitting at the head of the table, the man I idolized, the man I called Daddy, might have already been a murderer.

"You know when we first got married, your daddy was still working for Stiff," Momma began. "And you know how things are with them. He never told me one thing about what they did. And I never asked." She reached into her purse, pulled out a stick of gum, and stuffed it into her mouth. "He was so loyal to Stiff," she continued, smacking on her gum, "that I think he could have called your daddy on our wedding day, told him that he needed him, and your daddy would have probably canceled the wedding."

"Why is it like that," I prodded, twisting the top off my water bottle. "I mean, do you think the things they say about Stiff are true? Do people really disappear when they mess with Stiff?"

"I can't answer that," she said, "but I wouldn't want to test that theory."

"Well, do you think that Daddy ever helped him? Do you think that Daddy ever killed anybody?"

"I can't imagine your daddy ever killing anyone," she replied. "But I just don't know how much people say about Stiff is true and how much is just people talking. Why are you thinking about all these things anyway? Just remember your daddy as he was to you. He was a good father to you, your sister, and your brother. Remember him like that. Now ain't the time to be wondering about what he did in his past." She paused for a moment and pulled a tissue from her purse. "I can tell you this —when your daddy got saved, he changed. I know that. It was obvious."

"I know, Momma. I know Daddy loved us, and I know he was a good father. But I just can't seem to get it out of my head, wanting to know why they called him a legend. There must be a reason."

"Okay," she sighed dolefully, as if I had coaxed her into a confession. "I don't know if I can answer that question for you, son. But I guess I can tell you about something that happened a long time ago that seemed kind of strange. Now, I don't know whether this has anything to do with him being called a legend or not. But it did strike me as kind of strange." She grabbed a pack of cigarettes from her purse. "Do you mind if we walk outside," she asked. "I'm gonna need a cigarette to get through this story."

I followed her onto the porch. The July heat was sweltering, the temperature on the thermometer nearly touching 100. I leaned against the porch railing, turning my back to the sun, and watched Momma sit in the porch swing, lighting her cigarette as she did. Her eyes were not as beautiful as they once were. They were full of sadness and pushed into the wrinkled contours of her aging face. There was a time when her eyes were so beautiful that you could hardly stop looking at them, even if you wanted.

"Not long after you were born, you got real sick. Had to put you in the hospital. You couldn't have been more than six or seven weeks old. And you had to stay there for almost two weeks. They never did find out what was wrong with you. But you wouldn't nurse, and you kept running a fever. At one point, I thought you were going to die. You looked so pitiful." She took a drag from her cigarette and noticed the ashtray on the plastic table between the swing and the rocking chair. "Has Katie started smoking again," she asked.

"I don't know," I answered. "She was last night."

Momma just shook her head and took another drag of her cigarette.

"Anyway," she continued, "we were getting real short on money. I mean, I had birthed two children in two years, and I was only working part-time back then. Where your Daddy was working, things were slow. He couldn't get much overtime. So, he called Stiff and asked him if he could help him out some. Well, Stiff really didn't want him to come back to work for him. He knew that your daddy had been saved and was trying to live right. Stiff offered to lend him some money, but your daddy was too proud to borrow money, so he went back to work for Stiff. He promised me it would only be temporary, that he would only do it until we got caught up with our bills."

Momma paused for another draw of her cigarette, tapping the ashes into the ashtray.

"Then, one night, Floyd called the house and asked Daddy to come get Fudge. Said he was getting kind of rowdy down at the bar. Well, I didn't think too much about it because it wasn't unusual for Floyd to call the house and ask your daddy to go get Fudge. But this night, your daddy stayed gone for a long time—probably three or four hours.

"When he got back home, he looked like shit, like somebody had beat the hell out of him. One of his eyes was almost swollen shut. His nose and mouth were bleeding, and his clothes was ripped. I tried to get him to go to the hospital, but he wouldn't go. Just told me to bandage him up. When I asked him what happened, he said Fudge was fighting with some boys down at the bar, and when he tried to break the fight up, they started pounding on him, too.

"I probably would have believed that story had I not seen Fudge the next day. I saw him walking down the sidewalk, and he didn't have a scratch on him. I stopped by Floyd's and asked Floyd if there had been any trouble in the bar the night before. I asked him if what your daddy had told me was true and told him how your daddy had looked when he came home. But Floyd said there had been no trouble at the bar and that if your daddy got into a fight, it would have happened after he left there.

"I didn't know what to think. I asked your daddy about it when I got back home, but he never would tell me what happened. That evening, Stiff came over, and he and your daddy walked out to the garage and stayed out there for a long time talking. I never heard any more about it. After a couple of months, your daddy quit working for Stiff again, just as he promised. That was the end of it.

"I don't know if that has anything to do with him being called the Legend or not, but I have always wondered what happened that night."

Momma finished her cigarette and smashed it against the side of the ashtray.

"You think he and Stiff retaliated against whoever beat the hell out of Daddy?"

"I don't know, son," she mumbled, as if telling the story had worn her down. "I really don't know." She paused for a moment and flicked her lighter a few times, as if she were trying to find the courage to tell more or was regretting she had told me as much as she had.

"Do you want to know what I think? Do you really want to know what I think, and why I think they called your daddy the Legend?"

"Sure," I answered.

"Because he could tell stories better than anybody I ever knew. You have heard some of his stories. You know how interesting they are. I just think it was a combination of things he either did or things that happened to him and the way he told the stories that earned him the nickname Legend."

"Blake kind of felt that way too," I replied. "He took me out to breakfast this morning and said the same thing."

"First, there was the Ricky Swanson story, which is just a bunch of bullshit. Then, there were all the trespassing stories—how he and Gomez always got away, and how, one time, the game warden and a couple of policemen were looking for him, and he was watching it all while eating supper at somebody's house. How he never carried a flashlight into the woods. People started saying John Stiles could see in the dark and how, if John Stiles got into the woods, he would disappear, and nobody would ever find him. And there are even more stories, some that you have probably never heard. Like the time he got stopped for speeding, and they found a bag of marijuana in his car. Well, the pot belonged to Gomez, and even though Gomez admitted it was his, they issued a warrant for your daddy's arrest anyway because he was the owner of the vehicle. And the damn thing was, they didn't arrest your daddy that day. They asked him and Gomez to come to the station the next day, but all they wanted was for them to narc on somebody. You know that wasn't going to happen.

"Three months later, they arrested your daddy at work and handcuffed him right there in front of all the office people. Later, the charges were dismissed, but you can imagine the stories they began telling about him and all the rumors that began."

Momma pulled another cigarette from her pack and lit it.

"Then there was this time he got involved with this married woman. Apparently, he didn't know she was married. He met her at this party or something, and she asked him to come back to her place. Well, according to your daddy, he had not been inside for more than fifteen minutes when a car pulled into the yard and the woman started panicking, shooing your daddy out the back door, telling him that she was married and that was her husband. Well, by the time he got out of the house, her husband had seen him. Her husband gets his pistol and starts chasing your daddy through the woods shooting at him."

"What?" I asked, chuckling a bit. "No, I never heard that one."

Momma laughed.

"Can't you just see that?" she asked, still laughing. "Your Daddy running through the woods at night with some man shooting at him? And it was summertime, so he was wearing shorts, and the briers were scratching his legs terribly. Even worse, his shoes were still back at that married woman's trailer. She was rushing him so much to get out that he forgot to get them. So, he was running through the woods at night barefoot and wearing shorts while some man was shooting at him." She continued to laugh as she took another drag of her cigarette.

"Is that story true?" I asked.

"According to your daddy, it was," she said.

For about a minute, we didn't speak, just continued to laugh. It had been so long since I had heard her laugh, since we had laughed together. I wanted to frame the moment, to preserve it in that part of my mind where the things I never wanted to forget were stored—me and Momma laughing on the porch as if everything was how it used to be when we were a family before Daddy got sick and Momma became disillusioned with life. I didn't want the moment to pass because it reminded me of our yesterdays, and, for some reason, the yesterdays of my life seemed polished with a hard-to-explain innocence and tranquility and happiness that seemed absent in my days and that I did not believe I would ever find in my tomorrows.

Momma finished her cigarette and flicked it into the yard, forgetting about the ashtray on the table, I suppose.

"Do you see what I mean," she asked, reminding me of the purpose of her story. "Your daddy was always telling stories like that, and, when he told them, they were even funnier. He always added a little flavor to them is what he told me. For example, that story I just told you, that story about him running through the woods barefoot and in shorts while that woman's husband was shooting at them. Well, that story is true. But the part about him forgetting his shoes and being barefoot—that part was added to the story by your daddy. He confessed that to me. Everything else was true, he said." She paused for a minute and stared out into the yard, as if maybe she was missing Daddy a little bit, too. "And you know what else I believe?" she asked, turning her attention back to me.

"What?"

"Sometimes, I think your daddy's stories are why everybody is so scared of Stiff. Now, I may be wrong, and I certainly wouldn't want to test my theory, but I have been living in Turkey Creek all of my life. I have never once heard about Stiff physically hurting someone. Besides that Ricky Swanson story, I have never heard of your daddy physically hurting anyone. I know Fudge has been in fights. I have seen some of the people he beat up. And everybody knows that Huck has been in more than his fair share of scraps. But Stiff and your Daddy—I have never heard about them getting into any kind of fight. Of course, somebody beat the hell out of your daddy on that night I told you about. I just wonder sometimes if your daddy didn't make up stories about Stiff to make him sound tougher than he really was, to make him seem more dangerous than he really is."

"Do you really think so?"

"I don't know," she admitted. "But I certainly have wondered that. All those stories about people going missing when they mess with Stiff. How easy would it be for your daddy, as good as he was at telling stories, to read some article in the newspaper about a missing fisherman or a missing hunter in Black Bend Swamp and make up some kind of story to suggest that Stiff may have had something to do with that person's disappearance?"

"I guess I never thought about that," I confessed, puzzled by her startling theory.

Momma stood and walked back into the house, grabbed her purse, and returned.

"Guess I need to be going," she said, giving me a hug. "Yall will probably start getting company before long. And most of those folks ain't going to want to see me here," she said, releasing me and walking down the steps. "Call me if you need anything," she said, as she got back into her car.

I nodded my head and waved, watched her back out into the road, and watched her car disappear. Maybe she was right. Maybe Stiff wasn't that bad. Perhaps I was just thinking the worst. And maybe that is why those newspaper articles were in that box that Katie found. Maybe Daddy used those stories to fabricate yarns about Stiff Jenkins. I certainly wanted to believe Momma's theory. But what I was about to discover was just how real those stories were. Stiff Jenkins was just as dangerous as people said.

ASHLEY

I expected things to be different once Ashley arrived. I really did. I loved her so much, and I hadn't seen her in over a week. I expected that, once I was in her presence, all this shit I was feeling inside would subside.

She pulled into the yard about thirty minutes after Momma left, walked up the steps, gave me a kiss, and sat in the swing beside me. I didn't even want to look at her. Of course, I blamed my apathy on the passing of my father, so she really had no reason to suspect that anything was wrong with us. But I wondered privately if things would ever be the same. How could I not tell her about what I had seen in that box and put a wedding band on her finger? How could I marry the daughter of a man my father had perhaps murdered? I didn't know what to do. Nothing was making sense anymore.

I began thinking about Daddy again, remembering all the times Ashley had been with me at his house. Did he know then? Did he know then that she was the daughter of Cleve Astings, the man he had murdered almost twenty years ago? I was hoping so much that Momma was right, that Daddy had just made these stories up to validate Stiff's reputation. But how would I ever know? I regretted now even beginning this investigation into my father's past, but I had gone too far now. There were questions I needed answered—questions I believed I deserved to have answered. But who knew the answers? Did Fudge? Huck Strawhorne? Or was it only Stiff? I sure as hell wasn't prepared to just walk up to Stiff Jenkins and ask him if my daddy had ever helped him kill someone and expect him to give me a straight answer.

Ashley pressed her head against my shoulder. She smelled so

good. I couldn't remember what kind of perfume she used, only the way it smelled. I remember letting her wear my jacket one night at the county fair and how it smelled the next time I wore it. It smelled just like her, and I never wanted to wash it again because I didn't want to lose that scent.

"Gosh, it's hot out here," she remarked, as she pressed herself tightly against me.

She was wearing a pair of denim shorts, and her legs looked incredibly beautiful, tanned by the summer sun and toned by hour-long jogs she took almost every morning. I started remembering things about us, like our first date, our first kiss, the first time she told me she loved me, and the night I asked her to marry me. I started remembering things like that and wondering if those moments, which had once been such beautiful memories, could sustain their fond nostalgia now that I suspected my father may have been involved in the death of hers. Or would they just be moments I wished I could forget, moments I wished would have never happened? I placed my arm around her and began stroking the long tresses of her hair.

"Can I ask you a question?"

"Sure," she replied.

"How did your Daddy die?"

"Well," she began, "I really don't know, to tell you the truth. Momma always told me that he drowned when I was little. When I got older, she told me they never found his body, just the boat he and a friend had been fishing in. She said she would not have been surprised if someone had killed him and made it look like a drowning because, apparently, he was involved in a lot of things he should not have been. That's what Momma said anyhow. Why do you ask?"

"I was just wondering," I answered. "I knew he died when you were real young. Just didn't know how."

About that time, Pastor Tim pulled into the yard and walked onto the porch. He shook my hand and nodded at Ashley, then sat in the chair closest to the front door. I asked him if he wanted something to drink, and he said he wouldn't mind having a little water. Ashley walked into the house and brought us each a bottle of water. Pastor Tim began telling me the same stories about Daddy that he had been telling me since I had known him—how good of a man he was, how Christ had made such a change in his life, what a great testimony he had, how he went with him once a month to the nursing home in Saylors, how much the people down there thought of him, how much they were going to miss him, and what a great friend he had been to so many people. And, of course, there was the story of the car wreck.

About five years earlier, Pastor Tim had been involved in a serious automobile accident. They didn't expect him to live. He was in a coma for over a month and then had to endure maybe three more months of rehabilitation before he was able to return home. Pastor Tim reminded me of how much Daddy had done for him during that time, how often he visited him, how he always made sure his sons had a ride to ball games and ball practices, and how he often slipped twenty dollars into his wife's hand and paid for their meals when he saw them at Little Perry's. From what Pastor Tim said, you would have thought Daddy was the kindest man that ever lived. Maybe he was. I certainly remember him like that. But what was he like before he got saved, what was he like before he asked Jesus into his heart? That was what I needed to know, and that was something Pastor Tim would never be able to tell me.

"Do you believe in heaven?" I asked Ashley, after Pastor Tim's brief visit.

"I want to," she confessed. "I want to believe there is life after death, some kind of paradise we can live in forever. I can't say I am entirely convinced there is a heaven. I guess I just try not to think about it too much. What about you?"

"I don't know," I said, taking my arm from around her and leaning forward in the swing. "I guess I am about like you. I try not to think about it too much."

"Well, what do you think in your heart right now?" she asked. "Do you think you will ever see your daddy again?"

"I hope so," I answered. "I want to believe I will see him again. But I guess everyone feels that way when a loved one passes." I pulled a can of Copenhagen from my shirt pocket and took a dip. "For some people, believing in Jesus and God and heaven seems so easy. For me, it just ain't ever been easy. Don't know why."

"I passed your daddy's trailer on the way over here. Saw Katie's car down there. Is Carter down there with her?"

"Yeah."

"How is he handling all of this?"

"I am not sure," I answered. "None of us have talked about it too much. Seems like we have always had trouble sharing our feelings with one another in this family."

"I worry about him," she remarked. "He and your daddy had grown so close in the last few years. And he is only fifteen years old. I can't imagine what he is feeling like inside."

The afternoon sun had dipped behind the house by then, and a bit of a breeze began to ripple among the maple trees planted beside the house. I remembered helping Daddy plant them. I couldn't have been more than ten years old. I remember Momma bringing them home. She had bought them from this nursery that was going out of business. I remembered Daddy digging into the dry ground with the post-hole diggers, cursing the damn South Carolina summers and the heat and the way it never rained enough anymore. I remembered the way his muscles flexed every time the post-hole diggers hit the hard ground, and I remember wanting to be as strong as him one day.

Back then, I thought my daddy was the strongest man in the world. I wanted nothing more than to be like him one day. He was my hero, my role model. I guess that was why reading those newspaper clippings was so disheartening. I had this image of Daddy in my mind, this image formed from being around him so much and seeing the way he interacted with others and the loyalty he had toward his friends.

Now, this image of the man I admired so much was being shredded by bits and pieces of small-town folklore. I had to accept the fact that my daddy may have never been the man that I thought he was, the man I wanted to believe he always had been. I didn't even know what I would think about him once I saw him in that coffin.

"I love you, Ashley," I said, turning to look at her.

There were tears in her eyes, and I knew she was hurting just because I was hurting. I knew she was probably wishing there was some way she could better comfort me.

She leaned her head against my shoulder and wrapped her arms around me.

"I love you too, sweetie," she said. "I wish there was something I could say or do to make you feel better. But I know there isn't."

"Well, I am glad you came. You being here makes me feel better."

I wrapped my arm around her and held her close. How was I ever going to be able to marry her? This girl I had fallen in love with? Everything about my life seemed to be unraveling, every vision I had of my future, every dream, every goal. What was I supposed to believe? That Ashley and I would get married, have a big wedding, buy a house, have a couple of kids, and live happily ever after?

Hell, I bet Momma and Daddy had been sitting in this same swing at one time, thinking they loved each other just as much as Ashley and I believed we loved each other. Look at what happened to them. What assurance did I have that the same fate didn't await us? That one day, years from now, we would be sitting down with lawyers discussing the distribution of our assets and setting up visitation guidelines. I wanted to believe our love would last forever, but I wasn't sure anymore. I was beginning to think that love died just like people died, that love deserved a tombstone also, with dates separated by a dash: 1993–2011, the love between John Stiles and Sharon Mills.

What would be the year on the other side of the dash for the love between Ashley and me? 2025? 2035? When would she stop loving me? When would I stop loving her? Was there even such a thing as a happy marriage? Did anything last forever? I thought about all of that as I held my fiancée in my arms. And the July heat smothered us. I thought about just telling her right then what I had discovered, just to see what her reaction would be. I wondered if our love for each other could absorb such tragic news.

But I wasn't ready yet. In two days, I would be burying the man I called Daddy. All this other shit—well, it would just have to wait.

THE ARGUMENT

It was nearly dark when Cody arrived, lumbering up the steps in a sleeveless shirt with a Braves ballcap fitted backward on his brow, carrying a quart of strawberry-flavored moonshine in his hand. By then, all the church members had left, and we didn't expect anyone else would come for a visit.

The kitchen was full of casseroles and dishes of ham and pimento cheese sandwiches cut into halves and more damn pies than we could eat in a year. I never understood the abundance of food for families that had just lost a loved one. Was food supposed to make us feel better? Was eating one of those pecan pies supposed to liberate me from the sorrow of my father's death, from the memory of watching him die, from the haunting sounds of his final breaths? I didn't feel like eating anything, to tell you the truth. I didn't feel like doing much at all.

"I stole this from Daddy's stash," Cody said, handing me the moonshine as he crossed the porch and settled into the metal glider. "Your favorite flavor—strawberry."

I twisted the top off the mason jar and took a sip, grimacing as I swallowed.

"Been a long time," I said, as I felt the warmness of the liquor passing through my glands.

I twisted the top back on and set the jar of moonshine on the plastic table that separated the porch's two rocking chairs, remembering those days when Daddy ran shine for Stiff and how there would be cases of shine stacked up on the shelves in the laundry room. I remember hearing him load them at night sometimes when I was in my bedroom, supposed to be asleep. I missed that and had been missing it for a long time. Not just the sound of him loading the moonshine, but the sounds he made while he was in the house, the sounds that assured me he was there, that he would be there when I woke in the morning or when I got home from school. The home had not been the same since he left. It was too quiet and sullen, like even the walls and the ceilings knew something was missing, knew there was an absence not yet filled, an absence that never would be filled.

"Where is everybody?" asked Cody.

"Katie and Ashley are inside looking at some movie. Guess Carter is in there with them," I replied. "Do you want anything to eat? We have like a hundred sandwiches in there and any kind of damn pie you can think of."

"No thanks," Cody answered. "I ate some meatloaf before I came."

About that time, Carter walked onto the porch. He was tall, about a half inch taller than me, and only fifteen. I guess I already knew that, but standing on the porch that night, I realized, perhaps more graphically than ever, that he wasn't a kid anymore, that none of us were, that we were all being shoved into adulthood by moments that moved faster than we wanted them to move. I felt ashamed because I did not know how to comfort my little brother, like that was some skill I should have acquired during my maturation. Since Daddy had passed, Carter and I had barely spoken. Usually, if Carter was in the presence of Cody and me, we would be giving him hell, just like Daddy and Stiff used to give us hell when we were young. On the porch that night, however, there was just an awkward silence, none of us knowing what to say, none of us knowing what was right to say. I picked up the moonshine and placed it in my lap, preparing myself to take another sip.

"Sorry about your daddy, Carter," Cody finally said to terminate the silence.

"Thanks," Carter answered reverently.

"He was a damn good man," Cody added. "Done a lot for folks in this town. Done a lot for me."

His words made me remember when he and I were Carter's age, maybe even a little younger, and Stiff was out of town. Cody would spend the night with us during deer season sometimes. I remember riding to the hunt club in Daddy's old truck, Cody sitting in the middle, straddling that damn gear shift. I remembered how Daddy would take us to Little Perry's after we got through hunting, how Cody always ordered pancakes, and how just about everybody who walked into the restaurant would walk over and speak to Daddy. I remembered how grown up I felt sitting there beside him, dressed in my camouflage apparel, everybody knowing I had been hunting. I remembered how I felt as if I were a man, or, at least, on the way to becoming one.

Sometimes, I think I felt more like a man then than I did now. Sitting on the porch that night, I felt trapped somewhere between adolescence and manhood, as if there was this part of me that wanted to be a little boy again, that did not want to evolve into a mature adult with responsibilities and a fiancee, and that was warring with this other part of me that knew I had to become a man, the kind of man my daddy had been, the kind of man that Stiff was, or, at least, the kind of men I thought they had been. And that I needed to become this man quickly, not for me and not for Ashley, but for Carter. I needed to be his role model now, I needed to set an example for him now. I didn't know if I was ready for that. I was scared I would fail. I was scared I would disappoint him and Daddy and Stiff and all the other men around Turkey Creek who expected Luke Stiles to be as good of a man as his father had been.

"Can I get a dip," Carter asked, rousing me from the mnemonic stupor into which I had drifted.

"Sure," I answered, nodding to the can of Copenhagen that was on the porch table. He thumped the can a few times, then opened it and fingered a wad of tobacco into his jaw. Then, he set the can back on the table and leaned against the porch railing, staring down into what could be seen of Turkey Creek, South Carolina. The Little League all-star team was still practicing on one of the fields down there, practicing beneath those giant lights that cast a haze across the night sky. They had just won their region and were preparing to go to the state playoffs the following week. I missed those days, and I guess Carter did too, judging by the way his gaze seemed affixed to that field.

"Is there anybody worth a damn on that team down there?" I asked.

Carter just shrugged his shoulders, never allowing his eyes to veer from the field where he had played so many games, where Cody and I had played so many games.

"Do you know Hot Dog?" Cody asked, leaning forward a bit in the glider and glancing toward the field, although it was not visible from where he was sitting.

"Damn it, Cody," I said, taking another sip of shine. "How many times have I told you about that?"

"About what?"

"About asking stupid questions," I replied. "Of course, I know Hot Dog. We live in Turkey Creek, South Carolina. You can damn near see the whole town from our front porch. I know everybody in this town, just as you do."

Carter chuckled a bit at my response. I think it was the first time he had smiled since Daddy had passed.

"Well, anyway," Cody continued, "his boy is pretty good. Best pitcher they have. And he can knock the piss out of a ball."

"Have you seen him play, Carter?" I asked, wanting him to become a part of the conversation, wanting him to know I respected his evaluation of ball players now, wanting to make him feel the way I used to feel on those autumn Saturday mornings sitting beside Daddy in a booth at Little Perry's.

"Yeah," he responded softly, spitting a flume of tobacco juice into the front yard. "He can get it into the low seventies."

"Do you think they have a chance in the state playoffs?" I asked.

Carter shook his head, and, for the first time, took his eyes off the field. He turned toward Cody and me and leaned against the paint-chipped porch post.

"I don't think anybody else can pitch good enough to win a game in the state playoffs."

"Me neither," Cody agreed. "Nick Wilson's boy ain't bad, but, after him, you just looking for someone who can throw strikes."

"Who is coaching them?" I asked.

"Jim Wilson," Cody replied. "His boy plays center field all the time. He ain't a bad ball player, but he ain't no superstar either as Jim thinks he is."

"Why ain't Hot Dog out there coaching?"

"Hell, Hot Dog got arrested about a month ago for DUI. And he had a damn bag of weed in the car, too. He's been sitting in the county jail since then. His old lady said she is tired of his ass, ain't bailing him out anymore. This is about the third or fourth time he has got a DUI. I can't believe you didn't know about that. You suppose to know everything about this town. Ain't that what he just said a little while ago, Carter? Hell, I live in Greenville and know more about the damn town than you do."

We all three laughed at Cody's response. It was one of those moments in life that you wanted to preserve, that you wish you could take a photograph of and put it in a frame just to remind you every now and again that life wasn't always sad or unfair, that there were some moments sprinkled into your life that were good and enjoyable and made you believe that happiness and peace did exist and that experiencing those moments before you die was possible. I wondered what Daddy's moments were, what moments in his life he would have preserved in a photograph, what moments in his life he thought about before he died—the moments he regretted, or the moments when he was happiest.

Then, the front door opened. Katie appeared, holding the cordless house phone.

"Floyd just called," she announced.

I could tell she was nervous, the way she was shaking, and I knew there was something she needed to tell me, something she probably didn't want to have to tell me.

"What's the matter?" I asked.

"Damn Becky Strawhorne," she snorted angrily. "I guess her and Momma are fussing at each other down there at the bar, about to get into a fight. Floyd asked if you could come down there and try to calm Momma down."

"Damn," I said, as I rose from my seat. "Why did Momma have to go down there tonight?" I grabbed my can of Copenhagen and pressed it into my back pocket. "Come on, Cody," I said. "Let's go see what is going on down there."

"Alright," he agreed, standing and stretching, then following me down the steps.

We got into his truck, since it was the only vehicle that could be moved out of the drive without any rearrangement of other vehicles, and drove to the bar.

Becky Strawhorne was Huck's wife. She and my mother had been involved in several verbal altercations since my parents had split up. She didn't like the fact that Mom had left Daddy after he became unable to work. And she didn't mind sharing that opinion with others.

When we walked into the bar, Huck had Becky pinned into a

booth, and Fudge and some other guy I did not recognize were restraining Momma at the jukebox. But the two were still yelling at each other, hurling threats and obscenities at one another across the smoke-filled bar. Huck finally convinced Becky to leave, and the two exited the bar together, Momma still cursing even after the heavy wood door had closed. I walked over to the jukebox and asked Momma what happened.

"You know damn well what happened," she snapped. "All I wanted to do was come in here and have a few drinks, maybe shoot a little pool. Then, Becky came in with Huck and started running her mouth. That damn bitch. She needs to learn to mind her own damn business."

I could tell that Momma was intoxicated. I grabbed hold of her arm and led her away from the jukebox. We leaned against the bar. The man I did not recognize followed, and, by this time, I assumed he was Momma's boyfriend, the one she had been living with in Georgia. I had only met him once or twice, but his hair was longer and stragglier than I remembered. He asked Momma if she was ready to leave, and she nodded, gulping down what remained of her beer.

"I am tired of everybody in this damn town acting like your daddy was some kind of damn saint," she blurted angrily as she crushed her empty can onto the wooden countertop of the bar. "Some kind of fucking martyr." She was speaking loudly to ensure that the few people left in the bar were certain to hear her words.

"Calm down, Momma," I said, placing my arms on her shoulder.

"Well, it's the damn truth," she continued. "Nobody in this town knows what it was like to live with him," she added. "Tell them, Fudge," she yelled. "Do you want to know why your daddy was a fucking legend?" she asked me in a quieter voice. "Ask Fudge to tell you about Ginger Heath. Ask Stiff to tell you about her. Bet you ain't never heard about her, have you? They can tell you about all the good things your Daddy did, but they ain't going to never tell you about all the shit he put me through, all the shit he did, and I stood beside him all the way."

"Come on baby," her boyfriend said, grabbing hold of her hand. "Let's get out of here," he suggested, prodding her to stand. "Let's go home."

She followed him to the door without resistance, and I didn't know what to do. I didn't know whether to tell her goodbye, give her a hug, or sit silently as she exited the bar. Cody was standing behind me looking dumbfounded. He hadn't said a word since we had entered the bar. Guess he was tired of dealing with all of Turkey Creek's bullshit, probably ready to get back to Greenville, a city where people didn't have their nose in your business all the time. My eyes followed Momma to the door, and I could feel the sultry heat of the summer evening waft into the bar when her boyfriend opened it. Then, she turned around. I could tell she was crying. She motioned for me to come to her, so I did. She grabbed me and wrapped her arms around my neck.

"I'm sorry," she said. "I shouldn't have said all those mean things about your daddy. He was a good man. He loved you, Katie, and Carter. I have never known a man to love his kids more than he did. And I know this is hard on you all. You call me if you need anything."

She released me as she walked out of the door and into the parking lot with her boyfriend. I watched them get into a short bed Ford pickup truck and back into the street as the heavy wooden door slowly closed. Things were never going to be the same again. Relationships had crumbled, and friendships had dissolved. I remember looking around at the people in the bar. I remember looking at their faces, the way nobody wanted to look at me, not even Floyd, not even Fudge. It was like all the happiness that had ever been a part of my life and all the optimism I had about my future had been drained out of me. Whatever I thought my life was going to be like or whatever the people in that bar, at one time, thought my life was going to be like didn't matter anymore.

I was twelve years old once, standing on the pitcher's mound, throwing a ball so damn hard that nobody around here could hit it. Everybody patted me on the back after the games and told me how good I was. Hell, I had even out-of-town umpires speak to me after the game and tell me how impressed they were with my pitching abilities. I remember one.

We were playing a weekend tournament in Spartanburg. He approached me after the game and told me he had never seen a twelve-year-old pitcher that could get so much break out of his pitches. He patted me on the shoulder and told me he would be reading about me in the papers one day. So much for that shit. All I was now was a story in a small town, a college dropout, and a baseball has-been with a dead father I was beginning to feel I never knew and a mother who got into bar room brawls.

Cody and I walked outside and got into his truck. The Little League all-stars had gone home by then. There were only a couple of parents lingering in the parking lot. The night was quiet, and the town and all its decadent buildings swaddled me in some kind of false security, as if Turkey Creek was a town where there was only tranquility and peace, some kind of All-American town where all the kids were happy and there were no such things as affairs and drugs and people that died too early and dreams that did not come true. I put a pinch of Copenhagen into my mouth, then offered the can to Cody.

"I gotta ask you a question, Cody," I said, settling the pinch of tobacco into my jaw.

"What is it?" he asked.

"What do you think about our fathers? I mean, you know what people say about your old man, how people get to missing when they mess with him and shit like that. And you know how people were always calling my dad a legend. I just wonder where all that shit comes from. I never saw my daddy do anything legendary, and your old man—hell, I can't imagine why anyone would ever be scared of him. He has always been so nice to me and my family and a lot of other people in this town."

"I don't know," Cody sighed. "Guess I just don't think about it too much."

"Katie found this box underneath Daddy's bed. She showed it to me last night. Most of it was just full of knickknacks and shit—you know, pictures we colored for him when we were kids, some home run balls, some old photographs. But, at the bottom of the box, there were some newspaper clippings about people who were missing, people from out of town, people I had never heard of before. Just seemed kind of strange."

"That does seem strange," he agreed, handing me back the can of Copenhagen. "But my daddy don't talk to me about shit like that. And I guess I just ain't ever felt the need to ask him." He pushed the keys into the ignition, and I closed my door. "Why is that bothering you so much now?" he asked.

"I don't really know," I answered softly. "Just thought Daddy and I were so close, thought I knew all there was to know about him. And now it seems as if there was this part of him I never even knew at all."

"I wouldn't think on it too much," Cody suggested, cranking the truck, the gears spinning as the engine started. "Your Daddy was one of the best men I ever met. Hell, I still remember all those times he took us hunting and fishing and camping. He was the kind of man you wanted to grow up and be like. That is the way I remember him. Whatever he did in the past, or whatever him and my Daddy did in the past ain't going to change that."

He patted me on the shoulder, as he began to back out of the parking lot.

"I can't imagine what you are going through right now, Luke.

And I probably ain't too damn good of a counselor. But I wouldn't let a bunch of small-town rumors change the way you remember your dad because you don't ever know whether those rumors are true or not, and you probably never will know. But I do know this—I saw the way your daddy was when he was around you. I know he loved you. I know he was real proud of you, a lot more than he probably ever let you know."

"What about Ginger Heath?" I asked. "Have you ever heard of her?"

"Never even heard that name."

"I wonder why my mom would want me to ask your daddy about her?"

"I don't know," he replied, turning onto the empty highway. "Do you want me to ask him who she is?"

"I don't guess so," I said. "I'll go home and think on it for a while. If I decide to ask him, I will do it myself."

"Alright, just let me know what you find out."

"Are you going to stick around a while and help me finish off that moonshine?"

"I don't reckon so," he answered, pointing up the hill to my house. There was a police car pulled into my driveway. "Looks like you got company."

"I wonder what in the hell he is doing there."

"I don't know," Cody replied. "But I don't think we will be drinking any more moonshine tonight." He stopped at the edge of the road, and I exited the truck. "I will give you a call tomorrow," I said, as I slammed the door.

I stood there in the road for a minute. I stood there until the rumble of Cody's 350 engine waned to inaudibility. In the sky, I noticed flashes of heat lightning and clouds curling around a half-moon. There was a part of me that did not want to walk inside. There was a part of me that knew everything would change once I did.

JONAS WANNAMAKER

Inside the house, sitting at the kitchen table, drinking a cup of coffee, and talking with Katie, Ashley, and Carter was Jonas Wannamaker, the chief of police in Turkey Creek, South Carolina. Didn't seem like that difficult of a job to me being the chief of police in such a small town. Hell, there were only three police officers besides him on the force, and, truth be known, we probably didn't even need that many. In fact, the town council had suggested a few times that the number of police be reduced to two, but I guess the old-timers in town had gotten accustomed to four being on the force. So, even though the population had dwindled to less than a thousand, they always voted to keep it at four paid policemen.

Chief Wannamaker had only been chief for a few months. He was awarded the position at the first of the year when Ben Turner, who had been the chief of police for more than twenty years, dropped dead from a massive heart attack on the day after Christmas, I didn't know that much about Chief Wannamaker, other than he had grown up in Turkey Creek, that he was about the same age as Daddy and Stiff and Fudge, and that they grew up playing ball together.

Sometime after graduating high school, Jonas attended the police academy and joined the police force in Charleston. He returned to Turkey Creek about a year ago to help tend to his widowed mother, whose health was declining. He was married and had two elementary-aged daughters. They lived in a small house on Lampass Lane and attended the United Methodist church. I had seen him at some of the softball games but never had introduced myself to him.

When I entered the room, he stood from the table and stuck out his hand, a big fake smile on his face.

"Hey Luke," he said, as I extended my hand. "My name is Jonas Wannamaker," he announced. "I don't think we have ever officially met, but I have heard a lot about you."

"It's nice to meet you," I replied politely, placing my plastic bottle spittoon on the kitchen counter.

"I'm sorry about your father," he added. "I knew him all my life. He was a good man. Don't make many like him anymore."

"Thanks," I said, leaning against the counter.

"Did y'all get things straight down at Floyd's?" he asked with a wink.

"Yes, sir," I answered. "Momma and Becky Strawhorne were getting a little rowdy. We finally talked Momma into leaving."

"Do you want anything to eat?" Katie asked, munching on a pimento cheese sandwich herself.

"Sure," I said. "I'll take one of those sandwiches."

Katie handed me a sandwich, and I began to eat it while Chief Wannamaker wandered away from the table and angled toward me. He dumped what was left of his coffee into the sink, then placed the cup into the dish strainer.

"Did I scare Cody off?" he asked, almost chuckling as he did.

"I guess so," I answered, chewing on the sandwich and shrugging my shoulders.

"Well, maybe that is a good thing," he stated. "I wanted to talk with you in private anyway. Do you mind stepping outside with me for a minute?"

"No, sir," I replied, stuffing the last of my sandwich into my mouth, as I followed the chief through the screen door.

"Thanks again for the coffee, ladies," he said before letting go of the door. "And, again, I am truly sorry for your loss. If you need anything, let me know."

"We will," Katie answered. The screen door closed, and it was just me and Chief Wannamaker alone on the porch—us and the dim lights of the town of Turkey Creek, where most people were asleep by now. I felt sort of uncomfortable being around him and kept wondering why he wanted to talk to me in private. He had not spoken since we left the house—just kept looking around as if he was in search of something in particular.

"I tell you what," he finally said. "Why don't we go sit in the squad car?" he suggested.

"Am I in some kind of trouble?" I asked, following him down the steps.

"Oh no," he replied. "Just don't want anybody listening to our conversation," he explained.

I followed him down the steps and got into the passenger side without closing the door behind me.

"Do you mind if I take a dip?" I asked.

"No," he assured me, choosing to leave his door open also, the July heat still heavy in the night air. "Not at all."

There was some chattering on the police radio, so he adjusted the volume and stuffed a piece of peppermint candy into his mouth. I could tell he was nervous by the way he was shifting around in his seat. I looked down into the town of Turkey Creek as I fingered a pinch of tobacco into my mouth. The town seemed docile in the absence of activity and light, like nothing bad could ever happen there, like the town, in its evening tranquility, was quarantined against things like death and disease and divorce.

"Look," the chief finally began, "I know this may not be the best time to ask you these questions. I know you just lost your daddy.

I know the last few years have been tough on you and your family, so I don't want you to feel any pressure to answer these questions tonight or tomorrow or anytime soon. You take time to mourn the loss of your father and take care of your brother and sister. I just want to ask you a few questions, offer you a few of my theories, and maybe give you a few things to chew on for a little while. Hopefully, you might be able to help me out one day and help me answer some of these questions."

"Like what?" I asked, staring up at the light spurting from the kitchen.

I wanted to be in there with Ashley, holding her in my arms. I was tired of all these revelations about my father, now that he was dead. I just wanted to watch a little television and maybe drink a little more moonshine. I didn't want to be bothered by anyone. Seemed like since the moment my father took his last breath, I had not had any rest. I sure as hell didn't feel like sitting in Chief Wannamaker's squad car and talking to him.

"Have you ever heard the names Anderson Dill and Cleveland Astings?" he asked.

I remembered those newspaper clippings Katie had shown to me. I wondered if she had shown them to Chief Wannamaker. I couldn't imagine why she would have. She wouldn't have wanted anyone to make Carter believe his father may have been a murderer, so I took my chances and lied to him and told him I had never heard the names.

"Well," he said, "been a long time ago, but those two old boys went missing a while back. They were from Fulton, Georgia— a little old town right across the Savannah River. They found their boat floating in Lake Russell a couple of days later, but there was no sign of them. The rumor was that they had some kind of gripe with Stiff about something. Anyway, there were several people who believed Stiff had something to do with their disappearances."

"What does that have to do with me?" I asked.

"Well," he continued. "Really, it ain't got nothing to do with you. I just know that your Daddy and Stiff were real good friends. And I know that Stiff has done a lot for your family. But I do think you have heard of the name Cleveland Astings before, I believe that is his daughter sitting in there at the kitchen table, and I believe she is wearing a ring on her finger that you gave to her."

"Alright," I admitted. "I know that is her father, but he died when she was like a year old. She doesn't remember him, she doesn't even have his last name. What do you want me to do? Walk in there and tell her that my father's best friend, and maybe my own father is responsible for the disappearance of her own biological father?"

"No, son," he answered softly, shaking his head. "I don't want you to do anything like that. And, to tell you the truth, I don't think your Daddy had anything to do with the disappearance of those two men, but I do think Stiff did. And I do think your father may have had some knowledge of what happened."

"This is bullshit," I growled. "In two days, I will be burying my father, and now you are over at my house, damn near eleven o'clock, wanting me to implicate him in some twenty-year old case that has never been solved." I exited the patrol car and slammed the door. A breeze was twisting through the July night, like a thunderstorm was near. The wind chimes on the front began to heckle, a cacaphonous din slapping against the evening tranquility. I sat down on a front porch step, slapped at a couple of mosquitoes. Chief Wannamaker walked up to me, fanning at the mosquitoes and moths with his cowboy hat as he slowly approached.

"I want you to take a look at this," he said, offering me an envelope. Reluctantly, I opened it and pulled out a 4x6 photograph. I had seen the photograph before – the 1982 State Champions, Turkey Creek Panthers. My father was in the picture, so were Stiff and Fudge and, I suppose, Jonas Wannamaker.

"I've seen it before," I replied, handing it back to him quickly, after just a glance.

"Those were good times, Luke," he said, stuffing the photograph back into the envelope. "I enjoyed playing ball with your father and Stiff and all those boys. We were friends, good friends. And I know how much Stiff has done for you and your family. Hell, he has helped me out from time to time. So I can sort of overlook that Stiff has a still somewhere down there on his farm. I can even overlook the fact that he might be involved in some illegal gambling. But I cannot turn a blind eye to murder, Luke. I just can't do that." He stopped talking for a minute, combed his fingers through what little hair he had left. The dull, creamy light of the porch lights dripped across the porch steps, the breeze of the approaching storm cool against my face.

"So what do you want me to do," I asked.

"I don't want you to do anything right now," he insisted. "I just want you to bury your father, take care of your family," he said, placing his hand upon my shoulder. "Then, maybe we can talk a little more about it when you get ready." I nodded my head, hoping that he would interpret the gesture as an agreement that I would cooperate with him and just leave. That was all I wanted, for him to be out of the yard, for him to be out of my life.

"Well," he began, realizing that I was not in the mood for further discussion. "Guess I will be leaving now. See you around, Luke. And, again, I am sorry about your father."

I sat there silently, staring at the ground, as I listened to him get into his car and back out the driveway. Then, I heard the screen door open. "What was that all about," Katie asked, as she stepped onto the porch. She walked down the steps and sat beside me, placing her arm around me. Then, for the first time since my father had passed, I cried. I cried like I didn't think I ever would again. I cried like Katie and Carter had cried in that hospital room where he died. I cried because I realized how much I loved him and how much I would miss him, I cried because I would be seeing the lifeless shell of his spirit inside of a coffin tomorrow night. I cried because I wanted to believe that my father was a good man and now, I didn't know if I would ever believe that again. My world had changed, and I didn't like it anymore. I didn't like the idea of all the years to come, all the years I would have to live without Daddy.

"What did he say to you," Katie asked, as I attempted to control the banter of my sobs. I shriveled from her arms and wiped my nose with the sleeve of my shirt.

"Did you tell him anything about what you found underneath the bed," I asked, still sniffling.

"No," she answered. "What makes you think I would do that?"

"Because he asked about those two people that went missing in Georgia," I replied.

"What did he ask?"

"Just said that there were rumors that Stiff might have had something to do with their disappearance."

"Well, I never said anything to him about them."

"This whole thing is turning into a big damn mess," I said. I wanted to tell her about Cleve Astings, how he was Ashley's father, but I didn't know where Ashley was exactly or if she was eavesdropping on our conversation, so I just sat there quietly, as my sister massaged my back and flashes of lightning from an imminent thunderstorm illuminated the evening sky.

"It's going to be alright, Luke," she assured me. "Everything is going to be alright." But she didn't know the secrets I knew and she had no way of predicting the troubles that would fall upon our family in the following days. She just sat there and held me, like the passage of time would ease the sadness we now felt, would ease the pain of life without Daddy, not knowing what I already knew, that nothing would ever be the same again, that the passing of our father was only the beginning of our troubles.

THE BARN

Ginger Heath. I had not been able to get her name off my mind since Momma mentioned it during her rant at the bar. All that shit Wannamaker had come here and talked to me about—well, I cannot say I had not thought about it all, but I certainly had not thought about it as much as I had that name Ginger Heath. I wondered who the hell she was.

I had lived in Turkey Creek my whole life, but I had never heard of Ginger Heath. Hell, I had never heard of anybody with the last name Heath. I crawled out of the bed where I had slept for maybe a couple of hours, where Ashley was still sleeping, and determined my mission for the day: finding out who Ginger Heath was.

When I walked out to my truck, the sun had not risen, but you could tell it would be up soon, the way the sky was waning gray and the mists were rising from the asphalt streets still damp from the passing of an overnight thunderstorm, the transient coolness masking the imminent heat of the summer day. The soil would be crackling by noon, and the town of Turkey Creek, cloaked in the perpetual haze of heat that badgered it almost every day during the long months of summer, settled in between the old empty buildings and paint-chipped mill houses and suffocated every breath you tried to take.

I remember how Daddy used to say you only had a brief respite from the heat during the South Carolina summers, a transient and fragile few moments when you could actually enjoy being outside—before the sun rose, before the bugs started pestering you, before the fragrance of an evening thunderstorm faded. But those moments were so beautiful, Daddy said, that if you inhaled each of them, you would not mind the heat that would come because you knew the next dawn would be just as beautiful. He was always saying shit like that. I am guessing it was supposed to be some kind of metaphor for life.

But I didn't understand a lot of what Daddy said. I couldn't think that deep, I reckon. Even if I could, I probably would have chosen not to. I never could see the purpose of psychoanalyzing people or circumstances or looking for metaphors for life in the damn sky. But maybe Daddy could not help it; maybe Daddy didn't want to have the thoughts he had; maybe he didn't want to be an author or a poet or a songwriter. Maybe he wished he could have been talented at fixing cars or building houses or something like that. Maybe what we all thought was his talent was instead his curse.

I remember hearing Momma once asking Daddy why he couldn't ever write about anything happy or comical. Daddy said he didn't know how to write about things like that, said all the characters in his head were dark and arcane and that he knew more about sadness and failure than he did about happiness and success. He said he didn't know how to write happily ever after stories or stories where everybody's dreams come true.

So, those three novels that he wrote, those three manuscripts shoved beneath his bed, were morose and fatalistic novels, and the main characters were always fucked up in the head somehow. At least, that is what people told me. I never had read one of them. Not even one. But Daddy made sure I had one. In fact, he made sure all his children did.

Katie was the only one I knew who had read all three of them. The damn words were too hard for me to figure out. I could not even believe Daddy knew that many words. When he was around Stiff and Fudge, he talked just like they did—improper English and all. Still, I felt guilty for not reading them, or at least trying to read them. Daddy would have probably been thrilled if I did. But he never asked me if I had or not. Guess he already knew the answer.

I started my truck and backed, as quietly as I could, out of the driveway. Then, I headed towards Stiff's farm, which was about five miles outside of town. I knew he would be up at this early hour, even if he didn't have the day off. He always was. He would be checking on the cows or mending a fence or tinkling with the motor on that damn Allis-Chalmers tractor that he loved so much. He told me that his great-grandfather bought that tractor, and that tractor was the first one to ever till the land on the farm.

Hell, it was hardly ever running. It just stayed there in the back of the barn—like something that would never be used again, like something that never could be used again, like something dead, waiting to be buried. Just like the body of my deceased father sitting in that funeral home, closed up in that damn coffin with its pretty cloth material and inscribed Bible verses, ready to return back to the dust of the earth, ready to fill his spot in the dirt under which we would all lay one day.

I needed gas in the truck, so I filled my tank up and got a soda at the only gas station in town. Some of the old timers were already there, standing around Jake Barrow's pickup truck, smoking cigarettes, sipping bland gas station coffee from Styrofoam cups they paid a quarter to refill, and bickering about the weather and the price of gas and hay and cattle.

A couple of them spoke to me as I passed. One or two even offered condolences for the death of my father, reminding me again how great of a man he had been. I just said a quick thank you as I passed them. I didn't really feel like talking to anyone. Joe Reynolds, the owner of the gas station, didn't even have the kind of tanks that would allow you to pay with a debit card, but he turned the pump on whenever he knew who you were.

When I walked inside the store, I noticed that Joe's granddaughter was working behind the counter. She could not have been more than sixteen years old. I remembered her being in elementary school, playing with barbie dolls while

Mr. Reynolds tended to his customers. Now, she was filled out and pretty. And she would probably spend the rest of her life in Turkey Creek, South Carolina, raising kids, smelling cow manure, and managing this gas station that her grandfather would likely leave to her when he died since she was his only grandchild. I wondered if she ever had any dreams, or would she be satisfied with just this—Turkey Creek and the long summers and old timers sitting on benches and wood pallets outside the store, flirting with her when she walked outside to smoke a cigarette.

We exchanged pleasantries as I paid for the gas, a soda, and a can of dip. Then, I left the store and walked past the old timers again, thinking about time again and how swiftly it seemed to pass, how the people we knew as kids would evolve into adults a lot quicker than expected. I thought about how swift my demise had been. I thought about how quick my father's demise had been. I thought about all of that as the still-invisible sun began to bruise the edges of the eastern sky. On the radio, they were playing songs, and the damn radio morning disc jockeys were telling awful jokes and laughing like the world was a happy place, a good place to be. Yet, here I was riding down the backroads of Lincoln County, knowing my father would never breathe again, never see another sunrise. I couldn't think of any reason to be happy.

I pulled into Stiff's yard just as the first glimpse of the sun peeked above the horizon, spawning the first colors of the day. I didn't go inside or knock on the door. I just walked around behind the house and began looking for him. And, sure enough, there he was. Just where I thought he would be, straddled across the motor of that Allis-Chalmers, trying to get it to run.

"You ain't give up on that thing yet?" I asked, as I entered the barn.

"Hell no," he said. "I'll have it running before long."

"You been saying that for years," I replied.

He chuckled a bit as he scrambled through his toolbox.

"What brings you up here so early," he asked.

"Just couldn't sleep."

"Heard you had a visitor last night."

"Yeah," I answered, not really certain how much information to reveal about my conversation with the chief of police.

"What did he have to say?" he asked. "Make me sound like I am Al Capone?"

"Yeah, kind of," I replied.

"Look," Stiff said as he continued to work on the motor. "I ain't got nothing against Wannamaker," he said, twisting the socket driver as he spoke. "We went to high school together and played ball together. But I just think he always wanted more attention than he received. Like in baseball. He was a decent player, but we had a lot of good players. He never got to start. Think that bothered him a lot. And I think it still does to this day. And now he is trying to fill the shoes of Chief Turner. You know how much respect everybody had for him. And I think Wannamaker wants that same respect. I think he wants to do something incredible or spectacular that will bring him some attention, something that will bring him praise or recognition. And maybe he thinks that busting me for making moonshine or selling moonshine will bring him that kind of recognition. I don't know. That's just what I think."

"Do you think he will try?"

"I hope not," he answered, wiping his grease-blackened hands on a rag, then tossing the rag into a steel drum barrel leaned against the back wall of the barn.

I moved closer to the tractor. Morning light was seeping into the barn from the windows and the opened doors and spaces between the boards. You could feel the heat already, the humid air pressing against you. I leaned against the flat front tire and took a sip of soda.

"Do you know who Ginger Heath is?" I asked. Stiff sighed and shook his head.

"Where in the hell did you hear that name?" he asked, obviously frustrated.

"Last night at Floyd's. Momma and Becky Strawhorne got into a shouting match, and Momma said she was tired of people acting like Daddy was some kind of martyr. She said I should ask you who Ginger Heath was."

"Damn," he cursed. "I wish she wouldn't have mentioned her to you. You don't need to hear about that. Not now."

He paused for a moment and placed a pinch of Copenhagen into his mouth.

"But I guess since you here in my barn before sunrise, you want to know."

He jumped off the tractor and wiped his sweat-beaded brow with the sleeve of his shirt. The striated, dust-particled rays of sunshine brushed against the angled contours of his whiskered brow. He once seemed so young to me. Now, in the latent bows of morning light, his age seemed palpable and ostentatious—the dark wrinkles that encompassed his squinted eyes, his arms and hands riddled with bruises and scars that would never heal. He leaned against the back tire of the tractor, pressing himself into the receding shadows of the barn. And I could tell that he was reluctant to tell the story he was about to tell.

"Ginger Heath was your daddy's first serious girlfriend," he began slowly, spitting a few plumes of tobacco juice against the splintered and weather-bowed boards of the decrepit barn. "They started dating his senior year in high school. She was from some little town in Georgia, Clarkesville or something like that, and she was pretty. And your daddy was in love with her. But that girl was nothing but trouble. Drank a lot and partied a lot. Everybody always said she was messing around with other guys. I never knew any of that for certain, but I don't think it would have mattered anyway. Your Daddy was so much in love with her that I don't think he would have believed me.

"But, after about a year or so, something happened, I can't exactly remember what, and they broke up. A few years later, your daddy learned that Ginger had a baby about six months after they stopped dating. Found out it was his. Your Momma and him had only been married about a year or so, I guess, and it caused a little trouble for them. Your daddy wanted to meet the little girl, but your momma didn't think he should."

"Did he ever meet her?" I asked.

"Yeah," Stiff answered reluctantly, not looking at me, just staring at the dirt floor of the barn, as if he were trying to remember himself the details of the story. "We rode over there one Saturday afternoon and got to meet her." He removed his hat and scratched at his thinning hair. "But," he began slowly, fitting his greasy baseball cap back onto his head, "I don't really know how many times he saw her after that. I do know he thought about her a lot."

"Does she still live in Georgia?" I asked.

"Now that's a question I can't answer, Luke. Been many years since I seen her. Don't know where she lives. Last I heard, she married some guy from Savannah and moved down there. But I don't know for sure where she lives now."

I finished drinking my soda, waiting to see if Stiff would ever reveal any more information. But he never did. He turned and stared out of one of the barn's windows, his eyes squinting against the glare of morning light.

"Gonna be hot as hell today," he said. "I need to go fix a section of fence in that back pasture before it gets too hot. Tree fell on it during that last storm. Do you want to go with me?"

"No," I replied, chunking my empty soda bottle into the steel barrel they used for a waste bin. "I guess I better get back to the house. Got a lot to do today."

"Yep," Stiff agreed. "Going to be a busy day for you. That's for certain."

"Thanks for telling me about Ginger Heath, Stiff."

"Well," he started. "I didn't really want to, but I guess you had the right to know." He turned away from the window and stared at me, the morning light still caressing the contours of his face, a face that was once as young as mine. I could hear the cows lowing in the pastures, the passing of cars on the road, and a rooster crowing somewhere in the distance. Another morning. Another day. What would my daddy give to have one more day, to feel the sunlight on his face one more time, to have one more conversation with Stiff, to watch his sons play baseball one more time?

"Did you ever read any of the books my daddy wrote?" I asked Stiff.

He seemed a little surprised by the question. He grabbed a thermos full of coffee that he had set upon the top rail of one of the barn's stalls.

"I read the first one," he said, taking his first swig of coffee. "Had to take a damn dictionary around with me to read it, though. Don't know where your daddy learned all those big words from. We went to the same high school. I never learned those words."

"I never read one of them," I admitted sheepishly. "Not even one. I didn't even try. I feel bad about that now."

"No need to feel bad about that. I don't know many guys that like to read. Your daddy didn't know many guys that read. I am sure he wasn't too surprised that you never read one."

"Kind of wish I had. Think it would have made him proud of me."

"Look," Stiff replied, placing his arm around my shoulder. "There is nothing you could have done that would have made your daddy any prouder of you. He might of give you hell, but he had so much fun hanging out with you. I don't think anything made him happier than spending time with you—hunting, fishing, and working on that old Chevrolet truck he used to own. I wish I would have spent more time with my sons. Y'all grow up so fast."

He walked out of the barn and got into his old Chevrolet flatbed. I held the gate open while he drove into the pasture. A few breezes ruffled the ancient red oaks that swaddled the century-old barns. Stiff waved to me as I closed the gate, wrapping the chain around the railroad tine post and securing it onto a rusted hook.

"I will see you later," he hollered, as he waved and vanished beyond the rise in the pasture.

The empty pasture seemed so tranquil, the way the cows were following Stiff's truck. There was a pond near the back fence of the pasture—a big, creek-fed pond. I caught my first big bass there on a cool September morning. Daddy was there with me, standing about twenty feet away. I remember watching him pull it out of the water, I was so excited. I kept asking him if it was over ten pounds. He kept telling me, "Gonna be close, Gonna be close."

He was right. We weighed it behind Joe Reynold's filling station. It weighed nine pounds and four ounces. Not quite a ten-pounder. Daddy paid for me to mount it anyway. It was hanging on my bedroom wall. Every time I looked at it, I remembered that morning. Those were the moments I really missed, when it was just me and him before he got sick. I wanted to be just like him then. At least, I thought I did. Thinking back to that morning now, I realized that, even as he was smiling and pulling that fish out of that water for me, he was living with secrets he probably hoped I would never discover.

GINGER HEATH

I texted Ashley when I got back into my truck. I told her I would be helping Stiff on the farm for a while, and that it would probably be after lunch before I got back to the house. It was all a bunch of bullshit. I had no intention of helping Stiff on the farm that morning. My only intent for that morning was to find Ginger Heath, especially since I learned I had a half-sister I had never met. And, besides, Ginger Heath was someone who knew Daddy before he was married, before he acclimated to the quintessential small-town father who taught his kids to play baseball and took his family to church every Sunday.

I took a right when I left Stiff's farm and headed toward the Georgia state line. I crossed the Savannah River about mid-morning and saw vapors rising from the river, choking the interstate bridge. I stopped at the visitor center, looked at a map of Georgia, and found the town of Clarkesville. It was only about ten minutes away from the visitor center. Then, I noticed a short narrow trail that wound through a stand of pine trees down to an overlook of the river. I decided to walk it, still thinking about Daddy, still wondering if I really wanted to meet Ginger Heath or not.

Sometimes, the decisions I made always seemed wrong; sometimes everything in my life seemed wrong. I sat on a wooden bridge at the overlook, breezes from the river stirring up a coolness that almost made me forget the temperature would be nearly a hundred degrees by afternoon. I guess I forgot who I was for a moment—the son of a legend who lived in Turkey Creek, South Carolina, where the summers were always miserable and suffocating.

I sat there for a brief while, watching the mists break across the bridge. The scene seemed so serene and placid, the way the sunlight-dappled ripples of the river moved without a sound. Places like this overlook made believing in God easy, made believing in heaven easy. I always struggled with the whole God thing myself. Of course, I wanted to believe in heaven. I wanted to believe that Daddy would be there for me when I died, that he would be young again and strong, and that we could take walks together along the streets of gold.

Sometimes, it just seemed too good to be true. And you know what everybody says here in this mortal world: if it sounds too good to be true, it probably is. I always wondered why this adage was never applied to the existence of heaven. Anyway, after sitting there for a few minutes, contemplating the existence of heaven, I headed back to my truck, my thoughts again upon Ginger Heath and finding her.

I hoped my quest would be easy because I knew I didn't have much time. That evening, I would be standing in a line at a funeral home, shaking men's hands and hugging the necks of old ladies, who would assure me Daddy was in a better place— like they had been there already and been reincarnated as angels placed here on earth to be messengers of assurance for those who might doubt the existence of heaven. They didn't fucking know any more than I did. None of us knew. I wanted peace. But, sitting there alone beside the Savannah River that morning, peace seemed far away.

I bought a pack of crackers and a Pepsi from the vending machine before I left the visitor center and headed to Clarkesville. I was preparing to meet Ginger Heath and hoping she could provide some insight into my father's mysterious past.

The town of Clarkesville was just like the dead textile mills across the Savannah, cadaverous and forgotten, stranded among the corpses of empty brick buildings with walls covered in kudzu vines and broken windows, clinging tenaciously to the gossamer threads of life sustained by the few businesses that managed to survive the mass exodus of textile workers. It was a town dying, a town suspended in its final breaths.

There was only one gas station in the town, so I began my search there. A couple of old-timers sat on box crates outside the store, sipping on coffee. I parked my truck and asked them if they knew Ginger Heath. The old men scratched at their heads as if trying to remember something from a long time ago.

"Well," one of the old timers began. "There were some Heaths that used to live on Huckleberry Road." He dumped a cigarette into his hand and turned to the man sitting beside him for confirmation. "Ain't that right, Sam?"

"Yeah, I think so," Sam replied. "The man's name was Carl, I think, or maybe Charlie. I just remember it starting with a C. I think they moved, though, not long after the mills closed. They had a few kids. But I never knew their names."

He struck a match against the concrete frame of the convenience store and lit his cigarette.

"The only Heath I know of that is still living around here is Gretchen Heath. She lives on Huckleberry Road, too. Hell, she must be close to a hundred. I think she was Charlie's grandmother. She lives in that farmhouse up there on that hill. Do you know where I am talking about, Jim?" he asked the other man.

"Yeah," Jim replied, nodding his head. "I forgot about Mrs. Heath. She don't get out much anymore. Like Sam said, she has got to be near a hundred years old. She might know who you are searching for."

"Well, how do I get there?" I asked.

"Just keep straight here on 92," Sam began. "You will pass the old elementary school. Be the next road on your right. And her house is maybe, oh, I don't know, three or four miles down. You will know the house when you see it. It sits on top of a big hill—

an old white house with a few barns beside it."

I shook the hands of the old man and thanked them for their information, then returned to my truck and headed for Huckleberry Road, hoping the old lady might have the information that would lead to Ginger Heath and hoping Ginger Heath would have the information that would help me understand better the man my father used to be—the man I never met, the man I was desperate to know.

Those old-timers were right. That house where Mrs. Heath lived was easy to find. It was a big house, old and wan, with pecan trees all around it, perched on an enormous hill that rose ostentatiously from the flat pasturelands. You could tell it had been neglected for a while. A few shingles were missing from the roof, and some of the window shutters were loose and leaning. It had definitely been a while since the house had been painted. It looked like the kind of place where a hundred-year-old woman would live.

As I made my way up the precipitous drive, I noticed a woman with a cup of coffee sitting in a rocking chair on the front porch. There was an older model sedan parked beneath the shade of one of the pecan trees. Even it looked like it had not been moved in a while, leaves and pine needles bunched up against the windshield. The whole place seemed a caricature of the old South—the kind of place you envisioned when you watched *Gone with the Wind* or read a Faulkner novel.

I parked my truck beside the sedan and ascended the steps to the porch, the eyes of the woman on the porch watching me cautiously. I got the feeling that she didn't get many visitors.

"Good morning, ma'am," I said, as I stepped onto the porch.

She set her coffee on a glass table, then turned and looked at me.

"Good morning," she responded.

Her voice was soft and graceful and kind, and her blue eyes were mesmerizingly beautiful to be the Mrs. Heath described by the men at the gas station. But she was not young, either—probably about the age of my mother. I took my hat off as I approached, trying to think of what to say next.

"I was looking for a Mrs. Heath," I said, as the distance between us neared. "I was told that she lived here."

"Yes, she does," the lady responded. "She is my grandmother." She lifted her coffee cup and took a sip. "Ain't got much of her mind left, though," she added. "What did you need to see her about? Maybe I can help you."

"Well, I was just wondering if she knew somebody that my father used to know, someone that had the last name of Heath."

"Who was that?" she asked politely.

"Ginger Heath."

The woman chuckled a bit and placed her coffee back on the table. "I'm Ginger Heath," she replied. "Who was your father?"

"John Stiles."

"Yes," she responded excitedly. "I knew your father. I knew him well. You look just like him. But I haven't seen him in years. How is he doing?"

"He died a few days ago," I told her.

"What?" she asked, obviously shocked. She seemed she was about to cry. "How?"

"Well, he started having strokes a couple of years ago. They never could determine the cause. And a few weeks ago, he had a major stroke and never recovered."

"Oh my God," she said, rising from her chair and embracing me. "I am so sorry," she said, beginning to cry. "He was such a good man."

Reluctantly, she released me and wiped her tears on her sleeve. She picked up a pack of cigarettes from the glass table and lit one as she struggled not to cry.

"I'm sorry," she said, as she took the first puff of her cigarette. "I just haven't seen him in so long. I wasn't expecting this kind of news."

She took another drag of her cigarette and stared out across the pastures at the bales of hay glistening in the morning sun.

"I can't believe he is dead."

Morning light was scratching through the shade of the pecan trees, heat bubbling in the subtle movements of the day. I watched her standing there in the slants of sunlight. I tried to imagine what she looked like when she was young. I could tell she had been beautiful. Traces of that adolescent beauty remained in the features of her face, the way her eyes shined when she smiled, the dimples in her cheeks. I wondered what sort of games she played and what kind of dreams she had. I imagined the innocence of her adolescence—the innocence of mine.

She finished the cigarette, smashed it against the banister, thumped the butt into the yard, and then returned to her rocking chair. A breeze rustled the leaves of the pecan trees—a breeze without any coolness, a breeze as warm as the day would be.

Used to be, I liked the summers, no matter how hot the days were. Still did, I supposed. Now, however, I would always identify hot summer days with the death of my father. People were supposed to die in the winter, when the ground was frozen in the mornings and the trees were bare of leaves—not in the summer when you could hear the songbirds chirping in the morning and see bales of fresh cut hay and cornstalks high in the fields and watch young boys, still full of dreams, playing baseball in the evenings.

"Do you mind if I take a dip, Ms. Heath?" I asked, pulling my can from the back pocket of my jeans.

"No, I don't mind," she answered. "And you don't have to call me Ms. Heath," she added. "You may call me Ginger. Last name ain't Heath anymore anyway."

"Oh, I am sorry. I guess I should have known you were married."

"Well, I am not anymore, but I was," she replied. "Have a seat," she said, waving a hand toward the rocking chair on the other side of the glass table.

I put in my dip, sat in the chair, and stared at the fields of hay. How could a morning be so beautiful, I wondered? How could a morning be so beautiful and so sad at the same time? How could life fool us that way?

"You boys from Turkey Creek always have a ring on your back pocket," she said, smiling. "Guess you played baseball, too,"

"Yes, ma'am."

"You make me feel old when you say ma'am. But I guess I am old to you."

Her voice was kind and subtle, and the soft accent of her words seemed to amplify her beauty. I leaned back in the rocking chair and wondered what I would be like when I was fifty, what I would look like, and how many children I would have. For a few moments, I even forgot what I had come to see her about. It seemed like we were two friends, sitting on the porch on a summer morning, anticipating another day. But I couldn't forget why I wanted to meet the woman sitting beside me. I just had to figure out the way to ask her the questions I wanted to ask. I twisted the cap off my empty soda bottle and spit a bit of tobacco juice into my narrow spittoon.

"Do you remember Stiff Jenkins?" I finally asked.

"Yes," she answered, lifting her coffee mug from the glass table. "I remember Stiff Jenkins," she confirmed, taking another sip of coffee. "Guess you know then."

"Know what?"

"That your daddy, and I had a daughter."

"Yes, ma'am."

She lit another cigarette, then stared across the vast fields, stoic and aloof, the morning breezes passing softly across her face.

"What was her name?" I asked.

"Kansas," she replied.

"Kansas?"

"I know it is an unusual name," she said, "but I just liked it. My uncle once had this farm out there, and, sometimes, when I was a little girl, my parents would take us out there to visit him. I always liked it out there, so I just decided when I found out I was going to have a daughter to name her Kansas. I didn't care what anybody else thought. I thought it was a pretty name, and I wanted her to have it."

"I think it's a pretty name, too," I agreed. "Seems the more you say it, the prettier it becomes."

She chuckled a bit, then took another drag of her cigarette.

"So where is Kansas now? Does she still live around here?"

"She is dead," she answered somberly. "Been dead almost ten years now."

"How?" I asked.

She took another drag of the cigarette, then flicked the ashes of her cigarette into an ashtray on the glass table.

"When she was about fourteen, she started cutting herself. Cut up her arms and her legs and even her feet. I tried to handle it by myself at first. Took all the knives out of the house, but she always found some way to cut herself. I remember watching her one day from the kitchen window. She was sitting on a bench in the yard, just cutting herself. And I wondered to myself what in the world could be so wrong in the life of a thirteen-year-old girl that the only pleasure she got out of living was cutting herself?

"Finally, I took her to see a therapist, and she put her on medicine for depression for a while. At first, the medicine seemed to be working. Then, one day, I came home from work, and there she was, swinging from a rope she had anchored to a bough of one of the oak trees in the backyard. Her color was all gone." She was trying not to cry again, but I could see the tears gathering in her eyes. "Things ain't never been the same since that day."

"Did my dad know about it?"

"Yes," she answered, nodding her head slowly as she continued to sway in the wooden rocking chair. "He came to see me about a week after it happened. We met at the cemetery, and he put some flowers on her grave. I think it always bothered him that he never got to know her that well."

She pressed her cigarette into the ashtray and took another sip of coffee.

"We texted each other for a while after that, probably more than we should have—even met one day at that picnic area by the Savannah River. Then your momma got wind of it somehow, that we were texting each other and talking to each other again. She had a right to be mad about it, considering our history. But we never had an affair or anything like that, and we stopped communicating after she found out about it. Your daddy would never have done anything to jeopardize his marriage, and he really did love your momma. In a way, I was kind of jealous because I remembered when he loved me that way."

She placed her empty coffee mug back on the glass table.

"Sometimes, life seems to be nothing more than heartaches and disappointments and sadness."

"Did you still love my dad?" I asked.

"I don't think we ever stop loving our first love," she remarked. "He texted me some after he and your Momma split up. He told me he had been having some health issues. I guess I never knew he was as bad off as he was. I kept telling him I would come see him one day. But I was going through a divorce myself at the time and just never got around to visiting him."

She rose from the rocking chair and walked a few steps toward the front door.

"Now, I will never get to see him again."

"Do you think he still loved you?" I asked.

She leaned against the porch railing, the paint-chipped and weather-beaten banisters pallid in the mid-morning sun's glow. Her eyes were still swollen with tears that she periodically wiped with the sleeve of her T-shirt.

"I don't know, Luke," she answered. "I like to think he did. He told me he did after he and your mother separated. Like I said, I don't think we can ever stop loving our first loves."

"Mom doesn't think he ever got over you," I responded.

"I guess I never got over him, either," she said, continuing to stare out at the pastures.

There were squirrels scampering through the oak trees, storm clouds forming along the horizon, and the fragrance of jessamine and honeysuckle wrapped in the wafts of each fragile breeze. It was the beginning of another long summer day. Already, I was beginning to sweat.

"We just didn't meet at the right time," she continued. "We were both so young, and neither of us knew how to be in a relationship. I don't think he ever loved me as much as he did your mother. I never heard him say one bad word against her, even after they divorced." She turned toward me again, her face beautiful in the glow of sunlight. "Would you like some coffee or anything to drink?"

"No, ma'am," I declined. I rose from my seat and walked toward her. "I guess I need to be going."

"Wait," she said, lifting her hand in the air to stop me. "There is something I want to show you," she added, opening the door to the house.

I waited on the porch, trying to make sense of life, love, death, and time. I watched a pair of does walk through one of the hayfields, timid and sly, their beige fur blending into the colors of the grass. I wondered what life would have been like if Ginger Heath had been my mother, what it would have been like if this was my grandmother's house.

The breezes of the morning had been lost in the progression of the day. There was nothing now to hinder the heat—no breezes, no shade. Carpenter bees buzzed at the edge of the wood banisters. House flies and wasps badgered around the glass table. I took out my pinch of tobacco and chunked it into the yard, still wondering about all the things Ginger had told me, what she said about us never forgetting our first love.

I thought about the few girls I dated in high school. I thought about Missy Graham, the first girl I ever kissed, and wondered where she was, what her life was like, and if I would ever see her again. Then, I thought about Ashley, back there at the house. I thought about the way it felt to hold her in my arms. I thought about how scared I was to lose her.

I began questioning everything—all these ideas I had about my future, all these ideas I had about family and marriage, whether or not Ashley's first love still had a place in her heart, and whether or not the love I now had for Ashley would ever wane or dissolve. My mind idled in puddles of disillusionment. I was beginning to regret this visit to the house of my father's first love. Seemed like the more I attempted to analyze the past of my legendary father, the more questions arose. And not just about him, but about myself and what decisions I may have to make in my future, what I would do if my health faded, and what I would do if my children had to watch me waste away. I thought about running off the porch, getting into my truck and leaving and not stopping until I was in Turkey Creek again. Then, Ms. Ginger stepped back on the porch.

"Here," she said, offering me a photograph. "That is a picture of Kansas. It was taken maybe a month or so before she died."

I studied the picture, holding it at different angles to avoid the glare of the sun's rays.

"She looked a lot like your daddy," she commented. She did seem to have some of his features. All I could see was the sadness in her eyes, the sadness camouflaged by her counterfeit smile.

"Yes, ma'am," I agreed, offering the photograph back to her, "she did favor him."

"No, no," she said, refusing the photograph. "I want you to keep it. I want you to remember that you had a half-sister," she added.

"Thank you," I replied, offering her a handshake. "It was nice to meet you."

"It was nice to meet you also, Luke," she said, pulling me into an embrace. "Again, I am sorry about your loss. Your father was truly one of the greatest men I ever knew," she added, as she reluctantly released me from her embrace.

I began my descent of the steps, sliding my hand across the railing as I slowly walked away.

"Luke," she yelled, pausing me at the bottom step. "What day did your daddy die?" she asked.

"Two days ago," I answered." At two o'clock. Visitation will be tonight at seven."

"Could I ask you a favor?" she pleaded, walking down a few of the steps. "I don't think I would feel right attending visitation or the funeral. But I would like to see him before he is buried. Would you mind meeting me at the funeral home sometime today so I could see him?"

She lit another cigarette, and the vapors swaddled the contours of her face. In the sunlight, I noticed how blue her eyes were, how they looked just like the color of the sky.

"I know you will be busy today, and I will understand if you can't"

"No, ma'am," I answered, as I opened my truck door. "I don't have much to do. What time would you like to meet?"

"Well, I just need to take a quick bath and freshen up a bit and put on some decent clothes." She checked her wristwatch. "What about noon?" she asked. "Would that be good?"

"That will be fine."

"Thank you so much, Luke," she said. "I am going to start getting ready right now."

"I'll see you at noon," I said, as I started the truck and ambled back down the steep gravel drive, realizing there were so many questions I had not asked her, so many questions that remained unanswered. I pulled down my sun visor to try to hide the blinding brightness of the sun and headed back to South Carolina, just as confused as ever.

THE PARKING LOT

She was there just as she said she would be, at noon, parked at the back of the parking lot, beneath the shade of a massive white oak tree, the only shade that remained in the parking lot. She was sitting on the curb, her blonde hair pulled back into a ponytail, smoking a cigarette, wearing a denim skirt and a beige-colored short-sleeved blouse.

I wondered what she looked like when she was young and how pretty she must have been. I wondered if Momma had a reason to be jealous of her. I parked my truck at an angle just behind her and walked at a reluctant pace across the sun-scorched asphalt toward her. The wind wasn't blowing a bit. The air was still and stagnant and hot, as it always was during July—so hot that you could not even imagine it would be winter again one day or that you would be outside in the early morning scraping ice off your windshield.

I sipped on a bottle of water I had grabbed from a convenience store on my way to the funeral home, thinking only about yesterdays. Yesterdays were all I seemed able to think about since Daddy had passed, yesterdays filled with smiles and laughter and hope and dreams—things that seemed lost now, things that could never be replaced or simulated, things that were gone forever. Tomorrows, I didn't think about at all.

"Hey Luke," she said, as I breeched the shrinking slant of shade.

"Hey," I responded, taking another sip of water and wishing I would have bought one for her.

"I don't know if I can do this or not," she remarked, releasing the smoke from her cigarette into the hot July air.

Her legs and arms were tanned and smooth as if she spent a lot of time at a swimming pool or lying in the sun.

"I lied to you before," she revealed.

"About what?" I asked.

"About it being so long since I had seen your father," she confessed. "I actually saw him about a year ago. It was one of those times he had been in the hospital. He messaged me on Facebook, told me that he didn't know how much longer he would live, that he was tired of being sick all the time, and that he wanted to see me just one more time. So I went to visit him.

It was late when I did, almost midnight, way past visiting hours. I was hoping nobody would be there. I told one of the nurses I was his sister and had not seen him in quite a while since I lived so far away. I reckon they believed me because they didn't seem to mind me being there."

She took another drag of her cigarette. I didn't know if she was finished with the story or not, so I just remained quiet, waiting for her to speak again.

"He was asleep when I walked into his room. I walked over to his bed and touched his arm. You should have seen the smile on his face when he noticed it was me. It was so big that I just laughed. I could tell he did not expect me to come. I pulled a chair up close to his bed, and we talked for maybe half an hour."

"What did y'all talk about?" I asked.

"He talked about y'all a lot. He told me about Lydia. We talked about some of the things that we did when we were young. We talked about God. Seemed like we covered a lot of subjects in the brief time we talked."

She finished her cigarette and thumped it into the grass against the curb of the parking lot.

"I kissed him before I left, told him that I loved him and would be praying for him. And then I left. I started crying as soon as I left the room because of the way he looked that night. I didn't expect him to last much longer. I thought that would be the last time I would ever see him. And it was."

"What did he say when you told him that you loved him?"

"He told me he loved me too."

"So do you think my mom was right when she said he never got over you?"

"I don't know, sweetheart," she replied. "Could the answer be that simple? Could it be that he never got over me or that I never got over him, or just that part of all of us that wonders what things would have been like if we had made different decisions in life, married someone else, chosen a different career?"

She looked up at me. I guess just to see how I was responding to her revelations. But I wasn't showing any emotion, just sipping from my water bottle.

"God," she began again. "You look so much like him when he was your age—them broad shoulders, those beautiful brown eyes, that dark skin."

She yanked another cigarette from her pack and lit it.

"Did you know your daddy wanted to be a history teacher when he first graduated high school? That is what he told me anyway. Wanted to teach history to the poor children in Appalachia. That was what he wanted to do, besides write."

She took another drag of the Marlboro light, her eyes squinting against the bright rays of the afternoon sun, which was slowly melting the shade of the white oak tree.

"Did he ever tell you that?" she asked.

"No, ma'am," I answered. "But there was a lot he never told me."

She rose from the curb and stretched her arms as if she was just waking up. I didn't know whether I was supposed to like her or hate her. I just knew I felt comfortable in her presence.

"But y'all never had an affair, did you?" I asked.

"No, sweetie," she answered quickly. "I think your daddy spent most of the time he was married to your mom hating me," she added. "It was only after they separated that we began talking again. I was going through a divorce myself at the time. And I guess we both just needed someone to talk to. Your daddy was always easy to talk to. He always made me laugh."

"Then how did he know about Kansas' death?" I asked.

"I don't know," she replied. "Guess somebody told him."

She swatted at a horsefly that continued to pester her.

"I was driving by the cemetery about a year after she passed. And I saw someone putting some new flowers on her grave and taking the old ones out. It was your daddy. He told me he came and visited her grave every couple of months. He always did things like that."

"Things like what?" I asked.

"Things that let you know he really cared for people, things that let you know he really loved people."

"Well, why do you think that everybody in Turkey Creek called my daddy the legend?"

"Because, hell, he was a legend," she answered, puffing on her cigarette. "I guarantee you that there will never be another man born that will be like your daddy."

"But Katie found these newspaper clippings in a box underneath his bed. And there were stories of people that were missing or dead, people I had never heard of. In Turkey Creek, people believe that anyone who wrongs Stiff Jenkins will go missing. I always thought it was just talk, but, after finding those newspaper clippings, I just don't know. Do you think my daddy ever helped

Stiff kill anybody?"

"I can't imagine your daddy ever killing anybody, Luke," she answered. "Now, I can't explain those newspaper clippings. That does seem a bit strange. But I wouldn't dwell on them too much. Remember how much your daddy loved you and all the fun y'all had together, how proud he was that you were his son."

"I am trying, Ms. Heath," I replied, "but one of those newspaper clippings was about two men from Georgia who were missing. They found their boat, but no trace of them. It happened about twenty years ago. One of those men was the father of my fiancée. Now, every time I look at her, I think my father may have been responsible for the disappearance or death of her father. And it bothers me."

"Well," she began, "I can see where that would bother you. I wish I could give you some advice. I still can't imagine your daddy ever being involved with anything like that."

She dropped what was left of her cigarette to the asphalt and crushed it with the heel of her shoe.

"He was loyal to Stiff, though," she admitted. "Very loyal."

She grabbed my hand and placed it in hers. She held it while we walked across the parking lot, neither of us speaking, neither of us knowing what to say—me about to see my father for the first time in a coffin, and Ginger Heath about to see a man she once loved in her youth lying still and dead. He would never be able to make her laugh again; she would never be able to look into his dark brown eyes. It was all over—whatever existed between them eternally extinguished, whatever passion remained terminated by the unpredictable and indifferent spectrum of time.

Inside the funeral home, there was already a video of my father playing on a television, bolted to the outside wall of the room where his coffin was. There were also flowers in front of his casket and a book for visitors to sign.

Ginger and I sat on a couch together and watched the video. Tears fell slowly from the corners of my eyes as I watched the slideshow of my father's life, pictures Katie had picked from photograph albums stuffed into the back of a closet, pictures of me and him going hunting together, pictures of me playing baseball and him leaning against the fence like he always did, pictures of him holding me and Carter and Katie when were just babies, pictures of him and Gomez holding a stringer of fish. The memories were difficult to bear, the pictures reminding me of when my life was beautiful but stirring up doubt that it would ever be again.

Ms. Heath had grabbed a cardboard fan and was waving it in front of her face. "I am having a hot flash, Luke," she said. "I don't know if I can do this or not."

"I don't know if I can, either," I admitted, wiping my tears on the sleeve of my shirt.

She grabbed my hand again and squeezed it tightly. Her hands were so soft, so subtle.

"Let's do it together," she said, standing and stuffing a peppermint into her mouth.

I nodded and, together, hand in hand, this woman I had only known for a few hours and I ambled reluctantly toward the room where the coffin was.

She was the first to see him. When she did, her knees buckled, and she sank to the ground, sobbing intensely.

"No, no, no," she kept saying as she cried. "He can't be dead; he can't be dead."

But he was dead. Nothing made sense to me anymore. I didn't feel as if I could believe in anything ever again—not love, not God, not anything. The world was becoming a disorienting quandary, and I didn't want any part of it. I wanted to be in a place where everything made sense, where everything was as simple as it was in a little league dugout.

I helped Ms. Heath to her feet. She kept apologizing as she held me, still crying hysterically, her tears dampening the collar of my shirt. The funeral home director poked his head into the room, but I waved him away. There didn't seem to be any reason for another person to be in the room right then. Just seemed right for the two of us to be there together, two strangers, both crying over a man we both loved.

She must have held me like that for five minutes or more before releasing me. I grabbed her a tissue from a corner, and she wiped her tears, then took a few more steps to the coffin. She touched him on the shoulder, then leaned over and softly kissed his brow. We walked back out to her car without saying a word, the July sky filling up with thunderheads. I wasn't sure I would be able to handle visitation that night. A part of me didn't even want to go home, and a part of me never wanted to see my daddy in that coffin again.

I opened the door for her when we got to her car. She thanked me for meeting her there, then wrote her number on a piece of paper and told me to call her sometime. Then, I watched her drive away. I looked at the piece of paper where she wrote her number. Ginger Heath. I wondered what secrets she knew, what secrets she kept inside of her. I wondered if all of us were like that, inundated with secrets that we hoped were never unearthed, secrets interred not by dust but years. Maybe all of us were mysteries. Maybe all of us were like Daddy described Fudge—fighting our demons, fighting our vices, each in our own personal way.

STORMS

By the time I returned home, the weather forecast had become ominous. The entire state of South Carolina was under a tornado watch, as well as most of the state of Georgia. Seemed as if every few minutes the radio was announcing a severe thunderstorm warning for another county. But in Turkey Creek, South Carolina, there were only storm cloud skies and a slight breeze that appeased the heat of the usually sweltering July afternoons.

Ashley was sitting on the porch alone when I returned, swaying in the porch swing, her dark brown hair pulled back into a ponytail. I sat down beside her and stretched my arm along the back of the swing. The sun kept moving through the clouded sky, peeking out a few rays occasionally.

In the distance, I could hear the rumble of thunder. I thought about long-ago evenings, Momma and Daddy sitting in the swing together, us a family. I couldn't help but wonder how different things would have been if they had never been divorced or if Daddy had never gotten sick. Yesterdays kept running through my mind—me and Katie walking to Grandma's, sitting on the porch and eating ice cream sandwiches, me and Cody riding our bicycles down to the river. Yesterdays were all I wanted to remember—yesterdays when everything in my life made sense, when everybody in my life made sense.

"Where have you been, Luke?" Ashley asked, interrupting my reminiscing.

I pulled my can of Copenhagen out of my back pocket.

"I rode by Stiff's around noon, didn't see him there. Then, I knocked on the door and asked Cody if he had seen you, and he said he hadn't seen you since last night. What's going on, why are you lying to me?" she pleaded, almost in tears.

I tapped the can of Copenhagen against my thigh, then fingered a pinch into my mouth.

"I don't know, baby," I began. "Last night, when Cody and I went down to the bar, my momma started hollering about some woman named Ginger Heath, wanted me to ask Stiff about her, claiming that would prove that Daddy wasn't this good man that everyone thought he was. I thought about that all last night. I thought about that name Ginger Heath. And, this morning, very early, I rode over to Stiff's house and asked him about her."

I paused for a minute to spit. There was no longer any look of sadness on her face but a look of bewilderment, a look that implied she was as lost as I was.

"Did he tell you about her?"

"Yeah," I continued. "He didn't want to at first, but he did."

I rose from the swing and took a few steps across the porch. I looked down into the town of Turkey Creek and saw a few people walking down the sidewalks and cars passing on the street. What did this town know, I wondered. What did the people of this town know about my father that I didn't?

"Well, what did he say?" Ashley asked.

I shook my head and spit into the yard. The sadness was beginning to overwhelm me, the sadness I had been trying to hide from everybody since I watched my father take his last breath in that hospital room in Atlanta. Tears began to fall from my eyes, and, at first, I tried to conceal them from Ashley. After a few minutes of observing me, she could tell I was crying. She walked over to where I was and placed her arm around me.

"What's the matter, baby?" she asked in her tender, caring voice. "Can you tell me?"

"I just . . ." I began, struggling to speak through tears. "It's hard to explain."

"Try, Luke. Please tell me what is bothering you so much."

I wiped my tears on the sleeve of my shirt. The rumbles of thunder were getting closer now. I didn't know how to answer Ashley. I didn't know what she expected to hear. I watched a truck pull into Floyd's parking lot. An old man I did not recognize lumbered across the compacted gravel, looking up at the sky. I wondered what secrets he had, what secrets he was taking into the bar with him, and what secrets he would take to the grave with him. Did we all have secrets? Were the things I had learned today supposed to be secrets never revealed, not even to my fiancée, not even to the woman I wanted to spend the rest of my life with?

"I just grew up thinking my father was this incredible man. But, since he died, it seems as if I keep learning more and more about him and about who he was. And maybe he wasn't such a good man. Maybe Momma was right about him. Maybe I never knew him at all."

"But your daddy was a good man, Luke. What makes you think that he wasn't?"

"I met Ginger Heath today."

"You met her?" Ashley asked, surprised by my revelation. "Where did you meet her?'

"She lives in a little town in Georgia. Clarkesville. I met her there."

"I know where Clarkesville is," Ashley said, leaning into me closer, her breasts pressing softly against my left shoulder. "What did she tell you about your daddy?"

"She told me they had a child together," I confessed. "A daughter. I lived my whole life not even knowing I had a half-sister. I never even got to meet her."

I pulled the photograph Ms. Heath had given me out of my wallet and showed it to Ashley.

"Wow," she exclaimed, after studying the photograph for a few minutes. "She does favor your daddy quite a bit." She handed the photograph back to me. "But that doesn't make your daddy a bad man, Luke, just because he had a child out of wedlock when he was young."

"No, but what other secrets are there, Ashley? What other secrets did Daddy keep hidden from me, from everybody? What other secrets did he take to his grave? I mean, I thought my daddy and I were so close."

"You were close to your daddy," Ashley affirmed. "You had to know how much he loved you."

"I know he loved me, but since he died, I have been hearing all these stories about him, stories I had never heard. I guess I have begun questioning everything: God, love, life. I mean, is there really a God? Is there even such a thing as eternal love? Can people really love each other forever? Can two people ever know each other completely? My half-sister lived her entire life, never knowing her real father, never knowing she had half brothers and sisters. And the reason she never knew is because her mother chose to keep that secret. Hell, if you cannot trust your parents to tell you the truth, who can you depend on? It's like we are all make-believe characters, put together by what others believe about you and what you choose to tell others about you."

"What did you mean that your sister lived her entire life never knowing?"

"Because she is dead now. Killed herself a few years ago."

"Oh, baby," she consoled, wrapping her arms around the front of me. "That is a lot of information to absorb."

I could see the lightning by then—crooked spectrums

crisscrossing through the dark clouds.

"We better get inside," she warned. "There is a storm coming."

"What about us, Ashley?" I asked.

"What about us?" she countered.

"Do you think we will love each other forever?"

"I don't plan to ever stop loving you," she reassured me, squeezing me even tighter and kissing me on the cheek.

"Well, I am sure Momma felt that way about Daddy at one time, and I am sure Daddy felt that way about her. But they didn't last. Hell, a lot of marriages don't last."

"There are no guarantees in life, Luke," she replied, turning my face to look at her. "But I am willing to take that risk with you. Because divorce happens to other people doesn't mean it will happen to us. I still believe two people can love each other for the rest of their lives. I realize your father just passed and that you have been hearing a lot of shit since then, but don't let whatever you are feeling now affect what you and I have together. I love you, and I want to spend the rest of my life with you. I want to have your children and to sit on a front porch somewhere with you when we are old and gray-headed and watch our grandchildren running around in the yard. Isn't that what you want?"

"More than anything," I answered. "More than anything in this world."

"Good," she agreed, giving me a quick kiss. "Now, let's get inside before this storm comes."

I followed her into the house, wishing it was that simple—life and marriage and love. I sat beside her on the couch, and we watched some game shows while the storm passed. Katie and Carter were gone somewhere, so it was just me and her, holding one another and listening to the wind and rain. Already, even though we had not married, there was that secret I had yet to reveal to her, that secret I was afraid to tell her, that secret I was afraid would ruin whatever visions of the future she or I had of us.

I secretly wondered how long we would last, as I held her in my arms. I secretly wondered how many more times I would get to hold her. I privately wondered about all of this as she tried to guess the clues on Family Feud—innocent of what I knew, innocent and naive and beautiful. I wanted it to be this way forever, I didn't want time to move. I needed her so much. The way she smiled, the sound of her voice, the sound of laughter. But something inside of me already knew I would have to let her go one day because of something my daddy did—because I was the son of the legend of Turkey Creek, South Carolina.

MOM'S FINAL VISIT

It never stopped raining that afternoon. After the initial storm passed, the thunder and lightning ceased, and the stentorian deluges that fell from the stormy skies tapered to tranquil showers of rain. But the dampness remained—the dampness and the paleness and the sadness. All of that remained, and it was almost like a cloak of disconsolation had wrapped around Lincoln County, like the whole county was in mourning, like the sky itself was in mourning. Soft, silent raindrops drifted noiselessly to the ground.

I remember riding to the funeral home, the sound of windshield wipers scraping across the misted glass, the puddles of water in the road, and me and Ashley and Katie and Carter riding together. We were all silent, all of us dreading the two hours we would spend shaking people's hands and hugging people's necks, and listening to the bullshit condolences of people. People would tell us how great of a man my father was, how much he had done for them, how much he had impacted their lives.

All the while, I would be thinking how much they really knew of my father—if they knew him before he got saved, if they knew what he used to be, and if they wondered if he was responsible for the disappearance of people or even the death of people. I wondered what people would say when Stiff died, when it was him in that coffin? Would the same people who warned their children not to mess with Stiff be shaking the hands of his sons and hugging their necks and kissing them on their cheeks and telling them what a wonderful man their father was?

Was that just the way shit worked? When we die, all people remembered—or all people chose to discuss—were the good deeds we did. Everybody just forgot about our vices, our secrets, our mysteries, and our sins. And I wondered if God worked that way also? Would he be that forgiving? I guess I hoped he would be.

I didn't even know if there was a God anymore. I remembered some of the Bible stories Momma used to read us at night and the ones we learned about when we went to Sunday school. I also remember Daddy sitting up at night reading his Bible. There had been times in my life when I attempted to develop the habit of a daily devotion. But I never did stick with it, even though Daddy encouraged me to read the Bible.

In fact, during one of our final conversations, he admonished me not to forget about Jesus. I don't really know what he meant by that, but I nodded my head as if I would comply with his request. Since he and Momma separated, I had probably only been to church three or four times and read my Bible even less. I guess, in all the chaos of my life that followed their separation, any adolescent desire I may have had to draw nearer to God sort of dissolved into all the confusing feelings I was having inside of me.

Anyway, none of that seemed to matter now. I could not find consolation in any of the Sunday school stories I was taught or any of the Bible verses I had remembered. God didn't seem too concerned about me. Besides, if God was so full of love as they said he was, why had he allowed my dad to suffer so much during the final years of his life? Daddy was faithful in church attendance and probably knew more about God than anyone I know. So why was he never healed or spared the suffering? I don't know.

Maybe there is a God. Maybe, one day in my life, something would happen to make me certain of his existence. Riding to the funeral home that day, I didn't feel as if God was in any of this. All I knew was that my daddy was dead, and I was, once again, about to see him in that casket. That is all I could think about. All the other enigmas of life, those fears and anxieties,

I had to push those thoughts to the side for a while. I had to get through this evening, I had to get through visitation, and I had to learn how to bear this sadness before I would be able to move forward in life, whatever forward meant. At the moment, riding in that silent car and listening to the hiss of tires on wet asphalt, the future didn't seem too promising. The future seemed ambiguous and scary. I wasn't sure that I was ready for any of it.

When we got to the funeral home, Momma was waiting for us in the parking lot. The door of her car was open, and plumes from her cigarette spiraled into the silent slants of drizzle. We parked right beside her. The sky was still sad and gray and dropped mundane showers of rain on the earth in varied sequences of ferocity, sometimes as big drops of rain and sometimes as just a gossamer mist.

Carter was the first to exit the car after Katie parked. He bolted straight for Momma, burying his face into her chest and crying vigorously as if his tears had been waiting on her embrace for deliverance. Katie was the next to exit the car, opening an umbrella and holding it above her head as she approached Momma's car. She leaned against the opened door, as Momma continued to console her youngest child with back rubs and kisses on the cheek.

I sat in the back seat, holding Ashley's hand. I feared what was to come, of the days ahead. I was supposed to be the patriarch of this family now, I was supposed to take care of my brother, and I was supposed to be responsible for the welfare of him and my sister. I didn't know how to do that. I didn't even know how to comfort them.

Ashley let go of my hand and asked if I was ready for this. I didn't know how to respond. I didn't know if I would ever be ready for the days that would follow the funeral and burial of my father. I didn't know if life would ever be normal again for any of us. There was a part of me that wanted to run away, to go someplace where nobody knew me, where nobody knew I was the son of a legend.

Instead, I followed Ashley across the parking lot to where Momma continued to console Carter, still thinking about my yesterdays because my yesterdays were all I wanted to think about—the yesterdays before Daddy got sick, the yesterdays before he and Momma got divorced, the yesterdays saturated with peace and bliss and solace and tossed into some measureless abyss where retrieval was impossible. I sure as hell didn't want to think about my tomorrows because I couldn't envision anything in my tomorrows ever being as beautiful or as wonderful as the moments lost and buried in my yesterdays.

"I didn't know you were coming," I admitted to Momma.

She released Carter and dropped her cigarette on the asphalt parking lot.

"I want to see him," she stated firmly, smashing her cigarette with the sole of her shoe. "I want to see him before everybody starts coming."

She looked at me, then Katie, as if she needed some kind of affirmation. I didn't know what to say. I put my arm around Carter, who was still sniffling, and we walked toward the entrance to the funeral home. Ashley and Katie followed, both attempting to stay dry beneath the canopy of a single umbrella.

Momma followed behind them, walking through the rain without an umbrella, walking with apprehensive determination, walking to the place where the body of her children's father lay. She wanted to see the man she once loved, the man she once vowed to love forever, the man she once rejected. I wondered what sort of force was compelling her to walk inside that funeral home and view his body. Was it some kind of unrequited love? Was her love for him as great as Ginger Heath's love? Had it ever been?

When we reached the door to the funeral home, one of the Thompson brothers took the umbrella from Katie and led us to the room where my father's body lay in a burgundy casket. Ashley and I sat on the sofa, while Katie, Momma, and Carter viewed the body.

Momma didn't break down as Ginger Heath had. She just dabbed the corners of her eyes with a tissue while she stared into the coffin. Katie was beginning to cry vehemently, harder than I had seen her cry since Daddy had passed. Carter was crying, also, just a little more reserved. Momma put her arms around them, drawing them to her side. She then reached into the coffin and touched the corpse of her former husband. Then, she gave Katie and Carter a hug and walked back into the room where Ashley and I were. She bent down and wrapped her arms around my neck.

"Be strong," she whispered into my ear. "Be strong for your brother and sister."

"I will," I promised, as her arms released me.

I watched her walk away—a part of me wanted to go with her, wanting to walk with her back in time to the days when we were a family, and I could throw a baseball faster than anybody around here, and she and Daddy still loved each other. I wished I could go back that far in time before Daddy started having his strokes, before I messed up my elbow, before I read those newspaper clippings that Katie found in that wooden box, and before I knew I had a half-sister who decided to hang herself one afternoon because she could not bear any longer whatever it was that was eating up her mind.

I leaned my head against Ashley's shoulder and watched the video of my father—a superficial video of him that only showed the happy moments in his life, that wanted to deceive visitors into believing his life had been happy and rewarding. There were no pictures of him lying in that hospital bed, paralyzed by strokes that doctors could not explain. There were no photographs of him sitting in a lonely trailer on sleepless nights staring at pictures of children he missed. There was no mention of the depression he sank into after being rejected by a woman who vowed to love him forever, or the shock of being told he would never be able to work again. There were no photographs of a grave in Georgia where a daughter he never knew was buried.

I guess whoever made the damn video wanted us to believe life was only full of happy moments, wanted to deceive us into believing in the blissfulness of life. Well, I was tired of being fooled. I knew what possibilities awaited me in the future. Maybe, for a select few, life would be this incredibly fantastic endeavor where everything just fell into place as it should. But, for most of us, there were going to be a hell of a lot of hard times coming. Parents would get sick or so senile that you would have to put them in a nursing home. Friends and relatives would die, disease would ravage our bodies, and people who once loved each other enough to get married would transform into people who could barely stand the sight of each other. That is what awaited us in life, not this bullshit video fabricated with happy pictures and Daddy smiling and everybody around him happy. That wasn't life at all.

Life was full of years of sorrow, regret, and disappointments. In all of those years, there would only be a handful of happy moments, only a handful of moments when you really believed in the joy of life, only a handful of moments captured in photographs that would one day become a misleading video at your funeral—a video that would attempt to deceive the people who visited your body that your life had been one of bliss and joy, void of heartache. I grabbed a peppermint from the bowl on the end table then walked with Ashley into the room where the coffin was, preparing myself for the next two and a half hours of handshaking and neck hugging.

THE REVELATION

It was nearly two o'clock in the morning when Ashley woke me up, tugging at my arm and telling me that someone was tapping on the back door. I grabbed a pair of jeans draped across the footboard, slipped into them, and walked into the hallway shirtless. That was when I noticed Carter headed toward the door.

"It's Fudge," he said, turning back to look at me.

"I'll go see what he wants. You go on back to bed. He is probably just drunk and needs a place to crash."

"Alright," he said, passing by me as he ambled back into his room.

I patted him on the shoulder. He wasn't little anymore, not as I remembered him to be and never would be again. Those bat boy days, sitting in the dugout days, thinking life was going to be nothing but a series of dreams coming true days had all vanished. His first fifteen years on this earth had been marked with more sadness, disappointment, and confusion than I could imagine. It was hard to decipher the thoughts going through his adolescent mind.

Yes, he knew Ty Cobb retired with the highest batting average in the history of baseball, and he knew that Babe Ruth was and always would be the home run king no matter how many long balls Barry Bonds hit, and he knew that Satchel Paige was probably the best pitcher there ever was, even though nobody kept stats on him because he played in the Negro leagues. Hell, he even knew about Pete Rose.

But none of that mattered anymore. None of it ever had. I watched him disappear into his bedroom and close the door.

The old springs of the mattress creaked when he crawled back into bed. I wanted so much to walk in there and comfort him, but I wouldn't have known what to say. All I knew how to talk about was baseball and hunting and fishing and maybe a little about engines. Nobody had ever taught me how to comfort others. Guess nobody thought that would ever be needed in Turkey Creek, South Carolina—not from a man, anyway. I guess our fathers just assumed we would learn how to camouflage our emotions behind stories of baseball and fishing. Stories about where we were going to hunt on opening day and why we were having a problem getting a vehicle to start—like they had been programmed to do for generations, keeping their feelings inside so nobody ever knew how they felt.

Hell, even if I had known how to comfort Carter, I would not have been able to do it then. Fudge was still banging on the back door, his taps becoming more urgent and vociferous in my hesitation. I sauntered through the mudroom to reach the back door. A laundry basket filled with clothes sat atop the washing machine, clothes that Katie must have washed and folded during the day.

It still didn't seem real that Daddy was dead and that we would be burying him in about thirteen hours. Hell, sometimes, it didn't even seem real that my parents were divorced, even though they had been for nearly five years. All my mind seemed to want to remember were the years before the divorce and the years before Momma and Daddy hated each other. Seemed sometimes like the years since then didn't even count, didn't even matter.

There was once a coat hanger nailed to the wall by the back door. Daddy would hang his flannel shirts from the hooks, the ones he wore down to the shop if he walked down there at night. I remember the way they smelled, the sawdust and sweat mixed together in some musky scent that belonged singularly and eternally to him—an odor preserved in my memories, in the recesses of my thoughts, in those scarce but deep parts of your brain where forgetfulness could not reach.

There was nothing left here anymore that belonged to Daddy—no coat hanger, no flannel shirts, no scent of sawdust, no sign at all of the family we once had been—just some damn picture Momma had picked up from the flea market one Saturday morning because she thought it looked pretty and nailed it to the wall in the same place the coat hanger used to be.

I unlocked the back door and invited Fudge inside. But he just kept shaking his head, refusing to enter the house, telling me what he had to tell me didn't need to be told inside the house. I told him to walk on down to the shop while I put a shirt on. Ashley asked if everything was okay when I walked back into the bedroom. I just told her that Fudge was drunk and wanted to talk to me in the shop. Then I instructed her to try and get some more rest.

The house was dark, still, and sad with vestiges of old memories spawning in the nocturnal silence. Grandma coming to visit us on Sunday afternoons, Momma yelling at us for slamming a door, Daddy sitting in the recliner, watching the Braves play, maybe eating a piece of pie or a bowl of ice cream before he went to bed. God, why did life have to be so sad, so filled with encumbrances and letdowns and tragedies we never saw coming? I wanted to be alone, I wanted to be asleep, I wanted to forget that Katie had ever shown me those newspaper clippings. I wanted things to go back to the way they were before Daddy died. I may have been a little confused about life before he died, but, at the least, I could lay my head on a pillow and go to sleep without wondering whether my father had been a murderer or an accomplice to a murder and how many other secrets there were I didn't know about this man who had shaped my life.

I pulled a shirt from a hanger in the closet and walked back into the yard. There was a mist falling from the black, moonless sky —a silent wind-slanted mist that felt cool against the sides of my face. Fudge was already in the shop, already had the lights on—their paltry glow dripping delicately from the sawdust-covered windows. I gathered a few twigs that had blown into the yard from the earlier thunderstorm as I walked, tossing them into a brush pile I was supposed to have burned weeks ago.

Fudge was sitting in a chair near the front entrance, his cooler of beer on the floor beside him. He had this disconsolate look on his face, as if there was no hope left in him, no emotions left in him. I hoisted myself atop the workbench across from him, tracing the shop with mnemonic glances, remembering Daddy's voice, the whirr of the table saw, him and Fudge and Coach Blake laughing and swapping stories, and me just wanting to be a part of it.

Now, I didn't even like being in there. Hell, it didn't even warrant being called a shop now. There was nothing in the building except some of Carter's weights and a scattering of tools on the shelves and boxes of Christmas decorations stacked against the back wall.

"So what's up, Fudge?" I asked as I fidgeted with a measuring tape to appease my anxiety.

"Did your daddy ever tell you about any of the talks we had out here?" he asked.

I shook my head and began yawning, still trying to wake and wanting Fudge to get to whatever it was that had made him feel the need to rouse me from bed at two in the morning on the day that I was going to bury my father.

"I didn't figure he did," he continued, assuming, I suppose, I was not going to offer an oral response to his inquiry.

"If anybody could keep a secret, it was your daddy," he announced, opening another beer. He took a swallow, then continued. "It is my fault, Luke," he admitted bluntly. "It is my fault what happened to your daddy."

"What are you talking about, Fudge?" I asked, confused. "It ain't your fault my daddy died."

"Not talking about that," he answered, shaking his head. "I am talking about what he did, what folks suspected that he did, him and Stiff."

He set his beer down atop the cooler and started rubbing his hands together. Whatever he was about to tell me, I could sense had been troubling him for a long time. Sweat beaded upon his wide forehead, and he leaned toward me in the chair.

"I need to get it off my conscience," he confessed.

He picked up his beer and took another swallow, then surveyed the shop like he was afraid someone was watching him. I guess, as much as I longed to be that teenage boy sitting in the dugout during a baseball game, Fudge probably longed for those days even more. I wondered what thoughts were burdening Fudge's mind, what the demons were Daddy said he tried to slay with alcohol.

It was sort of sad, looking at a fifty-year-old man like Fudge become speechless in the presence of the twenty-year-old son of one of his best friends. It was like all the sadness in the world was settling upon us, right there in what was once my father's woodworking shop but that was now just a place to store things Momma didn't want in the house. I watched a pair of beetle bugs tapping against the yellowed blinds of the window. They would be dead by morning, having exhausted all their energy trying to get out of a place they should have never entered.

"Do you know that bridge on Walton Place Road, that bridge that crosses the Saluda River?" he asked, finally breaking the span of silence.

"Yeah," I replied. "I know the one you are talking about."

"Must be a thirty-foot drop from that bridge to the river," he said.

I could not imagine what that bridge had to do with my daddy, but I waited for Fudge to continue. He sipped at his beer slowly, thinking, I suppose, of the right way to tell me what he thought he needed to tell me or maybe wondering if he should even tell me at all.

"I cannot count the times I have stood on the ledge of that bridge and thought about jumping into that river. All it would take was one leap. Just one leap. Then, it would all be over, all the shit of this life. And, whether I went to heaven or hell, I would find out right then. Wouldn't have to wonder about it anymore."

"Don't talk like that, Fudge," I replied. "You're talking crazy."

"Well, it's the truth," he insisted. "I have done it many times. Did it tonight, as a matter of fact, right before I came over here."

He swatted at a horse fly with his Turkey Creek baseball cap, then set it back upon his balding head.

"I ain't shit, Luke. Fifty years old, got no kids, got no wife, never even met my father. Only know his name because Momma told me."

"Hell, you have people that love you," I rebutted. "My daddy loved you. Stiff loves you. And a lot of those boys I played ball with think the world of you. Hell, I always looked up to you."

"Well, I appreciate that," he mumbled. "I loved every kid I ever coached. But everybody knows I ain't nothing but a damn drunk. God gave me a life to live, and I wasted it on whiskey and beer and women who I wanted to love me."

He finished his beer and tossed it into the waste basket.

"You are right about one thing, though. I did love your daddy. Closest thing to a brother I ever had. That is why telling you this is so hard."

He reached into his cooler and cracked open another beer.

"One night, a long time ago, maybe twenty years or so, I was down there drinking at Floyd's. Well, there was these two fellows from Georgia in the bar that night, and we were just shooting pool and talking shit, you know. They seemed like pretty good old boys. They said they had heard of Stiff Jenkins and had heard he made good shine. They wanted to know if I knew him. Well, of course, I told them I did. After that, they just kept pestering me to tell them where his still was. But I couldn't tell them that. I didn't know where his still was. Still don't know where his still is.

"Well, about that time, your daddy walked over to the pool table. I never even noticed him coming into the bar. I guess Floyd must have called him or something. I was pretty drunk by then, and I guess I became a little loose-lipped. Anyway, as soon as I saw your daddy, I blurted out that he was the only man who knew where Stiff Jenkins kept his still." He paused for a moment, then took a few more swallows of beer. "I wish I would have never said those words. You don't know how many nights I have lain awake in bed, wondering how my life may have been different if I had never spoken those words."

"What happened?" I asked.

"After he took me home that night, those two old boys began following your daddy. I guess he suspected they were following him because he didn't go back to your house. He just went right through town. Maybe, he wanted to be sure they were following him. I don't know about that. He finally stopped somewhere out by the old rock quarry. Your daddy got out of the car, and those two boys from Georgia wanted him to tell them where Stiff's still was. Well, of course, you know your daddy wasn't about to tell them, so they ended up beating the hell out of your daddy. When Stiff found out about it, he was pissed. A couple of days later, those two boys went missing. Found an empty boat floating in Lake Russell that belonged to one of them. But they never found the bodies. Probably never will."

"You think Stiff had something to do with their disappearance?"

"Hell, I know Stiff had something to do with their disappearance. I just don't know how much of a role your daddy had in it."

"Ya'll never talked about it?" I asked.

"No," he answered softly. "It wasn't the sort of thing we wanted to remember. Guess we thought by not talking about it, the memory of it would just go away or that we could somehow convince our minds it never happened."

I jumped down from the table, checked my pockets for a can of Copenhagen, and then realized I left it atop the bedroom dresser in the house. I asked Fudge for a dip, and he handed me the can sitting atop his cooler. I grabbed a pinch, fingered it into my mouth, then handed it back to him. The mist continued to fall outside. I could see it in the slanted glow of light that dilated from the dusty shop lights into the yard. I leaned against a 4x4 post, my eyes becoming watery with tears.

"That is a hell of a thing to hear on the day you going to bury your daddy," I said, staring at the house, seeing the little bit of light that seeped from the curtainless window of the mud room.

We played hide-and-seek here when I was a kid almost every night—especially during the summer when Katie and I were still young, probably before Carter was born. We played hide-and-seek, kickball, and tag. We were able to laugh back then, and we were able to be happy.

I didn't know who to blame for taking all of that away. Was it Daddy's failing health and the ensuing depression? Or was it Momma, who wanted the divorce? Or was it God or just some sort of ill-fated destiny for our family? I stared up at the sky, allowing the sprays of mist to settle on the skin of my face. I shook my head. If there was a God, he sure as hell didn't seem to give a shit about me.

"I know it is, Luke," Fudge admitted. "And I been struggling for hours, wondering whether I should tell you tonight or wait until after the funeral or if I should even tell you at all. It's just been bothering me for so long," he continued, sniffling a bit as if maybe he had been crying.

But I didn't turn around and see if he was. I was too close to crying my damn self.

"I guess this was bad timing."

"No," I said, as I turned to face him. "No, I am glad you told me, Fudge. That answers a lot of questions."

"I have carried this guilt around for so long," he confessed, sipping slowly at his beer. "If I would have never spoken those words, your daddy never would have got beaten up so bad, and those two old boys from Georgia would still be alive. It's all my fault," he repeated. "It's all my damn fault."

"So is that why they called him the legend?" I asked.

"Well, that and the Ricky Swanson story and all the other stories he told and all the other stories people told about him," Fudge answered. "It just kind of snowballed from there, the things people believed your daddy could do, the things people believed your daddy had done."

He paused for a moment and took another swallow of beer. I guess he didn't know what else to say, and I didn't either. A harrowing discomfort festered in the silence of the shop, and there were no words to fill the empty spaces. Fudge finished his beer, as I just stood there, leaned back against the post, and spit tobacco onto the dirt floors every now and again. At least I knew the truth now. At least, I didn't have to wonder anymore. I suppose that was one positive outcome of our late-night conversation. I had been wanting to know anyway. And now I did. I just didn't know whether I was better or worse for it.

Fudge leaned over and picked up his cooler and began walking toward me.

"You have to remember, Luke," he implored. "This all happened before your daddy got saved. When he got saved, he quit drinking, and he went to church every Sunday. He tried to do right, and he tried to make sure you kids were in church every Sunday. He even tried to get me and Stiff to go. He never wanted y'all to know about this side of him. He never wanted anybody to know."

I shook my head, as Fudge put his hand upon my shoulder.

"Guess I am going to go now," he said, as he sauntered back into the darkness.

I watched him walk across the yard and get back into his truck. He was probably too drunk to drive, but I didn't try to stop him. I just let him go. It was only a mile to his mother's house anyway, and I assumed that was where he was going. Maybe he would make it that far.

About thirty minutes later, I got a text from Fudge: "Don't tell Stiff."

I hit okay and walked back into the house. I knew I would not be able to go back to sleep, so I didn't even try. I grabbed a sandwich and a can of Sprite from the refrigerator and sat at the table. I couldn't feel anything while I ate the sandwich, not anything —not sadness, not relief, not peace. I wondered if I would ever be able to anymore. I wondered if I would ever be able to feel anything again.

KATIE

Katie walked into the kitchen not long after I sat down, hair pulled back into a ponytail and wearing one of my old baseball jerseys that swallowed her petite frame. She looked so much like Momma used to look before she started dying her hair and wearing too much makeup and getting facials and manicures and all that shit.

I remember when Katie was a little girl and would come home and fuss at Momma for smoking every time somebody came to the school and talked to us about the dangers of smoking and passed around pictures of what a smoker's lungs looked like compared to the lungs of a normal person who did not smoke. Now, she was just like Momma. She couldn't even begin the day without a cigarette and a cup of coffee.

After turning on the coffee pot, she pulled a chair from the table and sat. I didn't know what to say to her, didn't even know if I should say anything to her. Words sort of floated around in my head, but I couldn't catch enough of them to make a sentence or a question.

She put her feet in the seat, pressing her knees against her breasts, yawning as if she were still half asleep. I wanted us to be little again. We were always happy then, before we knew about things like divorce and moonshine and people hurting one another. The world hasn't changed since then because I am sure bad things were happening when we were little, too. I guess when we are little, things don't seem as bad or depressing as they do when we grow older. Hell, all it took to get rid of sadness back then was an episode of SpongeBob Square Pants or Scooby Doo and maybe a bowl of vanilla ice cream covered in chocolate syrup.

It was easy to laugh back then, when we were little. Now, laughter seemed almost impossible to initiate. Seemed like we were engulfed in a sea of despondency, sorrows simmering in every subdued corner and hidden crevice of this century-old house that once felt like home. Now, it seemed like a place to lay your head down and sleep or maybe get a bite to eat. It was almost like the house itself knew we were not a family anymore, almost as if it felt as lost as we did, searching for answers in our now fatherless world.

"Why were you always number 8?" Katie asked, startling me a bit.

"What?" I asked, not because I had not heard her but because I guess I was not expecting that type of question.

"When you were playing baseball, you were always number 8. I was just wondering why."

"Daddy said that was Uncle Wade's number, so I guess he always wanted me to wear it."

"I never knew that," she admitted. "Do you miss baseball?"

"Sometimes," I said. "It's not so much the playing I miss but sitting in the dugout with your teammates, talking shit and laughing. I miss that. Life just seemed so easy then, so easy to live, so easy to understand."

Behind me, I could hear the coffee brewing, gurgling as the last drops dripped from the filters.

"What made you ask that question?" I asked.

"Been meaning to ask you that for a while, I guess. Just never remember to do it while you are around." She slid her chair from the table and rose from her seat. "Do you want me to pour you a cup?"

"Sure. "Can't sleep anyway."

"How much sugar?"

"Two scoops will do, and maybe just a little bit of creamer if we have some."

"Yeah, we have some," she said. "What flavor? French vanilla or hazelnut?"

"Hazelnut," I replied.

She stirred the sugar and creamer into a pair of cups, then returned to her seat.

"So, what did Fudge want?" she asked, slurping at the still-steaming coffee.

"Just told me something else about Daddy," I answered, shaking my head, hoping she would not ask me any further questions, even though I knew she would.

"What did he tell you?"

"Said Daddy got beat up by a couple of guys from Georgia one night because he would not tell them where Stiff kept his still. Said that a couple of weeks later, those guys disappeared. They found their boat unoccupied and drifting in Lake Jocassee but never found any bodies. Fudge said he was certain Stiff had something to do with their disappearance but didn't know how involved Daddy was."

Katie sighed and twisted at the band of her ponytail.

"Do you really think Daddy could have killed somebody?"

"I don't know," I answered. "Do you think Stiff could?"

"Yeah," she confessed, as she sipped at her coffee. "I could believe Stiff could kill someone."

"Why?" I asked. "What makes him different than Daddy?"

"I don't know," she began. "I guess because he has been in the military and probably had to kill people in combat before and, hell, there has to be some reason that everybody in this damn town is scared to mess with him."

"Momma said Daddy was the reason everybody in town was afraid of Stiff. Said Daddy would make up stories to tell about Stiff, to make folks think he was more dangerous than he was."

"Maybe," Katie pondered. "Hard to say. Just don't think of either of them as murderers."

"I know. Daddy was so mild-mannered, and Stiff has always done so much for us. Kind of wish I had never started trying to figure out what made Daddy a legend."

"Yeah," Katie agreed. "Kind of wish I had never found that box with those newspaper clippings in it."

She took another swallow of coffee and ran her finger around the rim of the cup.

"You haven't talked to Cody about this, have you?"

"Well, I mentioned it to him last night when we were sitting on the porch."

"Damn it, Luke. You know he is going to tell his daddy. And then what will happen to you?"

"What do you mean?" I asked, confused.

"What if Stiff thinks you know too much or that you are getting too nosy? What is he going to do to you?"

"Stiff would never hurt me."

"I want to believe that, too, but who knows what he might do if he is threatened with jail time or a dishonorable discharge from the Army?"

"I don't think anything would happen to me."

"Yeah, well, a lot of things have been happening that I never thought would happen. Momma and Daddy divorced and Daddy dead at the age of fifty. I don't know what I would do if I lost you," she said tearfully.

I stood and walked over to her chair and held her as she cried.

"Nothing is going to happen to me," I whispered into her ear, as she sniffled.

The strong smell of coffee filled the air, and light draped delicately from the light above the stove—the only light that was on. She had tried to be strong for so many years, for too many years. I realized that as I held her that night. I realized she wasn't just mourning the death of our father, but that she was mourning every sorrow we had endured since Daddy had his first stroke. I rubbed her back gently as her tears fell gently onto the sleeve of my shirt. I held her until she stopped crying, until there were no more sounds in the kitchen, except the humming of the refrigerator and the occasional crash of ice as it fell from the ice maker.

"Do you remember when we were little?" she asked, wiping her eyes with a napkin, "and Momma and Daddy would play hide and seek with us, and Daddy would always hide in the stupidest places?"

"Yeah," I answered.

"Do you think we will ever be that happy again?"

"I don't know," I replied. "Maybe. When we have kids of our own, I guess."

"Luke," she murmured, trying not to cry anymore. "We can't tell Carter about any of this, okay?"

"Okay, but, by not telling him, we will be doing the same thing to him that Daddy did to us. I mean, sooner or later, he is going to hear the stories, as small as this town is and as much as Fudge talks when he is drinking."

"Maybe you're right," she said. "But not now, okay? Not now."

I nodded and finished my coffee. The sun would be rising soon. Light would melt from the sky into the town of Turkey Creek. By the next night, Daddy would be buried beneath the dirt in the town cemetery. But what he did, all the good and all the bad, would remain, floating around Turkey Creek in bar room conversations and front porch gossip. The stories of his life would remain, just like the empty buildings on Main Street. Nothing would ever be able to bring those chipped brick, window-broken buildings back to life, but the stories of what they used to be would resonate in the memories of the people still living, the people who remembered what Turkey Creek was like before the mill closed, before the flood of 2000. For those people, the legend of my father would survive just a little longer.

BURIAL DAY

The next day began sad and stormy as the last one had ended. All the counties in western South Carolina were still under a tornado watch. Usually, in mid-July, the storms came in the late hours of the afternoon, but these storms didn't wait for daylight. They came rumbling through about an hour before dawn, and the wind was blowing like hell.

I stood on the porch for as long as I could, feeling the breezes brush across my face and the sting of wind-whipped rain against my skin. I stood there until the slanted sheets of rain became too harsh to bear, and then I stepped back into the house. Carter had woken by then. He walked over to where I was standing and peered out the hinge-sagging screen door.

"Looks pretty bad out there," he said.

"Yeah," I answered, latching the screen door so the wind wouldn't catch it.

"Is it supposed to be like this all day?" he asked.

"No," I replied. "Supposed to clear up by noon."

He nodded, then sauntered casually back into his bedroom, shirtless and barefoot, dressed only in pajama pants—my grown-up little brother. I remember when he was too short to ride the rollercoaster at the county fair. Now, he was damn near two inches taller than I was.

I watched as he disappeared into the shadows of his bedroom. I heard the door close. I thought about him in there, missing Daddy, listening to the radio, or trying to fall asleep. A part of me wanted to walk into the room and sit beside him, offer him some kind of comfort, some kind of illustration that would make him believe we could get through this sorrow together. I wanted to tell him some kind of story like the ones Daddy used to tell us when we were young and had an important decision to make or when we had done something wrong.

But I didn't know what to say to Carter. I didn't know how to comfort him. I didn't know how to counsel him through this sadness, through these dark days of his life. I should have known. I wanted to know. Instead, I allowed him to walk back into the shelter of his room without saying a word—knowing how much he was hurting, how much he was missing Daddy, and how much he was struggling with this aspect of life and death, which once seemed so abstract in his juvenile thoughts but was suddenly real and palpable and definitive.

Hell, I couldn't understand it myself. I tried sometimes. I looked in the Bible, I read some devotions from a devotional book that Daddy had given me a few Christmases ago, and I even read a few chapters of a self-help book one time. I was still as confused as ever about God and Jesus and whether there was a part of us that was immortal or not. I certainly didn't have any peace about Daddy's death—not now anyway, not since I had read those newspaper articles that Katie had shown to me and heard what Fudge had to say.

My thoughts were frazzled and erratic and insomniacally frequent—dashing through my mind randomly and frantically, disturbing any chance of clarity in my process of thinking. The moments passed in surrealistic staccato as if time weren't moving as it once did, as if time would never move again as it once had.

I tried to go back to sleep. After Katie left the kitchen, I went back to my room and snuggled up against Ashley. She was sleeping so soundly. Her left arm stretched around my chest, and her skin was so warm. I thought about how much she loved me and how much I loved her. I stared at the engagement ring on her finger, sparkling in the faint glow of streetlights that seeped through the dust-yellowed blinds.

I remembered walking into the jewelry store to purchase it. I remembered the night I proposed to her, how happy she was, how happy I was, how happy Daddy was when I told him about our engagement. None of that mattered anymore. Everything I once thought would make me happy, would catapult me into a grand and fulfilling life—all of that was gone. I couldn't play ball anymore; I couldn't love Ashley anymore. All of those visions I had in my mind of the future had vanished: buying a few acres of land outside of town, building a house with a wrap-around porch, raising a few kids, and teaching them to play baseball as Daddy had taught me.

All those thoughts had perished in the rumbling thunders of an approaching storm and the indelible knowledge of my father murdering the father of the girl who was lying topless beside me in the bed—the girl I wanted to love, the girl who had agreed to marry me. No matter how much I wanted to go to sleep, I couldn't. I just lay there looking at the ceiling.

Finally, I got out of bed, paced the floors of the house, and walked back and forth from the back porch to the front door— munching on a slice of poundcake and sipping from a bottled water while thunder rumbled in the dark skies and flashes of lightning cast shimmerings of light against the curtainless windows. I wanted life to be simple, I suppose. I wanted it to be easy and placid and barren of sorrow, as effortless as throwing strikes was when I was twelve years old. I wanted life to be that way forever, but I knew it never would. I knew it never could be again.

After an hour of pacing, I sank into the familiar comfort of the living room recliner. I held the television remote in my hand. The room seemed so strange, so sad, like whatever good that may have been a part of its past had been eternally extinguished. All that was left were a few framed pictures on the wall, pictures of us when we were young, pictures of my grandparents when they were young, pictures of me and Katie and Carter when we were still happy—before the divorce, before Momma stumbled into alcoholism, before Daddy began having his strokes.

That seemed so long ago now. I remembered Christmas mornings, sitting on the edge of the fireplace mantel, waiting to open my presents, and hearing the subtle rhythms of Christmas carols emanating from the corner stereo. That was the only time I ever remember Daddy listening to that stereo. We sat on the hardwood floors and opened our presents, little kids who still believed in Santa Claus, still believed in the deity of our parents, and still believed in the happiness of our future.

That all changed pretty damn fast. Seems like once I figured out that Santa Claus was a myth, I realized that the existence of a fat bearded man living at the North Pole wasn't the only lie parents told to their children. There were a lot of things that they hid from us. I guess they thought it was better for us not to know certain things.

Maybe they were right. I don't know. I guess kids want to believe so much in their parents, and parents want so much for them to believe in them that they try to camouflage all their flaws and weaknesses and stuff they did in their past, hoping their children will never discover what they were before they were parents.

Sitting in the recliner that night, alone in the darkness, listening to the thunderstorms, I didn't know what to believe in anymore or if I should even try. Daddy was dead, the girl I loved would never marry me once she discovered the truth, and those baseball dreams I once had were buried beneath a twelve-inch scar on my left elbow.

Seemed to me, the longer I lived, the less reasons I could find for living. There was nothing to motivate me to want to live, to cause me to be optimistic that the days to come would be any better than the days that had already passed. I wanted things to be the way they once were, but there was nothing I could do to change that. Can't change the past, everybody was always saying.

The longer I sat in that recliner, the more I was beginning to believe there was nothing I could do to change the future either. I used to stand out in the backyard with a bucket of baseballs every afternoon and practice my pitches. I would hurl the balls into this netted target that Daddy had built. When the bucket was empty, I would pick up the balls, drop them back into the bucket, and throw them again. Sometimes Daddy would sit on the steps and watch me. Most of the time, however, I did it by myself.

No telling how many hours I had spent on that makeshift mound, imagining myself in the majors, thirty thousand people watching me, cheering for me, and me sitting there with a ball in my hand, sixty feet away from Albert Pujols or David Ortiz. What did all that practice do for me? Not a damn thing. Woke up in a hospital, nineteen years old, with stitches in my elbow and a brace around my arm. They told me I could recover with proper rehabilitation, but I was tired of throwing baseballs by then. I was tired of all the practicing and all the believing in fairy tales. I didn't want to play baseball anymore. Guess I was satisfied with what I had been: Luke Stiles, the best damn left-handed pitcher ever to play for the Turkey Creek Panthers.

In fact, I think all of us had difficulty being optimistic about our future. And by all of us, I am referring to me and my siblings. The only one who seemed to be optimistic about the future was Momma. I guess she thought a lifestyle liberated from the bondage of marriage and commitments would lead her to some person or place that would provide whatever she needed to be happy.

Momma could not see what I did, or, if she could, she never would admit to it. She would come home with a new tattoo or a couple of new friends or a boyfriend and all of that would make her happy for a while. But that happiness never lasted long. Sometimes, I could hear her crying in the kitchen late at night after she thought we were all asleep. I never knew what she was crying about. Maybe she regretted asking Daddy to leave or maybe some guy had broken her heart again, some guy she wanted to be her Prince Charming and give her all the things Daddy never had.

All I know is that she hadn't seemed happy since Daddy left, not for long anyway. I guess she still believed she would be one day —that one day she would find the happiness that had eluded her all her life, the happiness that would wipe away all those late-night tears, the happiness she felt she deserved. Wish I could say the same for me. All I expected out of life was more trouble, more sorrows, and more disappointments because that was all it had ever brought me.

I sat there until the black skies became gray and dawn sank into the town of Turkey Creek. Just another day for some people. Another day to go to work; another day to go to school. For me, the day would be different than any I had ever experienced. That day would be the day we buried Daddy.

GOING TO THE FUNERAL

By noon, the storms were over, just as the weatherman had predicted. The water in the puddles and drain ditches had dried up, as if it had never even rained. The familiar heat and humidity that suffocated Turkey Creek in the summer returned with little resistance.

And there I was in the back seat of Katie's car, wearing a suit coat, long-sleeve shirt, tie, and Sunday dress pants. I was about as uncomfortable as I could be. Ashley was sitting beside me, wearing a dark blue blouse and a black skirt that stretched to her knees. She was beautiful, her long black hair had been straightened and lay perfectly across the knobs of her shoulders. We had barely spoken since she arrived at the house, just a few little words here and there. She hadn't asked me for an explanation yet. Guess she just thought my silence was due to the passing of my father. I knew it wouldn't be long before she would question my silence and apathy. I knew the day would come. Just didn't know what my answer would be. She stretched her hand into my lap, and I fitted my fingers between hers. But I couldn't look at her, not knowing what I knew. I didn't know if I would ever be able to look at her again.

Katie asked Carter for a cigarette, and he reached into the glove compartment and handed her a pack of Marlboro Lights. She yanked off the Styrofoam wrapper, tapped the pack of cigarettes against the door a few times, and lit one up. Then, he rolled the window down just a bit so the scent of smoke would not permeate throughout the car.

The wind hissing through the open space felt soft and cool on my face. I tilted my head against the windowpane, staring out at places I had seen a thousand times: the IGA grocery, the old elementary school, the Dairy Queen, the Jiffy Lube, the train depot, Wilkins Feed and Seed, the empty buildings on Main Street, crumbling brick structures with cracked window panes and For Sale signs hanging from pegs on the front door.

Time had changed this town … and us. For some reason, nothing seemed the same. I don't really know why. Those places, I once passed without giving a thought. Now, those rundown, forsaken buildings suddenly seem resurrected, inundated with ghosts and spirits and sounds, and I could see the town the way it once was before the mill was closed and the flood caused everybody to move. A time when people had money in their pockets and walked down the sidewalks of Main Street on Saturday afternoons to go window shopping, a time when people bought sodas and ice cream cones from Hodges Pharmacy. I could see the town the way Daddy said it was when he was little, pedaling his bike from place to place with nothing to worry about or fear. And I wished it could still be that way.

Hodges Pharmacy was now a halfway house for recovering addicts, and the JCPenney store, where Daddy said Grandma used to buy all her Sunday dresses, was just another empty building with a For Sale sign on the pad-locked front door. Most of the people walking the sidewalks were addicted to meth or crack or painkillers. People were afraid to leave their doors unlocked and to let their children walk around unsupervised or go up to the IGA or Dairy Queen. At night, people stayed home and watched television, and kids just sat in their rooms and played video games. I could not imagine how different the town must have seemed to Daddy, or, for that matter, even the world.

I remember once when we were hiking somewhere in the mountains of North Carolina, we stopped by a creek with a small waterfall. We sat on a boulder and ate some peanut butter and jelly sandwiches Daddy had prepared that morning. Daddy started talking about God and Jesus and what it meant to be saved. I guess he was trying to collect my thoughts on the matter. All I did was offer vague answers to the questions. Right before he left, he told me something I never forgot. He said that being in the woods, being on a trail somewhere in the mountains or just sitting beside a creek as we were doing was the only place he could understand God. He said he struggled with believing in God when he returned to town and heard about all the things people were doing to each other—how kids were dying of cancer and how marriages were falling apart and how siblings would not talk to one another anymore.

In the woods, he claimed everything made sense to him, and believing in God was easy. Maybe that was what I needed. A hike in the mountains or some kind of getaway from everything, from Turkey Creek, from Katie and Carter, even from Ashley. Maybe then I could convince myself there was a God, that there was some reason or purpose for us being here on this earth, some subliminal meaning for our life. Riding to the funeral home that afternoon, I couldn't feel a damn thing. Maybe it wasn't exactly correct that I couldn't feel anything. Maybe it was more like I couldn't explain what I was feeling or the lack of feeling that swelled inside of me. Whatever it was inside of me didn't stem from sadness or remorse or grief. I didn't know where it came from. It was as if I were walking in a dream, sleepwalking, and everything that was happening around me didn't matter.

I put it in a pinch of tobacco as we neared Saylors, spitting a flume every now and then into an empty Coke bottle. Nobody had spoken since we left the house, not enough words to make a conversation anyway. Guess none of us knew what to say. The trip was leisurely and morose, knowing what we were going to do. Katie had already thrown up twice before we left the house. I guess she was taking it hard too. I guess we all were. Hell, nothing in this life can prepare you for the funeral of your father, nothing I had ever experienced anyway.

When we reached the funeral home, one of the Thompson

brothers escorted us into the family room. Nobody was supposed to be in there except immediate family and the pallbearers and, of course, the casket where the corpse of my father lay. It was still open. The attendant said they would leave it open until they were ready to move it into the chapel.

Katie began feeling sick again, so she rushed to the bathroom, and Ashley followed her. Carter and I sat in a pair of hardback cushioned chairs separated by a sofa. Uncle Randolph was already there. He was talking with Pastor Tim and the Thompson brother. They walked over and talked to us for a little while, but, as soon as Stiff and his entourage arrived, they wandered back over to the corner near the casket.

"Have you seen Fudge?" Stiff asked, as he grabbed a peppermint from the bowl on the table and stuffed it into his mouth.

"Not since last night," I answered.

"Where did you see him last night?"

"He came by the house."

"What time was that?" he asked.

Huck was standing beside him, his wife trying to pin a flower on the chest pocket of his suit.

"I don't know for sure," I answered.

"What in the hell did he want at that time of night? He knew the funeral was today."

"He said he just wanted to talk," I said, shrugging my shoulders.

"What in the hell did he want to talk about?"

"A bunch of shit," I answered carefully, aware that Carter was listening to our conversation. "You know how Fudge gets when he begins drinking."

"Damn," Stiff mumbled, moving the peppermint around in his

mouth. "I bet his drunk ass is still passed out somewhere."

About that time, Huck's wife turned her attention to Stiff and began pinning a flower to his suit pocket.

"Be still," she warned, as she slipped the needle into the fabric of his coat.

"I figured he would pull some shit like this," Stiff proclaimed. "I made Cody dress in a suit. He can take Fudge's place as pallbearer if that's okay with you and Katie."

"That's alright by me," I answered.

I had not noticed that Katie and Ashley had returned. Katie came over and hugged Stiff's neck.

"I don't know if I can handle this," she said, placing her head on his shoulder. "I should have visited him more," she confessed, sniffling as the tears began to drop from her eyes.

"Hey, don't beat yourself up over stuff like that," Huck consoled her. "Your daddy was proud of you, and he knew that you loved him. Be strong. Try to remember the good times y'all had together."

"I just wish I could see him one more time," Katie said, as she drew away from Stiff and wiped at her eyes with a tissue. "I just wish I could hear his voice once more."

"We all do, sweetie," Stiff agreed. "We always will wish that." He spit what was left of the peppermint into a tissue and dropped it into the trash bin. "And you will see him again one day. We all will. He is in a better place now."

Katie wiped her nose and eyes one more time, then asked if Carter and I wanted to see Daddy one more time before they closed the casket. The three of us, hand-in-hand, walked up to the coffin and looked at the corpse of our father. He had lost so much weight in the last few weeks of his life that he barely resembled the man who taught me how to play baseball, skin a deer, and bait a hook. Only his face seemed the same. Katie placed her hand on his chest and told him that she loved him. By that time, Carter was crying. I put my arm around him, as he placed his hand on Daddy, too. Then, we walked away, the three of us, and the Thompson brothers closed the casket. That was the last time I saw my daddy. That was the end. The end of life. The end of a relationship. The end of us.

UNCLE RANDOLPH

After the funeral, we assembled back at the house. By we, I mean the family and Pastor Tim and some of Daddy's closest friends. Aunt Marilyn, Chelsea, and Ashley began pulling out sandwiches and casseroles from the refrigerator and setting them on the kitchen countertops. Katie attempted to help, but they shooed her away and told her to sit down and relax. She finally heeded their instruction and sat on the sofa between Carlie Johnson and Savannah Clark, two of her closest friends.

Already, I was beginning to sense how easy it was to forget somebody. Even though he was supposed to be some kind of legend in this town, Daddy's death didn't seem to alter the affairs of many people who were at the house that afternoon. People were scooping out spoonfuls of casseroles and nibbling on sandwiches and talking and laughing, the same people that were sniffling and crying just a few hours earlier. Those same people now didn't seem to have any burden of loss at all.

I snaked my way through the throngs of people and slipped out the back door. I was tired of people, tired of listening to futile condolences. I wanted to be alone. I still missed my daddy. Life wasn't going to fall back into place for me. I wasn't ready to talk about baseball or listen to somebody tell me a funny story. I was hollow inside, broken down by sleeplessness and a heartache that hurt more than any pain I had ever experienced. I wanted the day to be over; I wanted the visitors to be gone. I didn't think there was any way I could ever heal in the company of others.

I walked out to the shop in the backyard, the voices of people inside waning as I neared my hiding place. I loosened my tie as I walked, sweating in the afternoon sun, my feet aching in the uncomfortable Sunday brogans I had borrowed from Coach

Blake. When I entered the shop, I leaned against the wooden table and removed them from my feet. I didn't even notice that Uncle Randolph was already in the shop. He was sitting on a paint bucket, smoking a pipe.

"Shoes a little uncomfortable?" he asked.

"Yeah," I answered, as I kicked them under the table. "Too damn tight."

He chuckled a bit as he puffed on his pipe, wisps of smoke pirouetting against his face.

"I suppose your father spent a lot of time out here, didn't he?"

"Quite a bit," I replied.

Uncle Randolph just nodded, scanning the corners and shelves of the building as if he were looking for something. He seemed so different than Daddy, so different from any man I had ever met in Turkey Creek really—the way he spoke, the words he chose, the clothes he wore.

"How did you ever make it out of here without playing baseball?" I finally asked him.

It was a question I had always wanted to ask him, a thought on which I had often pondered.

"Well," he began hesitantly. "I did play baseball. Played through Little League anyhow, but I wasn't very good at it and not interested in playing it, to tell you the truth. Your grandfather didn't seem to mind too much. As long as I made good grades in school, he didn't heckle me too much about playing baseball."

He took another long draw from his pipe and sighed as if he was pondering what to say next or even if he should say anything more.

"Now, I don't mean to imply that I do not enjoy watching the game," he clarified. "There is a certain beauty to baseball that seems absent in other sports, a certain aura that seems to emulate from the dusty fields, a particular camaraderie that seems to develop among the players."

"Did you ever watch my daddy play?" I asked.

"Perhaps a few times."

"Was he any good?"

"Not really," he answered, chuckling a bit.

Hell, I think his answer even made me smile a little.

"But you were," he added. "And your father was proud of that."

"Hell, everybody was proud of me when I was playing baseball. Wish it was that easy to please folks now."

"Baseball is a bit exaggerated in this town," he agreed. "But you were the best pitcher I ever saw."

"I never even knew you had watched me."

"Yes, I watched you pitch a few times," he said softly. "It helped me overcome the guilt I felt for never watching Wade play."

"So, you never saw him play?"

"I am afraid not," he confessed. "Never even knew what he was like. I was so busy with school at that time."

I could sense the sadness in his words as he spoke, even in his eyes, as he revealed this apparent guilt he had carried for so many years. I thought about how much he had lost in his lifetime. His father was dead, and both of his brothers were too. All that remained of that family was his mother, who was so afflicted with Alzheimer's that she could not even remember the names of her own children.

"How does it feel, Uncle Randolph?" I asked. "How does it feel to be the only brother left?"

He tapped his pipe against the scrap bucket, watching the wad of tobacco settle among empty beer cans and plastic Gatorade bottles.

"Makes me feel old," he replied. "Nature deals with us and takes away our playthings one by one and by the hand. Leads us to rest so gently that we go, scarce knowing if we wish to go or stay. Henry Wadsworth Longfellow. From the poem 'Nature.'"

"I believe you're the first person from Turkey Creek I ever heard quote from a poem," I stated.

He chuckled again, as he rested his pipe on the side of an old end table Momma had gotten from somewhere and didn't have room for in the house. I wondered how alike he and Daddy might have been. And I wondered why I wasn't like that at all. I wondered why Daddy seemed to have this dark side stuffed deep down inside of him somewhere and why Uncle Randolph's life seemed to be absent of such meanness.

"Did you ever read any of the books Daddy wrote?" I asked.

"Certainly did," he answered. "They were worthy of publication, in my opinion," he declared. "Especially the first and third one. Your father was a gifted writer."

"Then, why didn't he ever have one published?"

"Hard to do," he revealed. "I tried several times to get the attention of a literary agent. But I was never successful."

"But you have had your writings published, haven't you?"

"A few poems," he replied. "And a few short stories. Never a novel. Very difficult to get a novel published."

"I never even read one of the books my daddy wrote," I shamefully admitted. "Never even tried."

"Well, you still have time, Luke," he consoled. "You have copies of them, don't you?"

"Yes sir, I have copies of all three. I just don't like to read."

"Not many boys your age do," he assured me.

"Daddy sure did like to read."

"Yes, he did."

"Well, explain to me something, Uncle Randolph. How did Daddy have friends like Stiff and Fudge and Huck?"

"Not sure exactly," he admitted. "I really don't know much about Huck or Fudge. Only know a little about Stiff. But I do know this —Stiff Jenkins is no idiot."

"How do you know that?"

"Well, as I am certain you have already discovered, word travels quickly through these small towns, even to those of us who no longer live here, especially with the development of social media like Myspace and Facebook. And I am certain of this fact— nobody attending Turkey Creek High School now or in the past has ever made a SAT score higher than Stiff Jenkins. Not me, not your father, not anyone."

"What was his score?"

"1430."

"But he told me he didn't have a good vocabulary, like Daddy did. He told me he couldn't understand many of the words Daddy used in his books. How could he have made that high of a score."

"Well, he is either a remarkable guesser, or he compensated his inferior vocabulary with an unusually high mark in mathematics."

I chuckled after that answer. Perhaps for the first time since Daddy's death, I believed I could be well enough to laugh again, to smile. Uncle Randolph stood and walked to the back of the shop, perusing through the few tools that remained and all the junk Momma had stored in boxes piled up against the walls.

"Do you have anything that your father made, Luke?"

"In my bedroom, I do. He made me a baseball nightstand and a wooden bench where I keep my ballcaps and tennis shoes. And, over at his trailer, there is a glass case he made to display some of my baseballs. Guess I will get that now."

He nodded as he continued to amble slowly through the shop, seeking perhaps something that would remind him of his brother or maybe even his father.

"Ain't nothing out here that he made," I assured him. "Do you have anything he made?"

"Yes, I actually do," he confirmed. "Made me a wooden box for firewood. It was a long time ago. Almost forgot he made it."

He gathered his pipe from where he left it and began walking toward the open entrance, as if the memory of that firewood box satisfied his search. As he passed me, he patted me on the shoulder.

"Guess I better get back inside before your Aunt Marilyn begins to search for me."

"I guess so," I agreed.

I watched him walk back across the yard, stoically and regally like he always walked, his fedora perched carefully on his brow, tilted to the right side a bit, his wood pipe dangling from his left hand. I wondered what it would feel like to be the last of your siblings. I wondered who would be the last to go of my siblings and me. I wondered who would be the first.

I unwrapped the tie around my neck and set it on the work table. There was so much gone from this place that it didn't even feel like home anymore. Felt more like a place we had visited sometime in the past and took a liking to. So much had been lost —so many dreams, so many expectations. I kept trying to put it back together in my mind, the happiness that used to be here, the peace, the comfort. It had not felt right to me since Daddy had left.

Now that Daddy was dead, those memories seemed even more difficult to resurrect. Seemed like everything I wanted to hold onto was crumbling in my weakened grasp. And what scarcity of hope did remain in my spirit or mind or wherever hope was stored, what little of it remained, was waning quickly. I was ready to surrender. There was no fight left in me. Time was decimating everything I once thought it would give me, eating up all my dreams and ambitions, like some kind of vociferous monster. It just kept eating and eating, like it could never get full.

HIT AND RUN

I don't remember too much about what happened after Uncle Randolph left the shop. Ashley texted me that Cody had left earlier and that there weren't but a handful of people remaining in the house. She said Uncle Randolph and Aunt Marilyn had left.

I reluctantly walked back across the yard and into the house. Carter was sitting at the kitchen table with a couple of his buddies. I walked right by them, without speaking. I opened the cabinet above the refrigerator and pulled out the jar of moonshine that Cody had brought me the night before. I carried it into my bedroom and closed the door. I could hear Ashley and Katie and a few other girls talking in the den and, every now and then, the voice of Carter or one of his friends. I turned on the clock radio to muffle the sounds, took a couple of swallows of moonshine, and went right to sleep. I was so tired that I don't even remember getting undressed to go to bed.

The next thing I remember is hearing Katie hollering my name and pounding on my bedroom door. And Ashley was shaking me, trying to get me awake. For a few seconds, I had to look around my room and couldn't even speak. Took me a little while to be certain where I was or even who I was or why Ashley was sleeping in the bed beside me. I rubbed my eyes, squirmed from beneath the sheets, and slipped on a pair of shorts that were draped across the foot of the bed. I could tell by the way the curtains were tinted with the paleness of morning that it was already daylight outside. I could even hear a few birds chirping in between Katie's frantic knocks. I ambled across the room, still half asleep, and opened the door.

"What is it?" I asked Katie, who looked like she had just woken up. Her hair was all messed up, and she was wearing one of my old tee shirts and baggy pajama shorts. She had no makeup.

"Fudge is in the hospital," she said, beginning to sob.

"What for?" I asked.

"He was hit by a car last night," she said, wiping her nose with a tissue.

"How bad is he hurt?"

"I don't know," she sighed. "I don't even know if he is still alive. Nancy Bowen just texted me. Said it happened right in front of her house."

"Shit. Well, I'll get on up there then. Do you want to go with me?"

"No," she clarified. "But Carter might."

"Is he up?"

"Yeah," she said. "Sitting in there on the couch."

"Tell him I will be ready in a few minutes."

I walked across the hall and into the bathroom, brushed my teeth, and took a leak. I could hear the television in the den, the early morning news and weather reports from familiar voices of the local media stations. I was still trying to grasp what Katie had told me—my mind slow to rouse from sleep, my thoughts struggling for clarity. When I walked back into the bedroom, Ashley was sitting on the edge of the bed, combing her hair and staring into the narrow wall mirror that hung atop my dresser.

"Do you want me to go with you?" she asked.

"No," I answered, fitting my legs into a pair of khaki cargo pants, stained with grass and mud and grease. "When I get to the hospital, I will let you know what is going on."

I slipped a tee shirt on and gave her a kiss. As the gaunt light of morning breached the windows, her face became more lucid. I remembered the night we first met, how beautiful she was to me then, sitting on the tailgate of my pickup truck, just talking, both of us a little sedated by alcohol. I remember the moon being half full and how the clouds looked as they drifted in front of it, how you could see them for just a little while before they disseminated into the darker spaces of the sky. I remember how easy it was to talk to her and the sound of her laughter. I knew that night that I wanted to be with her, but I was so damn shy that I waited two weeks to ask her out. I opened the bedroom door, trying not to think about that night anymore, trying not to think about how much I loved her.

"I love you," I said, as I exited the room, closing the door behind me.

Once I was in the hallway, I noticed the front door open and Cody standing outside on the porch. I walked into the kitchen to get me a drink. Katie was pouring herself a cup of coffee.

"Do you want any coffee?" she asked.

"No," I answered, opening the refrigerator door. "I will just grab one of these sodas."

"Luke," she said softly. "Please be careful."

"What are you talking about?"

"Don't you think it strange? Fudge talks to you in the shop, and then, two nights later, is hit by a car and maybe killed."

"Who hit him?"

"According to Nancy, they don't know. She said it was a hit-and-run. Just seems kind of strange to me. All the times he has walked the sidewalks of this town and nothing ever happening to him. Maybe there is some truth to what people say about Stiff."

"You think Stiff had something to do with it?"

"I don't know," she mumbled, beginning to cry. "I just don't want anything to happen to you or Carter."

"Nothing is going to happen to us," I assured her.

I walked over to where she was standing and gave her a hug. I held her for a minute while she tried to stop crying. The scent of coffee wafted through the kitchen. I thought about those ancient days, when Momma and Daddy were still married, how the kitchen always smelled like coffee in the morning. How I would walk in there and Momma would always have my pancakes waiting for me, sliced into small pieces and drowned in Aunt Jemima maple syrup. She was always in a hurry, Momma was, or, at least, she seemed to be, especially in the morning. But she always had time to make us pancakes. She always had time to do a lot of things for us back then. Now, when we needed her, she wasn't even around. I wondered if Katie ever dwelt on those days as I did, or if I was the only one who remembered random shit like that?

I heard the front door open, and Carter walking back into the house. He walked down the hall and into the kitchen.

"Are you about ready?" he asked.

"Yeah," I said, releasing my sister from my arms. "I am ready."

I turned and looked at him, standing there at the kitchen's entrance, silhouetted against the shadows of the dark hallway. He was so tall, so grown up looking. I had to keep reminding myself that he was only fifteen, and I didn't have any idea how his adolescent mind was absorbing all this shit that was happening. And now this with Fudge.

For some reason, Carter had always taken a liking to Fudge and Fudge to him. I assumed their adoration for each other stemmed from the fact that he and Fudge were both catchers. When he was just a little boy, just starting to play for the little league team, Fudge would come to the house sometimes and teach him about catching—how to squat on his toes, how to block a ball, how to frame a pitch. Fudge spent a lot of time with him. I always thought Fudge thought of him as the son he never had.

Since the divorce, Fudge didn't come to the house very often. Every now and then, he would come to one of his games, though. I could tell Carter appreciated him being there. He always seemed to play better when he was there as if he were trying to impress him—as I always tried to impress Daddy when he came to one of my games. I couldn't imagine how he was feeling, having just buried his father, and, now, maybe about to lose a man that had meant so much to him.

"Do you want some coffee or a soda?" I asked.

"No," he replied softly.

He turned and walked back out of the house, grim and silent, as if there was a sadness in him that couldn't be remedied, a sorrow he didn't know how to bear. I gave Katie one last hug and kissed her on the forehead.

"It's going to be alright," I assured her, even though I wasn't even sure what that meant anymore.

Nothing was ever going to be all right again. Our daddy was in the ground, and now one of his closest friends was lying in a hospital bed or maybe even dead himself. I turned and walked out of the kitchen and back down the dark, windowless hallway. What if Katie was right? Hell, what if Chief Wannamaker was right? What if Stiff was behind all of this? What if Stiff was a murderer? What if he was planning to murder me because I knew about what happened? I didn't want to think that could be true, but I couldn't be certain about anything at that moment. Seemed like everything just spiraled into chaos after Daddy died.

I grabbed my keys from a wall hook near the front door and walked onto the porch. Carter was already in the yard, leaning against the hood of my truck. He was wearing a sleeveless shirt and his wiry, muscled arms glistened against the bright reflections of sunlight from the metal hood. I wanted to be his age again, to still be in school, to still be able to play baseball, to still be able to dream.

I wondered what his dreams were. I wondered if he had any. Suddenly, I became aware of how little I knew about my younger brother and how little I knew about his life. All I ever talked to him about was baseball. I didn't know what his favorite subjects were in school or whether he wanted to go to college or if he even thought at all about the future. I had been conditioned, just like all the other males in Turkey Creek, to only be concerned about his ability to play baseball. Conversations about anything else didn't really seem important.

I glanced over at the morning sky as I entered the truck. It was so beautiful, with all kinds of colors bulging from the parts of the sky. I could see between the vacant buildings and the weathered wood houses. Didn't seem right that everything seemed so normal, that everything seemed the same. I don't know what I expected to be different, but it just seemed as if something should have been awry—as my father's death should have made something change in Turkey Creek. But it hadn't.

The sun was still rising; Parker Hantel was mowing the grass of the Little League field, Mrs. Grant was trimming her shrubs, and people were getting in their cars and going to work. It was just another day, just another morning in Turkey Creek. I flipped the truck keys to Carter and asked him to drive. He had just received his permit. I remember Daddy and me taking him down to the back pastures on Stump's farm and teaching him how to drive a stick shift, laughing at him every time the damn truck shut off. I remember Daddy and Stiff doing the same thing with me. I didn't want those memories to go away, I didn't want those memories to die or be poisoned by truths I never wanted to know.

"Do you remember how to drive a stick?" I asked Carter, as I settled into the passenger seat.

"Yeah," he answered, pressing on the clutch and starting the engine.

"Let's go then," I said.

We drove onto the highway towards Saylors, where the nearest hospital was—windows rolled down, morning breezes blowing against our faces, and country music playing on the radio. We passed by the same brick buildings, the same worn-down houses, the elementary school, the Little League fields, and the First Baptist Church. Everything was still the same in Turkey Creek, but, for me and Carter, nothing would ever be the same.

THE HOSPITAL

Wouldn't you know that the first person I saw when I got to the hospital in Saylors was Stiff? That's just my luck, I guess. The first person I saw was a man I didn't know whether I could trust anymore.

Stiff was sitting in a chair beside Fudge's mother. He wasn't trying to comfort her or anything, even though she was crying like hell. He was just sitting there staring at the wall, as if her sobbing didn't bother him a bit. He didn't even notice that Carter and I had entered the waiting room until we were five feet in front of him. Then, he stood and offered Carter his seat. He knew Fudge and Carter had been close and maybe that he would be more of a comfort to her than he could. I sure as hell didn't know what to say to her.

After Carter sat down beside her, Stiff gently grabbed my arm and asked me to walk outside with him.

The soft gray color of the early morning sky forged a fragile tranquility inside of me, as if everything was all going to be well. Even if Stiff was planning to kill me or tell me Fudge was dead or something, it would still be okay. It was a weird kind of feeling, like peace or something. But, hell, I didn't even know what peace felt like, not even before Daddy died. Maybe that is why the feeling was so strange.

Stiff was walking slowly, his fingers fidgeting for the can of Copenhagen in the back pocket of his faded blue jeans. When he finally got it out, he fingered a pinch between his lips, then sat on the iron bench underneath the hospital cupola. He offered the can to me, but I declined and told him that I had some of my own. He shrugged his shoulders and fitted the can back into the rear pocket of his jeans.

"How did you find out?" he asked, as he spit his first plume of tobacco into the hedge of bushes that wrapped around the cupola.

"Somebody called Katie," I answered. "One of her friends saw the whole damn thing."

"It was never supposed to be this way," he confessed, leaning slightly forward on the bench.

"What are you talking about?" I replied.

"All of this shit that is happening: Gomez dying, your Daddy dead at fifty, Fudge lying in there in a coma, not knowing whether he will live or die. Feels as if it is my fault. I know some people will be thinking that I did this to Fudge, including that dumbass chief of police we have now."

He turned to look at the parking lot. It must have been a shift change because there were a lot of nurses walking through the lot—some leaving, some coming, some stopping to talk with each other. I just leaned against one of the porch beams, waiting for Stiff to continue the conversation because I sure as hell didn't know what he wanted me to say. Then, I felt someone touch me on the shoulder. It was Tara Solomon. I had known her since we were kids. Now, she was all grown up and pretty looking in her nurse's uniform.

"Hey, Luke," she said, as if she was so happy to see me, smiling the whole time like everything was perfect in her world.

"Hey," I replied, trying my damnedest to smile like she was, trying my damnedest to act like everything was perfect in my world too.

"I was sorry to hear about your father," she remarked.

I had heard so many people tell me that in the past few days I was sick of hearing it. I shrugged my shoulders and nodded. Didn't know how else to respond.

"I had intended to go to visitation, but we have been so busy around here. And with the new baby, it is hard to go anywhere."

"You have a baby?"

"Yeah," she said, tapping her fingers on her cell phone. "Look," she said, handing the phone to me. "There's a picture of her. She is six months old."

I gazed at the picture, then handed the phone back to her, noticing the wedding band on her finger.

"Looks like you," I commented, as I placed the phone into her palm.

She stuffed it back into the pocket of her loose nurse's blouse.

"How about you?" she asked. "Are you still playing ball?"

I lifted my elbow and showed her the still visible scars from my surgery.

"I haven't even picked up a baseball in years."

"Oh," she sighed. "I'm so sorry. You were such a good pitcher."

"Don't be blowing his head up too much," Stiff said from his seat.

"Oh hush, you old grouch," she answered, furtively slapping Stiff on his shoulder. "How is Cody by the way?"

"Doing alright, I guess," Stiff answered apathetically.

The sun had crested the horizon by then. Tara pulled out her sunglasses and fitted them onto her face.

"Well, what are y'all doing up here anyways?"

"Fudge got hit by a truck last night while he was walking down the sidewalk," I answered.

"Oh my God," she gasped. "Is he okay?"

"Don't know yet," Stiff answered. "He's not responding to

191

anybody. They're getting him ready to be transported to Greenville."

"I guess that was his mother in the waiting room crying?"

"Yeah," Stiff said, his words drifting lethargically into the humid morning air, like pieces of my life, like pieces of my dreams, all mixed up and hovering around me intangibly.

Tara stood there for a few more seconds, as if she were waiting for Stiff to say more. But he didn't say anything else. He just sat there stoically, lost in some kind of dark memory from his past or something, sitting there silent and serene.

"Well . . ." Tara finally started, sensing Stiff was not going to continue the conversation, "I'll be praying for him. It was good seeing you again, Luke," she added, then she walked into the parking lot, stopping to chat with a few nurses as she walked toward her vehicle.

I watched her drive away, back into the world, back into her world where everything was perfect and utopian, the way mine had once been, the way I wanted mine to still be. My world had changed forever, and nothing I could do would ever make it better.

"I won't tell your girlfriend about that," Stiff commented jokingly.

"About what?" I asked.

"About you flirting with Tara Solomon," he answered.

"Shit, I wasn't flirting with her," I replied. "Who in the hell did she marry anyway?"

"One of the Gamble boys, I think. Don't remember which one."

"Are you shitting me?" I asked.

"No," he responded. "Sometimes, it happens that way. The ugliest mother fuckers get the prettiest girls."

I sat beside him on the bench.

"Did any of them Gamble boys ever graduate?"

"I don't know," Stiff chuckled. "Maybe one or two of them did. They all know what they are going to be doing after high school anyway. Working at their dad's lumberyard."

The sun was beginning to warm our backs. Slants of light leaked through the beams of the cupola, forming swaths of shadows across the cemented entryway. I couldn't stop thinking about Tara Solomon and how happy she seemed. I wondered if I would ever be that happy again and if I had ever been that happy before. I remembered the hospital where Daddy had died and the way life had been before he started having the strokes. Life seemed so safe then, so carefree and fun. Now, it was just chaotic and full of enigmas, and I didn't know how to handle it.

"What did you mean when you said it was never supposed to be this way?" I asked, interrupting the gap in our conversation.

"We were just some country boys looking to make a little money on the side by making moonshine. I never thought it would get to this level. People dying, people thinking I killed people, people thinking your daddy killed people. That's what I meant," he answered reluctantly, spitting another flume of tobacco into the hedge bushes.

About that time, Carter walked through the hospital doors. I knew then that whatever information Stiff was about to reveal would have to be postponed. He walked over and stood beside me, his gait reserved and cautious.

"They just put him in the ambulance. Taking him to Greenville," Carter revealed. Stiff nodded his head and leaned back against the bench.

"Well," Stiff began, "I guess he is lucky to be alive. Guess the good Lord wasn't ready for him yet."

DRIVING AROUND

After dropping Carter off at the house, I didn't feel like going in, even though I could see that Ashley's car was still in the yard. I wasn't ready to see her yet. I didn't know if I would ever be ready to see her again. Carter asked where I was going. I told him I would be home after a while and watched him walk up the steps to the porch and into the house. Then, I took off and drove around for a while.

I rode to the cemetery and stood in front of Daddy's grave, the dirt still soft and fresh beneath my feet. I knelt and picked up a handful of it and watched it sift through the fingers of my hand, falling furtively back onto the mound of dirt beneath which my father lay.

I remembered a conversation we had not long before he died. He was telling me about when his grandfather died. He said he didn't know if he gave up or not. He said living just became too hard. He said we would all reach that point one day unless we died suddenly and that we would all reach the point when the thought of death seemed less frightening than living another day.

I stayed there for a little while, crying for some damn reason. It wasn't just because Daddy had died and that I missed him. It was more than that. Everything was changing—everything about my life, everything about my hometown, everything about my relationships. And I didn't want it to change. I had, in my mind, a picture of how my life would be. Now, that vision was becoming all blurry and abstract. And what once seemed credible now seemed impossible. I didn't believe in happiness anymore or love everlasting or any other of that bullshit. I just believed in sorrow because that is all I had ever seen: the sorrow that filled the shop the night Fudge told me about Daddy, the sorrow of Fudge's mother sitting in that hospital waiting room crying, the sorrow of Ginger Heath sitting on her front porch alone, the sorrow I imagined Ashley was feeling because I had not responded to any of her text messages or phone calls. How was I to expect my life would be any different or that the years I had to live would lead me in some other direction?

I stood slowly and rubbed my hand against Daddy's tombstone. The world seemed like such a sad place. I wondered if anybody was happy. Were we all just walking around underneath this false facade, trying our damnedest to hide the dark secrets we cunningly concealed? Why did it even matter if my father might have murdered Ashley's father? What did anything matter? No matter what, the world would still be full of sadness and death and people walking around with dreams that never came true. I walked back to the truck carefully, slithering through the maze of tombstones. I still wasn't ready to go home, though. I only wanted to be alone, to be away from Turkey Creek and all the sadness interred in the somber and, sometimes, reprobate history of the town.

I didn't know where I wanted to go next, so I just rode through the country for a while. It is what I used to do when I was in high school and couldn't figure out what to do. Seemed like the world was easier to understand in the absence of people—seemed like believing in God was easier.

I pulled into the gas station at Crystal Crosswords to get a drink and a can of Copenhagen. There didn't seem to be many people there at the time, but, just my damn luck, the first person I saw was Huck Strawhorne. I pretended as if I didn't see him, but he yelled at me from across the store, so I just couldn't walk away.

"Have you been to the hospital yet?" he asked, as he walked toward me. "I know you have heard about Fudge."

"Yeah," I answered. "I stopped by there earlier this morning. Stiff was there. Carter said they were getting ready to move Fudge to Greenville."

"Let's walk outside," he suggested, holding the door open for me.

He placed a hand on my shoulder and led me back into the parking lot. I opened my can of Copenhagen as I leaned against the hood of my truck, stuffing a pinch in before Huck made it outside.

"How's Carter handling all of this?" he asked.

"Pretty shook up, I guess," I replied, spitting onto the hot asphalt. "I don't know what to say to him."

"What about you?" he added. "What's going on inside your head?"

I shrugged my shoulders. I didn't know how to answer him. I didn't know what he wanted me to say or if he wanted me to say anything at all or if he just wanted to yank out of me my authentic sentiments about Stiff Jenkins and all the stories I had been hearing since my Daddy's death. I just stared into the distance, wishing he would just go away, wishing I could just go away.

"Listen to me, Luke," he began. "I know there have been a lot of bad things happening in your life lately. But you can't keep all that shit stuck in your head. It will drive you crazy. If you ever need to talk with someone, come talk to me. I may not be able to answer all your questions, but I will sure as hell listen to you."

I wanted to say, 'Really, Huck? Are you going to tell me how I should feel after watching my father die? Or how I should feel after discovering my father was a murderer and probably murdered the girl I just asked to be my wife. But, as always, I didn't say anything. I just shook my head as I opened the door to my truck. I got inside and started the engine. I suppose by then Huck realized I didn't want to talk. He put his hand on my door.

"Remember what I said now. Don't keep all that shit in your head," he reminded me, as I backed out of the parking space.

I nodded my head and drove away. I wanted to get as far away from Turkey Creek as I could, to find a place where nobody knew my name, where nobody knew me as the son of a legend.

Somehow, I felt drawn back to Ginger Heath. I remembered seeing her that first day, how she was sitting contentedly on the porch with tranquility exhuming from her presence. And I thought about that day at the funeral home and how much she was crying. It was almost like in all his life Daddy had never had someone love him as much as she did. Likewise, Ginger never had someone love her as much as Daddy did. And their inability to have a relationship somehow sealed their destinies. Once they separated, their lives were destined for sadness and failure.

I wondered if it was like that for all of us and if there was a certain path we were supposed to follow. Would variance from that path, no matter how small or even if it wasn't our fault, seal our destination? Maybe I wasn't supposed to marry Ashley, and maybe this whole thing about my father and her father was just God (or whoever was in charge of the universe) attempting to keep me on my predestined path. Or maybe I was supposed to marry her. I felt as if I were in that damn Robert Frost poem—the one with the man in the woods where two roads diverged, and he didn't know which one to take.

I crossed the state line, and by lunchtime, I stood on the porch with Ginger Heath. She had walked into the house to bring me a cup of coffee. I wasn't much of a coffee drinker, but, for some reason, a cup of coffee seemed like what I needed at the time, even though it was hot as hell outside.

Two massive water oak trees shaded the front yard and made the heat more tolerable. But I could still feel the sweat beading on my forehead and underneath my arms. I flipped my pinch of Copenhagen into the yard, wondering what I was doing here, wondering what I would say to her when she returned. Every now and again, a car would pass on the highway, but, besides that, there was nothing but silence. Empty fields wrapped around the farmhouse, desolate, bramble-choked fields of undulating hills that dissipated into distant woods. I heard the screen door open, and Mrs. Heath walked back onto the porch, handing me a cup of coffee.

"Thank you," I said as I took the cup from her hands. She returned to her chair and began crocheting whatever she had been crocheting when I arrived.

"Have a seat," she offered invitingly.

"Thank you, ma'am," I replied. "But I ain't much for sitting."

I took a sip of coffee and glanced around the vacant fields.

"Does all this land belong to you?"

"No," she answered, smiling. "It did at one time. But Mom sold the field on the right after Daddy died. The one to the left still belongs to us. My brother once used it as a hay field, but he doesn't come down here anymore. That field probably ain't been cut in four or five years."

"So, you live here alone?"

"Just me and Mom" she replied. "But she ain't got much of her mind left. My son stayed with us for a little while, but he moved out last summer. Been just me and Momma since."

I nodded and took another sip of coffee. The breezes moving across the fields felt cool on my face. I leaned against a porch banister, struggling for words to extend the conversation.

"Is that the reason for your visit?" she inquired. "To ask me about my land?"

"No, ma'am," I answered.

"Then what's troubling you, Luke?

198

"A lot of things," I replied. "But mostly things I have been learning about Daddy since he died."

"Like what?" she asked curiously.

"Well, I still think he killed at least one person."

"What on earth would make you suspect that?"

"Stories people have told me. And that stuff Katie found underneath the bed."

I paused for a few seconds, thinking Mrs. Heath might have something to say. But she never spoke at all. Just sat there quietly, waiting for me to continue my response. I took another sip of coffee, swallowed it slowly and felt the warmth of the liquid soothing my vocal glands.

"I told you about those newspaper clippings Katie found underneath the bed, didn't I?"

She nodded.

"Why would Daddy keep an article about something like that in a box beneath his bed? There had to be something significant about it."

"That does seem kind of curious," she admitted. "But what makes you think your daddy had anything to do with it?"

"Because of what Fudge told me," I answered. "He came over to the house one night and told me what happened. He thought it was his fault for running his mouth, for telling everybody down at the bar that Daddy was the only one who knew where Stiff's moonshine still was. He said two guys were down at the bar that night, listening to him, and that those two guys beat up Daddy pretty bad later that night when he wouldn't tell them where the still was. Then, he said Stiff and Daddy found those guys later. Next thing you, they were dead."

The coffee had turned bitter by then, and I dumped what

remained into the yard. Why I had chosen to tell all these things to Mrs. Heath, I did not know. Maybe, I needed to talk to someone and thought she would be safest. But I did feel better, just as Huck said I would—getting all that shit out of my head.

"Well," she began, "I can't imagine your daddy killing anyone, Luke."

"I can't either," I confessed. "But there must have been some side of him I never saw."

"Just remember all the good times sweetie," she consoled. "Remember all the ball games and the times he took you hunting and fishing. Remember him that way, Luke. Don't think on such things as you just told me. Those stories you have been hearing may not even be true."

"Wish it was that easy," I replied, gazing into the vast, empty, and forsaken fields. "But there's more to it than that. One of those men was the biological father of my fiancée."

"Have you told her yet?"

"No. I don't know if I should or not. But how can I marry someone whose father may have been murdered by mine? Every time I look at her, I think about it. Can't get it out of my head."

"I wish I knew what to tell you. I wish I had the answers, Luke."

"I know," I mumbled. "I don't even know why I am telling you all this shit. Guess you are just easy to talk to."

"Well," she began softly, "I'll take that as a compliment, I suppose. And I'll try to always be here for you if you need to talk to someone."

"Thanks, Mrs. Heath," I replied. "Thanks for listening and thanks for the coffee," I said, handing her back my empty coffee cup. "Guess I better be getting back to Turkey Creek and figuring out what I am going to say to my fiancée."

I walked back down the porch steps slowly, allowing the breezes that originated from the empty fields to wrap around my body. I could feel Mrs. Heath's eyes on me. Since everybody had always told me I looked exactly like my daddy, I wondered, if she was thinking about him as she watched me walk away—if she was thinking about the way Daddy looked when he was younger, if she was thinking about how her life would have been different had she married him.

"Good luck," she hollered, as I neared my truck.

I turned and waved then climbed into my truck. It was so damn hot that a quivering haze clung to the empty fields and the asphalt roads. The whole world was a blur, just like my life, just like my daddy's life, just like everybody's fucking life—a big damn blur where nothing was clear and nothing was certain.

BALLFIELD

By the time I got back to Turkey Creek, it was nearly dark, but I could still see the yellow police ribbons quivering in the slight breezes beneath the gaunt and frail light of streetlamps.

I stopped by the ballfield. Hot Dog was out there pitching balls to his son, and some other man was behind the plate collecting the balls the kids missed and dropping them into an empty paint bucket. I walked out onto the field, remembering the many times my father had done the same with me. He would get so mad when I had a bad game or if I didn't do as well as I should. I could still remember the sound of his voice, hollering at me as he pitched to me, telling me I had to learn to wait and also learn to hit a change-up.

Sometimes, Stiff would stop by and start picking up the balls I missed. The mood always became better when he was there. He'd start giving Daddy a hard time, ragging him about how he couldn't hit a change-up or fastball when he was my age. His presence always relaxed me and made me feel better about myself. I wondered how things might have been different then if I had only known that the man pitching to me and the one behind the plate had already murdered the father of the woman I would one day want to marry. Then, I wondered how they could just be there, joking around as if the murders had never happened. Did my father really not have a soul, was there some wicked, malevolent side of Stiff I had never seen?

"Here comes an all-star," Hot Dog hollered when he noticed me walking through the gate. "Why don't you come up here and throw my boy a few of them nasty pitches you used to throw? My arm is about to give out."

I smiled, waved at him, leaned against the chain-link fence, and watched his boy take a few swings. Cody was right. He could knock the piss out of a ball. I looked up at the bright lights that wrapped around the field and the swarms of bugs hovering in their haunting illumination--remembering my yesterdays and how it felt to be standing on that mound. I was a fucking hero in this town at one time. All over the county, people knew who I was. Every damn boy that stepped up to the plate was scared of me.

Now, I was just another good ball player from Turkey Creek—the remnant of a kid that coaches and spectators and even umpires had believing was good enough to have a shot at the majors—watching another kid that was being fed the same lies, the same bullshit. One day, he, too, would realize the impotence of those dreams.

It was like when your parents finally told you the truth about Santa Claus, that he wasn't real but some fictional character they made up to help kids behave. Then you remembered all those Christmas evenings you had lain awake in your bed, hoping you would hear somebody come down the damn chimney, or listened for the pitter-patter of reindeer hooves on the roof. When you realized it was all a farce, you felt like a damn fool for believing in such an incredulous story in the first place.

After tossing a few more pitches to his kid, Hot Dog ordered him to go pick up the balls. Then, he turned and walked toward me.

"Last I heard, you were in jail," I jokingly remarked.

He didn't respond immediately, just kept walking toward me. He tossed his glove on the ground and leaned against the fence, wiping the sweat off his brow with a rag he yanked from his back pocket.

"Well, I've been out a couple of days now," he answered. "Finally talked my old lady into paying my bail."

We both watched his boy jogging around the outfield, throwing the balls back to the man I didn't know, standing at second base and putting the balls into the bucket.

"Trying to make up for missed time, brother," he sighed, breathing heavily. "Just trying to make up for lost time."

"How do y'all think y'all are going to do in state?" I asked.

"Well, I don't know. Could use some more pitchers."

"Your boy looks like he is a pretty good hitter," I remarked.

"Yeah," he confirmed. "He ain't bad. Wish we had more like him on the team."

By then, his boy had collected all the balls, and he and the man I didn't recognize were walking toward me.

"Hey, JC," Hot Dog hollered, motioning for his boy to come over to where we stood.

I noticed Hot Dog's arms were wiry and covered in tattoos. He looked like someone who had been in prison and someone who expected to return.

"Do you know who this is," he asked his son when he arrived.

He patted me on the chest, I suppose to clarify he was speaking of me, even though there were only the four of us present. I smiled at the kid, hoping he could interpret my smile as confirmation that it was perfectly alright if he didn't know who I was.

"Yes, sir," he answered his father. "I know who he is. He is Carter's brother."

"That's right," he agreed, nodding. "Damn Luke Stiles. There was a time when nobody in this county could hit off this son of a bitch."

"Do you still play?" the boy asked me, looking at me as if I were some kind of damn superhero.

"Hey," Hot Dog scolded. "Don't be so nosy."

"It's all right," I replied.

I lifted my arm to show the boy the scar on my elbow.

"Messed up my elbow in college. Ain't played since."

The boy kept staring at me, expecting me to say more. But I had told him all that I wanted him to know. He still believed in the fairy tales his father was telling him, and I didn't want to be the one to break the news to him that this time right here was probably going to be the pinnacle of happiness in his life—when he was the town hero, the kid who could hit the ball farther and throw the ball harder than any other boy on the team. Life would never be this kind to him again. He would be like all the other baseball heroes in this town—like Stiff Jenkins and like me. We were forgotten and invalid but remembered the days when we were heroes—wishing the memory wasn't even there for us to forget, wishing we never had been the heroes of Turkey Creek.

"Well," Hot Dog said, "we best be getting out of here. I'm getting hungry and it's getting late."

Hot Dog placed his hand on my shoulder.

"Sorry about your old man," he whispered, as he lifted the bucket of balls and led the trio out the gate.

"Hey, Mr. Stiles," the boy called before climbing into his father's truck.

It was the first time anyone had ever called me that.

"Are you coming to any of our games next week?"

"I might," I answered, smiling.

"I'll see you then," he added, tossing his bag into the bed of his father's truck and climbing into the cab.

I watched them leave. The lights went out, and the darkness

enveloped me. I walked into the dugout, stepping on empty bags of sunflower seeds and cigarette butts. I closed my eyes for a moment and tilted my head back. Memories began stirring in my mind—Daddy leaned against the outfield fence, spitting tobacco juice on the ground, people hollering my name, clapping every time I struck somebody out, every time I hit a home run. What was I now? A nobody? A nothing? The son of a man I didn't even fucking know.

I found an old, waterlogged ball beneath the dugout bench and walked out to the mound. There was nobody in the stands cheering for me now, nobody standing at the plate, nobody hollering my name from the dugout. It was just me, all alone, melting into eternal obscurity on a damned pitching mound, the place that had once made me a hero, now swallowing me into its heartless bowels.

I took the ball and threw it at the chain link fence and listened to the echoing clang—wishing I could wipe clean the slate of my life and start all over in a different time and place where baseball wasn't that important, and fathers didn't take secrets to the grave.

I looked up toward my house. There was a light still burning in the kitchen, and the front door was open. Someone was sitting on the porch, looking this way, as if they had been staring at me the whole time. I couldn't tell who it was, only that it was someone, and I didn't want to see anyone. I sat on the mound and began to cry. The world was too damn sad. Just too damn sad.

THE PITCHER'S MOUND

I guess I must have been wallowing in my self-pity pretty damn hard because I didn't recognize Ashley until she had passed through the open gate and was walking across the infield. I tried to wipe the tears from my eyes before she saw me crying, but I could tell that she knew I had been crying by the way she acted. She sat beside me and rubbed my back.

"What's the matter baby?" she asked. "Is it that your father passed, or is it something else? I mean, you have barely spoken to me since the funeral."

I finished wiping my eyes, looked at Ashley for a moment, and then turned back toward home plate.

"I used to be a hero out here," I admitted sheepishly, even though she had already heard all this shit before—the twenty strike-outs in one game, the records I had broken, my scholarship to college.

"I know you were," she agreed, leaning against my chest. "What's changed?"

"Well, for one thing, Daddy ain't leaned against the fence watching me. And I sure as hell don't feel like a damn hero now nor the son of some damn legend."

"Why are you still so concerned about that?" she asked.

"About what?"

"About finding out why they called your daddy the legend," she replied.

I shook my head a bit, never changing my gaze, just staring at home plate as I used to do when I was pitching. I was in charge of the game, in charge of the hitter, and in charge of the whole damn world as far as it mattered to the people sitting in the stands that day. I was nothing now. Just a twenty-year-old kid, saturated with a bunch of what ifs and what could have beens, sitting beside a girl that, just a few weeks ago, I was certain I wanted to marry.

"I don't know," I replied. "Just damn curious, I suppose."

I grabbed the can of Copenhagen from my back pocket and fingered a pinch into my mouth. It was nighttime, but I couldn't tell any difference in the temperature. During the months of July and August, it was sometimes like that in Turkey Creek. Didn't matter if the sun was shining or not. The heat and humidity were suffocating day and night. And the mosquitoes made it worse—some of them as big as a damn bat it seemed. The more you swatted at them, the more they swarmed. When I was a kid, they never bothered me, or, at least, I don't remember them bothering me. They aggravated the hell out of me now, like everything else. I took off my ball cap and swatted at them in vain, Ashley's hand still on my back.

"I can understand," she agreed sheepishly.

I wondered if she would understand if I told her I suspected my dead father was responsible for her own father's death. I wondered what her reaction would be then.

"I want to understand at least," she added. "That is what I meant to say."

"You can't understand, Ash," I revealed.

"Why?"

"Because I can't even understand my damn self," I snapped back. "I mean, I want to tell you, but . . ."

I stood and spit a plume of tobacco into the hard, dry, infield dirt. The American flag behind home plate sagged still in the windless night.

"But what?" she asked. "What is it that you can't tell me? I thought you and I could talk to each other about anything."

I sat back down and embraced her, held her as tightly as I could and broke into tears again as I did.

"Please tell me what's wrong, Luke. I want to help. I just don't know how."

I was embarrassed that she was seeing me cry. I wanted to be tough and apathetic, void of emotions like Daddy, Stiff, and Huck Strawhorne—men who never cried, men who couldn't cry.

"I'm sorry," I said, lifting my head and wiping my eyes.

"Sorry for what?" she asked.

"Sorry for crying like a damn baby."

"Luke," she consoled. "Your daddy ain't been in the ground but a day. I expect there to be some tears. You're still grieving."

Seemed as if she always knew the right words to say. I wondered what her father must have been like. There had to have been some good in him, being the biological father of such a kind and loving person.

I couldn't imagine that she was the progeny of some wicked or mischievous man, a man who deserved an untimely death. Then again. I guess people would find it hard to believe I was the child of a murderer. Even I had trouble believing that. A soft breeze began to stir in the ballfield, rippling the flag a bit, just enough that it clanked against the metal pole. I stood again and began walking across the infield.

"Where are you going?" Ashley called, as I neared the gate.

"Going home," I said, turning back to look at her.

"Can I ride with you?" she asked.

"How did you get down here," I responded.

"I walked," she said, smiling.

She was so beautiful, standing there in the gaunt light. I couldn't stop loving her because of what my father did. I couldn't stop wanting her to be my wife. I waited for her to reach me. Then, we got into my truck together. She scooted out a place for her feet among the pile of empty soda bottles and cans of Copenhagen.

"I guess you were the one I saw on our front porch earlier," I said.

"Yeah," she admitted slamming the heavy door. "That was me. I followed the path that runs alongside the old furniture shop to get down here. It's still pretty clear. Somebody's still walking it."

I cranked the truck and watched the headlights spread a creamy glow across the old ballfield. The radio was playing country music. Ashley leaned over and turned the volume down.

"How do you listen to that depressing shit?"

"I don't know," I remarked. "Grew up listening to it, I guess."

Ashley slid across the seat to be nearer to me, straddling the gear shift with her legs. The fragrance of her perfume wafted through the humid air. She rested her head against my chest.

"I have to leave tomorrow," she revealed.

I didn't know how to respond. Whatever bond there had been between us seemed frayed and pliable now, a fragile remnant of our once indelible passion for each other. A horsefly flitted in through the rolled-down windows, and I shooed him away with my hat, following him until he disappeared into the darkness.

"And I don't want to leave without knowing what is bothering you."

I pulled the wrinkled and yellowed newspaper clipping from my back pocket and gave it to Ashley. She read it beneath the glow of her cell phone flashlight.

"What is this?" she asked. "Is this about my daddy? Where did you find this?"

"Katie found it," I said, staring out into the layers of darkness, afraid to look at Ashley. "She found it in a box beneath Daddy's bed."

"I don't understand," she admitted. "What would this be doing in a box beneath your daddy's bed?"

"That's what I have been trying to figure out," I answered.

She crumpled up the clipping and gave it back to me. I crumpled it up even more and tossed it out of the window.

"What did you do that for," she exclaimed.

"Tired of looking at it," I replied.

The town's darkness swelled around the truck ominously, the moonless sky bulging against my idling engine. A silence had enveloped us, a strangulating silence sated and bowing from the weight of unfulfilled dreams and fragile promises—things and words you wish you could take back but knew you never could. Seemed like neither of us wanted to speak anymore. The silence seemed more comfortable, more amiable, wrapping around us like a blanket. I put the truck into reverse and began to back onto the empty highway. I reached for the radio dial, but Ashley grabbed my hand.

"I still don't understand what any of this means," she confessed. "What does any of this have to do with us?"

"I think my daddy killed your daddy," I blurted. "I think Stiff and my daddy murdered him."

"Why? What makes you think that?"

"Fudge told me," I replied. "The other night when we were out in the shop. That's what we were talking about."

"So, Fudge was a witness?" she asked.

"Not exactly. But he pretty much told me about what happened."

"What did he say happened?"

"According to Fudge, he was down there at Floyd's that night, running off at the mouth, like he always does when he starts drinking, telling folks that nobody but John Stiles knew where Stiff had his still. And I guess your daddy and one of his buddies followed my daddy when he left the bar, thinking he might lead them to the still. When he didn't, they just beat the hell out of him for some damn reason. Stiff found out about it, and that's when it happened."

I put the truck back in neutral and shut it off. The dark became complete again. She scooted back against the passenger door, becoming a silhouette in my peripheral vision.

"I'm not sure how to process all of this," she remarked.

"I'm not either," I admitted. "Been eating me up inside."

The words of condolence I expected never developed. We just sat there in the silence and the darkness. Once, we had been in love. Now, we didn't even know how to speak to each other. The darkness swallowed us up and separated us with chasms too wide to cross. I heard her door open and listened to her footsteps as she walked away. I didn't even try to stop her; I didn't even know if I could.

THE GUN

She was gone by the time I got back home. According to Katie, Ashley walked into the house, grabbed a bag, and left. Hell, she didn't even take all her shit. There were piles of pajamas, panties, and shirts piled up in a corner beneath the bedroom window. The fragrance of her Chanel perfume lingered in the humid evening air.

I sat on the edge of my bed and pressed one of her shirts against my face. I thought about our first real date. It was October, and I took her to the county fair. We rode the Ferris wheel and the Pirate's ship. We sat at the picnic table and shared a funnel cake as the sun set and the wind began to blow. The coolness of an autumn evening settled on the town of Saylors. I remember offering her my jacket and then draping it around her shoulders.

It could have been a thousand years ago, the way time just seemed to keep taking things away from me, whittling away at the pieces of my life I wanted to preserve, leaving me with only delicate and opaque memories—memories of first dates and kisses and Saturday morning deer hunts with Daddy. The world I had been holding onto for so long crumbled through the gaps between my calloused fingers. Katie walked into the room and sat beside me on the bed.

"Why is everything changing?" I asked.

"What do you mean?"

"I thought we would bury Daddy and everything would get back to normal, but it seems to be getting worse," I explained, dropping Ashley's shirt on the floor. "I've got a mind to go over there right now and shoot Stiff Jenkins myself."

"Don't talk like that," she responded. "How would that make

anything better?"

"I don't know. What am I to do? Just sit here on my ass and watch my whole world fall apart?"

I stood up and began shuffling through the wrinkled shirts in the top of my dresser.

"What are you looking for?" Katie asked.

"My gun," I shouted. "I am looking for my fucking gun."

Katie screamed for Carter, then stood and attempted to pull me away from the dresser. But I was too strong and pushed her back on the bed. By the time Carter responded to her screams, I already had the gun in my hand.

"What's going on?" he asked, entering the room.

"Your brother is about to do something stupid. That's what is happening," Katie screamed. "You have to stop him, Carter. Don't let him leave the house."

But there was nothing he could do, and he realized that. I nudged him out of the way as I entered the hallway.

"Where are you going?" he asked.

"I'm going to kill Stiff Jenkins," I answered. "Maybe then I'll be the fucking legend in this stinking town," I added, slamming the screen door behind me.

But someone stopped me on the porch, the last person in the world I wanted to see: Jonas Wannamaker, the chief of police.

"Slow down, son," he said, placing a hand on his holster. "Where are you going with that gun?"

"Don't worry about it," I barked, passing by him and tramping into the yard.

By that time, Katie and Carter were on the front porch. Katie was crying loudly, and Carter was trying his best to console her.

"I tell you what," Chief Wannamaker said calmly. "Why don't you put that gun down and let's all go back inside and talk about this thing?"

Reluctantly, I tossed the loaded pistol onto the seat of my truck and followed them back into the house. Katie made a pot of coffee, and we all sat around the kitchen table. The darkness seemed more tangible than usual, the gaunt light above the table impotent against the bulging of darkness. I felt as if I no longer existed—as if I was some sort of spirit moving around the room devouring all of the sadness and confusion that remained from the absence of Daddy. And not just from the time of his death but from the time of his departure from the house on that Sunday afternoon Momma asked him to leave.

Nothing had been right since then—nothing about me, about us, about life. We sat there comatose, like lifeless caricatures, the sediment of what had once been a family, void of emotions and hope and dreams. All of us except Jonas Wannamaker, of course. He looked like the happiest mother fucker in the world, sitting there with this big damn smile on his face, as if he were the protector of our family or something like that. As if we were all so excited and blessed to be in his presence as if were Jesus Christ himself sitting there at the kitchen table. As we listened to the coffee brewing and the sound of ice dropping into the ice tray, he took off his cap and placed it on the table.

"So tell me what's been happening," he commanded, his eyes settling on me. "Tell me where you were going with that gun, Luke."

Katie poured us all a cup of coffee, even Carter, whom I had never seen drink a damn cup of coffee in his life. She set the sugar and creamer onto the table, then sat back down. Her eyes were still swollen from crying. She dumped a bit of sugar into her coffee, then offered the sugar to Chief Wannamaker. He waved a hand at her, saying he preferred to drink his black. Then, he shoved the sugar toward me.

I still hadn't been able to look at him. I just stared at my coffee, like the answers were down there somewhere, buried among the alabaster, spoon-shaped swirls of creamer and sugar I had added to my coffee.

"What about it, son?" he repeated. "Where were you going with that gun?"

I looked up at Katie, and her head was bowed, too. Then, I turned towards Carter. He was looking from side to side as if he were lost or in some strange dwelling where nothing seemed familiar. Sometimes, I felt that way myself—that I was lost in some peculiar place, living in a home where I had never been, even though I had spent most of my life between these nostalgic walls. Nothing seemed familiar since Daddy had been gone. Not the walls. Not the rooms. Not even the hallways and furniture.

Once, there had been photographs of us in the hallway, photographs of us as a family, photographs of Momma in her wedding dress on the day she married Daddy. Now, nothing remained. Momma took all the pictures down, packed them up somewhere, I suppose, and replaced them with bland pictures of mountains and waterfalls and sunflower fields—almost as if she didn't want us to remember that Daddy had ever been a resident of this place. But taking down the pictures couldn't extinguish memories. They held tightly to this house—pasted to the walls and furniture, still vibrant in the grasses that surrounded the antiquated mill house.

"I always keep a gun on me," I finally answered.

"Do you have a concealed weapons permit?"

"Yeah," I responded. "Probably one of the few people in Turkey Creek who does."

Chief Wannamaker took his first sip of coffee and grimaced.

"Whew," he exclaimed. "Coffee's a little strong, Katie."

"Do you need some creamer or sugar?" Katie asked.

"No, no," he replied, shaking his head. "I need a little more hair on my chest," he chuckled, canvassing the room, as if he suspected all of us to be laughing at his sterile endeavor with satire.

"I could make some more," she offered.

"No," he insisted. "I will get used to it." He labored through another swallow, then turned his attention again to me. "I tell you what," he said. "Why don't you and me take a walk down to the shop? Maybe you can come with us, Katie."

"Whatever you have to tell us, why can't you tell us right here?" I asked.

I could tell my response bothered him a bit. He struggled with another swig of my sister's coffee.

"Well," he began, struggling for words to repel my unexpected response, "I just thought there may be some things you didn't want Carter to hear."

"He was Carter's daddy as much as he was mine," I countered. "Whatever you have to tell us about him, Carter is going to hear about it anyway sooner or later, whether I want him to or not. Might as well tell him now."

He scooted his chair away from the table, like he was about to leave, which I was privately hoping he would. But he didn't. He stretched his arms out and clasped his hands together. There was silence for a few moments, nobody wanting to make eye contact. Perhaps Katie and Carter were as surprised at my response as Chief Wannamaker had been. I took my first sip of coffee, then leaned against the table. In the afflictive silence, sadness seemed to engulf the room and all of us sitting at the table, even our unwelcomed guest.

"I'll go to my room," Carter said, rising from the table and ending the unsettling silence.

We listened to him walk down the hall to his room, shutting the door behind him. I tried to imagine how he was feeling, having just buried his father, and now not knowing whether the man he most respected was going to die or not. I wanted his life to be happy, to be void of troubles, but no matter how much I wanted that happily ever after life for him, I realized eventually he would unwillingly be exposed to the inequities of this harsh and challenging life and become familiar with words like dishonesty, heartbreak, betrayal, disease, and death. Then, he would be just as fucked up in the head as the rest of us, not knowing what to do or say or even how to react. A part of me wanted to walk into the room with him, sit on his bed and play video games, give each other a hard time, and laugh as we once did, as we once could. I sure as hell didn't want to be sitting at the kitchen table entertaining this dumb-ass Chief of Police.

"Well, Miss Katie," Wannamaker began, perhaps sensing my disinterest in whatever he wanted to say, "Luke and I have already talked about this a little bit."

He took another sip of coffee, then continued. "I know that Stiff and your father were good friends. And I know that Stiff has helped ya'll out a lot, especially after your parents split. As a matter of fact, he has helped many people in this town, including me, so I can overlook a little moonshining, but murder is different. As much as I like Stiff, I don't feel as if I can do my job without investigating a few unsolved murders or missing person cases. And, in most of these cases, I believe Stiff was somehow involved."

"So how do you think we can help?" Katie asked nervously, her head still bowed. "Do you really think Luke can just go over there and ask Stiff about these unsolved cases, and Stiff will just nonchalantly confess to these murders?"

"No, but I do think he may be able to get him to confess to one."

I knew which case he was referring to, and, by the way Katie was looking at me, I realized she did also.

"But," he said, rising from the chair, "y'all talk about it amongst yourselves for a little while and see what you think. I will tell you this, though, if Stiff did have anything to do with what happened to Fudge—well I would certainly be careful around him."

And that was all he said. He put his hat back on, thanked Katie for the coffee, and then walked wordlessly out of the house.

"What if he's right?" Katie asked, as soon as she was certain Chief Wannamaker was out of hearing range. "What if he's right about Stiff? What if he's planning to kill you, too?"

"Nothing's going to happen to me," I answered calmly. "Especially if I kill him first, as I am planning to do."

"That's not going to help anything," she angrily retorted. "Just get to spend the rest of your life in jail."

"And what happens to me if I just sit here, and he sends somebody over to kill me or you or Carter?"

Katie bowed her head and began to cry.

"I don't know what to do anymore. Daddy's gone, and everything is falling apart."

I finished my coffee and walked out of the house. Nobody followed me, and nobody attempted to stop me. I left the yard unbothered, a loaded 9mm beside me.

THE ENCOUNTER

Summer kills everything in Turkey Creek—the grass, the trees, hopes and dreams, even lives. On the first of April, everything is so beautiful around here—the oaks and hickories budding out, the dogwoods and redbuds throwing color into the forests, the jonquils blooming alongside the road and in the cattle pastures, and azaleas blooming in people's yards. By the end of July, everything is different . . . dead. Ain't no color anywhere, and everything is fried brown.

There isn't any wisteria or jessamine to smell, not even any honeysuckle to pull off a vine and taste. Just brown grass and brown trees dropping leaves before they ever had a chance to show color in the fall. In most places, the cold of winter kills off things, but in Turkey Creek, the cold doesn't kill anything but kudzu. It's the heat of summer that slays everything around here and makes you struggle for every breath you take.

With windows rolled down, I drove to Stiff's farm, ready to kill him, rage sizzling in the July heat that swirled in the window-down breezes fanning my face. I drove through the town like a stranger, as if Turkey Creek were just a town I was passing through on my way to visit someplace else.

It sure as hell didn't feel like my hometown anymore—the place where I was born, the place where I would most likely die, the place that held all my memories and swallowed all my adolescent dreams. I leaned my head out the window a bit, so that I could smell the stench of the dying town, so that I could take just one final aspiration of this wretched place. This was a place that melted people as the July heat melted candy bars left in a car, the abandoned brick buildings that used to be stores, the ruins of the burned-up cotton mill, and the decrepit elementary school. All of it merged into one final and perilous aroma that pirouetted in the peripheral silhouettes slanting against the hood of my truck as I navigated the winding streets of the empty town that most people had given up on a long time ago.

Nothing would ever be the same after this night—not for me anyway and not for my hometown. I was prepared to deliver a punch more lethal and detrimental than the flood of 2000 or the closing of the cotton mill or the end of every damn baseball season. I was prepared to kill Stiff Jenkins and register his name to the burgeoning list of men who had died too young in this town—men such as my daddy, Justin Gomez, and my Uncle Wade, whom I had never even gotten to meet.

They could put Stiff's name on a monument if they wanted. Hell, they could even build a fucking statue of him for all I cared. But I was prepared to extinguish the last languishing flicker of whatever optimism remained in this God-forsaken town. Whatever glimmer of hope that persisted among the desolate fractures of this forgotten place and this forgotten time, whatever glorious glaze lingered from its venerable past, I purposed to quench this night—infinitely and resolutely. In my nefarious thoughts, corrupted by small-town stories and incredulous rumors, I believed it could all be resolved with a single, malevolent shot, a lone bullet that would pierce the forehead of my deceased father's best friend.

Of course, as I neared Stiff's farm, my tenacity began to subside. An uncertainty, swelled by memories, began to settle on me as the darkness of pine forest-shouldered roads began to engulf me, and the gaunt light of Turkey Creek faded in my rearview mirror.

I remembered the state championship game, being down by one in the final inning. The other team had some kid on the mound who could throw in the low 90s. He struck the first two batters out. Then, Cody busted one to the gap between the centerfield and right fielder and got to second base. And there I was, the last hope for our team, staring down a kid who was throwing harder than any kid I had ever played against. I took a few balls, fouled off a couple, and worked him into a full count.

The next ball he threw, I smoked it into right center, Cody scored and tied the game, and we won in extra innings. That was the first time I ever heard my dad cheer for me. Usually, he just leaned against the chain link fence, spit tobacco, and stayed quiet. Not that night. That night, I heard his voice rising from the bleachers. I remember standing on the bag at first, looking up at him in the stands. He was so happy then. He was clapping his hands and smiling, and the people around him were high fiving each other. I was so glad I made him smile. I was so glad I made him proud.

At Stiff's farm, the darkness settled on me like a weight, a burden I could not bear alone. A summer breeze rattled the heat-withered leaves of the live oak trees, and every now and again, a spiny ball would drop from the sweet gum tree onto the tin roof barn. And the sky—hell, I couldn't even see the moon, just galaxies and galaxies of stars and more stars than a man could ever count—more stars than the sky could even hold.

When I was younger, I thought this place was paradise. Me and Cody would play all day in these pastures and barns. In the summertime, if we weren't playing baseball, we would be out here, playing cowboys and Indians or swimming in the pond, goofing off like kids do. Those days seemed so long ago. I wish I would have been able to bottle them up and put them in a time capsule or something, something I could open whenever I wanted and feel the bliss of adolescence again. But, as the old saying goes, man cannot stop time. And, if we cannot stop time, then we are unable to stop whatever time brings to us—good or bad, right or wrong, joy or suffering. Whatever time brings, we must accept. There is no other choice.

I softly closed the door to my truck, hoping to restrain the raspy creak of its rusted hinges. A slash of light sloped from the barn window and trickled banners of light across random thickets of wiregrass and brambles. I could hear people talking inside, maybe two or three. I couldn't really tell. Then, I heard a laugh, a bold, distinguished laugh that I recognized as belonging to Huck. I also noticed his truck parked against the back side of the barn.

I tucked my pistol into the back of my jeans and entered. Darkness still lingered where I walked, carefully monitoring my steps in a futile effort to mitigate the noise. But, in the anemic light at the back of the barn, I could see Stiff and Huck leaning against that old Allis-Chalmers tractor. Someone else was there also, buried in the darkness so well that I could not discern their identity. I stepped meticulously around old tools, empty bottles of beer, and burlap feed sacks. The person in the darkness noticed my furtive approach and leaned forward. It was Becky, Huck's wife, the one who had been arguing with Momma that night at the bar.

"What in the hell are you doing?" she asked, with her raspy, cigarette-hoarse voice. "You trying to sneak up on us?"

"Yeah," I answered, smiling. "Trying to sneak up on Stiff."

I thought my response would appease the sudden awkwardness of my flawed approach. But nobody said anything. I kept walking toward the subtle globe of light, my gait hindered by the anxiety of not knowing what would happen. Was I really prepared to kill Stiff, or was he going to kill me? Or was nothing going to be settled in this familiar barn? Would I walk away with questions still unanswered, hidden truths that kept me up at night? I was determined not to let that happen, no matter the consequences.

"You been choosing some really strange hours to visit me lately," Stiff finally said, reaching over the tractor for a wrench that Huck was holding.

"Well," I began cautiously, "I keep getting distracted."

"Wannamaker been to visit you again?" he asked.

"Yeah," I admitted shyly. "He just left."

"What did he tell you this time?"

"Same old shit," I said.

"Yeah," he agreed. "His story never changes. He wants people to think I am Al Capone, and he's been sent directly by the FBI to disrupt my moonshine operation. Carries around a list in his back pocket of people he thinks I have killed."

Stiff shook his head and spit into the iron drum barrel leaning against the back wall.

"That son of a bitch has been jealous of Stiff ever since high school, ever since we played baseball together," Huck agreed. "Son of a bitch has been holding a grudge for that long. It ain't Stiff's fault he wasn't worth a shit."

Huck had an angry look on his face, and I could tell that he had a strong dislike for Jonas Wannamaker and didn't even like talking about the man.

"He's an asshole," Huck's wife said. "Plain and simple, just like that. He's a grade-A asshole."

Stiff continued to work on the tractor, swapping sockets every now and again with Huck.

"Don't really bother me too much," Stiff said, straining to loosen a bolt. "But what does bother me is that he has you and a bunch of other people believing your daddy did some bad stuff he never did."

He jumped from the step of the tractor and handed the ratchet to Huck, wiping his soiled hands with a greasy shop rag. I continued forward, breaching the barn's grim glow of light, which trickled from a single 40-watt bulb that drooped precariously from a wooden beam. I temporarily forgot about the pistol I had tucked in the back of my jeans until Huck saw it.

"What are you doing with that pistol?" he asked, yanking it from my pants and examining it. "Stiff," he called, "Luke has done come in here packing."

His wife giggled as she puffed on a cigarette. Stiff looked at the gun, then back at me.

"Did you think you might have to use that tonight?" he asked.

"I thought I might have to," I answered, taking the gun back from Huck.

"Who were you thinking about shooting? Me?"

"I don't know what to think anymore," I responded. "I thought you might try and shoot me."

"For what?"

"I don't know," I replied, shrugging my shoulders. "Maybe because of what Fudge told me."

"And what did Fudge tell you?"

"Told me about how he was running his mouth one night down at Floyd's bar to these two strangers. For some reason, they followed Daddy around that night, jumped him somewhere, and beat the hell out of him."

"Well," Stiff agreed, "that did happen."

"Then he told me that those two fellows disappeared and that their bodies were found later. He suspected you might have had something to do with their disappearance and maybe Daddy too. He said he just wanted to apologize because he thought the whole damn thing was his fault."

"Well," Stiff responded, shaking his head like he was aggravated, "Fudge was right about something. He does have a pair of loose lips, especially after he has had a few beers. But your daddy and

I didn't have nothing to do with their disappearance. Only thing I did, when I found out who those fellows were, was bring Huck here with me. Then, we went to Georgia and beat the hell out of them two guys like they did your daddy. It was a couple of weeks later when we heard they were missing, wasn't it, Huck?

"Yeah," Huck confirmed. "Probably at least that long, maybe longer."

"And I can tell you this," Stiff added. "Guys like that probably had several people who wanted them to disappear."

"'Why do you say that?" I asked.

"They were dickheads," Stiff revealed.

"Damn bullies," Huck said. "And I hate a fucking bully."

"Why you so worried about them two fellows anyway?" Stiff inquired.

"Because one of them was Ashley's father."

"Ashley? Your girlfriend Ashley?"

"Yeah," I answered. "That's what I come down here to talk to you about. I didn't think I could marry her if my daddy had anything to do with her daddy's murder."

Huck grabbed a beer from the cooler and then offered one to Stiff. Stiff pulled the wad of tobacco from his protracted lower lip and peeled back the lid of his beer can. He sighed as he gulped his first swallow.

"Well," he began, "I am real sorry that one of those assholes was the father of your girlfriend. But neither me or your daddy had anything to do with their disappearance."

Stiff took the first swallow of his beer, his face just a shape in the struggling light, an anonymous contour that melted impeccably into the swelling shadows of the barn.

"I think maybe you and Huck need to take a ride," he suggested. "And, no he ain't going to kill you. He just needs to explain some things to you. Be easier for you to understand during a ride around town than standing here in this old barn, swatting at mosquitoes."

Huck reached out his hand and nodded at the pistol, implying for me to hand it back to him. "Just so I feel better," he explained, as I reluctantly placed the gun into his hand.

"Don't need a damn pistol anyway," Stiff said. "Not when you have Huck."

Huck turned, and I followed him out of the barn, tracing the steps of his mud-clotted boots into the yard. The air was thick and heavy, and I was sweating like hell. I stood there for a moment just looking around, getting caught up in memories again.

Seemed like the memories were coming from every direction, bouncing off each plank of wood that shaped the old barn—each strand of barbed wire, each cedar post, each pungent smell. Huck didn't speak a word. He got in his truck and cranked the damn thing up, as if he were ready to get the hell out of there. I wasn't quite as anxious to leave but afraid that any delay might rile Huck or Stiff.

I trudged through the muddy yard toward the truck anyway, put in a pinch of Copenhagen, and got inside. Huck finished his beer and chunked the empty can into the bed of his truck. I slammed my door and settled onto the torn cloth seats, shoving floor trash around so I could set my feet comfortably. The thought of what might happen to me didn't bother me too much anymore. I seemed unusually barren of emotion, and, as Huck guided his 75 Chevrolet truck back onto the highway, a strange kind of peace settled upon me—a peace I had not felt in a while, the kind of peace I used to feel when I was little and a bad storm came and Daddy would lift me into his lap. That's the kind of peace I felt.

That was exactly the kind of peace I felt.

THE RIDE

I have spent my entire life wanting to believe in God, trying to believe in God—especially the kind of God that Daddy believed in after he was saved, the kind of God that could change a man's thoughts or behavior, even when nobody else was around.

I remember being over at Daddy's trailer one evening, right after he and Mom had split up. This guy named Charlie Garth came to visit. I didn't know him well. He lived in the town of Banks, which is about five miles south of Turkey Creek and an even smaller town, if you can believe that. Nothing there but a trailer park and a post office, as far as I could remember. Didn't even have a damn church.

Anyway, Charlie had worked with Daddy a long time at the meat factory, same shift and all, so Daddy had grown used to him, I guess. To me, he seemed like an odd kind of fellow, the kind I wouldn't have wanted to be around long. Just something about him, I guess, something that kind of made me nervous. Daddy didn't seem to mind his visits, so I acted as if I didn't either.

Well, apparently, Charlie Garth was having a hard time believing in God himself because I walked in on one of their discussions that night. It was one of those deep, profound discussions that Daddy had a way of tricking people into, talking about the origin of the universe and all the different kinds of theories about its formation and all that shit. Where did we come from, where did the stars come from, and where did the fucking water come from?

I just let them talk because I didn't feel as if I had enough damn sense to be a part of their cordial arguments. I do remember what Daddy asked Charlie that night. Sometime, near the end of their discussion, Daddy asked Charlie if he had ever seen anything that made him wonder if there was a God or some higher form of being. Charlie answered, "Not that I can remember." Then, Daddy said he would pray for Charlie that before he died, he would see something that would cause him to know there was a God.

I guess, in a way, I was just like Charlie, still looking for that one thing, that one miracle in my life that would assure me of God's existence. My only problem was that the more I searched for proof of God, the more evidence I found to stimulate Charlie's theory that there was no God at all. We really didn't know why we were here or who in the hell started this fucked up thing called life. I guess that's about the way it was with me and God after Daddy died. I wanted there to be a God; I wanted to believe there was someplace up in the sky where Daddy was walking the streets of gold.

Hell, I guess we all think that way, wanting to believe our deceased friends and family are still alive somewhere, still breathing, still looking at us from some heavenly chamber. Easier to believe that way, I suppose, than to believe they are just there, lying beneath six feet of dirt, skin being eaten and torn away by ants and worms and maggots. Nobody wants to believe that way.

Huck Strawhorne hadn't said a word since we left Stiff's house. He just kept driving—road after road, turn after turn, looking more comatose than Fudge Pickens did in that hospital bed with all those tubes attached to him. I finally convinced him to pull over somewhere and let me take a piss. The thought crossed my mind, while I was whizzing into the high grass along the side of the road, to take off running. Wasn't any way Huck would have been able to catch me. I could have put ten or twenty yards between us before he even realized I was gone.

But I didn't do any such thing. I just climbed back up into the truck and sat there, waiting for Huck to do whatever he was going to do. I looked over at him while I buckled my seatbelt.

He was squeezing together another pinch of tobacco, his fingers thick and peeled white in some places.

"Where are we going?" I finally asked. He pretended not to hear me as he yanked his lip forward and fitted another glob of Copenhagen behind his poked-out lip.

"You know what?"

His words hung heavily and still in the night air, and I knew he didn't expect any response from me. I sat still, trying not to look at him, waiting for him to continue.

"I spent five years in the penitentiary," he finally responded, "and I think I missed this shit here," he added, tapping his can of Copenhagen to assure there was no misinterpretation, "more than my old lady's pussy."

I had to laugh a little at his surprising response. Seemed so long that there had been anything to laugh at in my life. He looked at me, grinned, and patted me on the knee.

"Why did you have to go to prison?" I asked cautiously.

"Well, I was young and stupid, as you are now," he responded.

"They don't put you in jail for that."

He screwed the top off an empty water bottle that was rolling across the seat between us and made it his spittoon. With the truck turned off, I could hear the whippoorwills and katydids and, every now and again, the hoot of a barn owl. Some things survived the hot South Carolina summers, and they boasted about it at night when everything else went silent.

"No, you're right about that," he answered, spitting. "The truth is, I got caught with some shine and beat the hell out of the damn cop who tried to arrest me."

"They will send you to jail for that," I agreed.

"Yeah," he said, nodding and giggling just a bit. "They will send you to jail for that."

"Then why do you still do it?"

"Do what?"

"I don't know," I began. "You know how folks talk around Turkey Creek. I hear stories about you beating up people that owe Stiff money, breaking their legs, or fucking them up in some kind of way."

"Yeah, I have heard a few of them myself," he responded. "But truth is, I haven't hurt anybody in a long time."

"Is that why you are having second thoughts about me?"

"What would I want to hurt you for?" he snarled. "Because you believe all that bullshit Wannamaker feeds you?"

"I guess so."

He sighed and spit into the water bottle again.

"Let's take a walk, kid," he demanded, stepping out of the truck.

"Where in the hell are we walking to?" I asked boldly. "I ain't walking nowhere to get shot. If you are going to shoot me, just do it right here."

"What am I going to shoot you with?" he responded. "Ain't got a damn gun."

I opened the door carefully and allowed my feet to fall onto the dew-wet grass. I shut the door and walked to where Huck was standing, holding onto a flashlight.

"There's something I need to show you," he announced with gruff words he tried to turn into a whisper. "Follow me," he said, climbing over a gate and cursing his age.

I hesitated at the back of the truck and could tell Huck was becoming frustrated.

"Damn it, Luke," he growled. "I told you that day when I saw you at the gas station to come and talk to me if you started having crazy thoughts."

"I'm not having crazy thoughts," I said.

"You're not? You brought a damn gun into Stiff's barn. What were you planning to do? Shoot your daddy's best friend? Are those not crazy thoughts? If you would have just come to me first as I asked, none of this shit would be necessary. And we could have both been sleeping in a bed by now."

Warily, I advanced toward the gate. All sorts of thoughts were stirring around in my head. It was like my whole life had abated to this one decision—did I trust Huck Strawhorne or not? I reluctantly placed a foot on the gate, trying to be as subtle as I could. The gate moved just a bit, making a whistling noise that caused Huck to turn and give me the hush sign.

"Where in the hell are we at anyway?" I asked, as I cleared the gate. "I don't recognize this place at all."

"Probably ain't never been in this way," he said, wanting his words to be whispers again. "You'll know where you are in a little while."

We began walking a wide forest service road between woods that had been recently cut. There were puddles and dips everywhere, but Huck never stumbled, just me.

"Why don't you turn the damn flashlight on?" I asked.

"Hell, your daddy could see in the dark. Just figured you could, too."

I didn't say anything else. I followed him down the craggy road until we came to a space where the woods opened up, and I could see the lights from a house in the dip.

"Do you recognize this place?" Huck asked.

I squirmed closer to him and peered into the yard. Some things seemed familiar, but others didn't. There was a playground at the rear of the house. Nothing outlandish. Just a couple of swings and a slide. I couldn't see into the house, and I couldn't make out what vehicles were parked under the metal carport. They all blended into a patch of darkness. The only source of light was what fell from a street post lamp, and it perished about fifty yards from the home.

"I don't know, Huck. Can't be sure," I whispered.

"It's Chief Wannamaker's house," he revealed.

"Well, what in the hell did you bring me here for?"

"We need to get in that barn down there."

"What for?"

"Because I think that son of a bitch is the one that hit Fudge last night."

"What makes you think that?"

"Because he reckons people will suspect that Stiff had something to do with it."

"What do you expect to find in that barn that will help you prove that?"

"I'm hoping to find a red pickup truck with a messed up front bumper," he said. "Let's try and sneak down this hill and slip in from the back."

I followed him through the used-to-be woods, my arms getting scratched by bramble patches and thistle weeds and pine saplings with thorny leaves and grass burrs. Beggar's lice stuck to my jeans. I was amazed at how swiftly Huck was moving through this shit and me, thirty years younger, struggled with every step. I managed to keep pace with him, and, in only a few minutes, we were standing there at the edge of Wannamaker's yard, staring at the shape of a barn big enough to hide a pickup truck.

Huck placed his arm across my chest, then stepped into the yard. When he reached the barn, he motioned for me to proceed, and I cautiously walked into the yard. By this time, my adrenaline was rushing because I had gone from being frightened to having fun. I stood close to Huck as we crept around the edge of the barn —stealthlike and calculating each secret step. My glands were beginning to sweat, though. It was so damn hot. My tee shirt was sticking to my flesh.

Huck pushed open the front door. There was the pickup truck, but it was too dark for me to tell what color it was. I edged up against a plywood table littered with bolts and sockets and nuts. The barn smelled like grease and paint and mildewed wood. As soon as I was far enough into the barn, Huck closed the door and turned on the flashlight he had been carrying the whole time.

"Son of a bitch," he mumbled as he inspected the front bumper. "I never thought he would go this far."

BLUE LIGHTS

Huck might not have said much on the way to Wannamaker's house, but damn if he didn't talk on the half-hour drive back to Stiff's farm. And he was right. I should have come to him first. He explained everything that didn't make sense to me—the reason they called my daddy the legend, the paper clipouts in the box beneath the bed, the reason we were sneaking around in Chief Wannamaker's barn. He explained all of what I had been trying to figure out since I watched my daddy die in that hospital in Atlanta, all the rumors and stories I had heard. All of it began to make sense to me as Huck and I drove the lightless country roads back to Stiff's farm.

According to Huck, all this nonsense began with Jonas Wannamaker. I always thought he went from the police academy straight down to the Charleston County Sheriff's Department. According to Huck, that's not the way it happened. After he graduated from the police academy, he came back to Turkey Creek and worked on the police force here for about a year before he moved to Charleston.

And that is when all this shit started happening. Huck said that grudge Wannamaker developed during high school because he wasn't worth a shit at anything had deep roots. When Wannamaker came back to Turkey Creek, he wanted to prove to the whole damn town that he was a good cop and that people should be afraid of him because he had graduated from the police academy and was wearing a badge.

He soon learned, however, that nobody treated him any differently than they had before he left. Hell, some people even thought less of him when he pinned that badge to his shirt. Seemed to make him cocky, Huck said. He started giving people citations and pulling them over for stupid shit. Huck said he wanted to be the badass in town, but despite graduating from the police academy and wearing a badge, people were still more afraid of Stiff than they were of him. People knew not to cross Stiff but didn't give a damn if they crossed Wannamaker.

Huck never thought many people were afraid of Stiff. He said people just respected Stiff. It didn't matter how many badges Wannamaker pinned to his shirt or how many lapels he attached to his sleeve. He never would gain the respect of the townspeople as Stiff had. Respect, Huck said, was one trait that could not be given to a man. It had to be earned.

Then, he started talking about my daddy, telling me how much he respected him and how much Stiff did, too. He said that's why Stiff and him beat the hell out of them two fellows. Said it didn't have nothing to do with money.

"Your old man knew that he was being followed," Huck said. "So he pulled over in this cul-de-sac. Well, those two guys lit into him and wouldn't let up, kept asking him about Stiff's still, wanting him to tell them where it was located. But your daddy wouldn't give them any information—just kept telling them that he didn't know where it was and that he had never even seen the damn thing. I guess, at some point, when they figured out he wasn't going to tell them nothing, they just decided to kick his ass. And I mean, they beat him up badly. Broke his nose and blackened both his eyes. He looked like shit by the time Stiff and I seen him.

"Your daddy wouldn't tell Stiff what happened at first—told him not to worry about it. But you know Stiff has a way of finding things out. And, when he found out the names of them two fellows, he called me over to his house, and we went over to Georgia and gave them boys the ass whipping they had coming. We didn't leave until their faces looked as bad as your daddy's did the night they beat him up. But we never killed anybody.

"Wasn't until a few weeks later that we found out those same two fellows was missing. Your daddy read that newspaper from Augusta, Georgia. Don't know why. But he showed that story to Stiff, and Stiff showed it to me that evening."

Huck stopped talking long enough to spit into his tobacco-stained water bottle. In the silence, his words hovered thick and sincere, bronzed bits of information desiring to be ingested. The music playing on the push button radio was soft and kind but only audible enough to be a sound when we paused at stop signs.

"It was because of the crossword puzzles," I finally said, disturbing the stillness.

"What?" Huck asked grumpily, as if he was surprised I even spoke at all.

"It was for the crossword puzzles," I explained. "That's why Daddy had that paper from Augusta. He said the ones in the Saylors paper were too easy for him, and, plus, the Augusta paper always had two crossword puzzles. Took him longer to complete them, I guess."

Spitting again, Huck responded, "I suppose you're right."

I didn't say anything more, hoping Huck would feel the urge for conversation again and sensing that Stiff's farm was nearing.

Finally, he continued, "A few months later, two more fellows went missing that supposedly had some kind of beef with Stiff."

He paused, and his stare fixed on empty space, like he was thinking really hard about something.

"Hell, I don't even remember what it was about now," he continued, surrendering to the absence of memory. "But anyway, we had just beat the hell out of them two guys, too. Maybe a month or two before. Well, your daddy got to thinking that was a hell of a coincidence, that something wasn't right. He began investigating, and somehow, he reached the conclusion that Wannamaker was responsible for these four missing people whose bodies happened to be discovered a few days after they were reported missing.

"Before your daddy had time to collect any more evidence, Wannamaker accepted that job in Charleston. And I guess your daddy's investigation just stopped. Wannamaker moved to Charleston, your daddy got married and started having kids, and I guess he just didn't have the time or motivation to keep playing Sherlock Holmes anymore."

"I wonder what made him suspect Wannamaker?"

"Hell if I know," Huck answered. "I'm sure he had his reasons, but I can't remember them. Stiff might. All I know is, from what we saw tonight, I am starting to believe your daddy was right."

"Yeah," I said, then sat silent again.

The air was filled with the clashing melodies of katydids and bullfrogs and the distant cries of whippoorwills and barn owls. I listened as Huck drove—even tilted my head out the window a bit to hear them better.

Finally, the burden had been lifted. I no longer had to worry that my father had something to do with the murder of my fiancée's father. I could begin to believe in the integrity of my father again. He didn't die with murder on his conscience. He died a forgiven and exonerated man, barren of secrets—at least, none as awful as murder.

I almost wanted to laugh. I was so happy. I placed my arm on the rubber sill of the truck's window and tapped my fingers against the metal door, searching for a rhythm in the turbulent symphonies of night. *Three more stop signs*, I thought in my suddenly tranquil mind. Three more stop signs before we turned on the road to Stiff's farm.

I could not wait to tell Katie. She would be so relieved. Thinking of Daddy as a murderer had been hanging on her like a lampshade since she found those newspaper clippings. What Huck told me would allow her to be happy again—happy like we used to be, happy like I thought we would never be again. Not happy about Daddy dying, but now we could remember him as we had wanted to remember him all along.

As we passed the last stop sign and turned towards Stiff's house, everything changed. Blue flashes danced against the night sky, and the sound of sirens whined in the once-silent air. I couldn't hear the katydids and bullfrogs and whippoorwills anymore—only the screech of sirens and the howl of nearby hound dogs.

As we rounded the final curve of our drive back, our greatest concern was verified. There were two Lincoln County police cars in Stiff's yard and one ambulance. Huck parked alongside the road and opened his door quickly. I could see Cody and his mother standing beside the barn. They were hugging each other, and it appeared that Mrs. Jenkins was crying. Suddenly, I saw Huck's wife running along the edge of the barn. She ran right into him, then sagged limply against his broad chest. His thick hands stroked her long, graying hair.

"What in the hell happened?" he asked.

"Stiff's dead," she replied.

"What?" Huck asked gruffly to be certain he heard the words he thought he did, that he heard the words I thought he heard.

"Stiff's dead," she repeated. "He's dead."

"How? What happened? Are you sure?'

"Yes," Becky shouted. "I'm sure that he is fucking dead. I'm not a moron."

I finger-tapped Huck's shoulder and pointed to the barn. Then, he saw what I saw: paramedics loading a tarp-covered body into the back of an ambulance while the two county policemen began wrapping the barn's borders with yellow tape. Huck nudged his wife and began walking toward the yellow tape.

"Wait a minute," one of the deputies declared. "You can't cross this line, sir."

But Huck wasn't listening to his orders. He ducked beneath the strand of tape and approached the ambulance with slow, resolute steps.

"Hold on," the second deputy said. "I know this man. Let me talk to him."

After jogging a few paces, he grabbed Huck's arm.

"Huck," the deputy began after reaching Huck, "I know you and Stiff were good friends, but I can't let you go any farther. This is a crime scene now."

Huck pulled loose from the deputy, turned, and stared at him.

"I want to see him one more time, Johnson," Huck told the deputy.

Reluctantly, the deputy nodded at one of the paramedics. Huck kept walking and prodding the paramedic out of the way. He pulled back the tarp a bit and caught one final glance of his friend.

DEATH IN A BARN

The scene became even more confusing after the ambulance left, carrying the corpse of Stiff Jenkins. I was still attempting to assimilate all I had just witnessed—my thoughts caught up in some kind of whirlwind, twisting and evolving and spiraling through what was left of my damn mind. How could Stiff Jenkins be dead? How could my daddy be dead?

I watched the way the blue lights flashed and swirled against the rotting boards of the barn, brushing reticently against the bereaved faces of Cody and his mother with each helicopter wave, the wind still and the night sky speckled with a million stars. In the distance, I could hear the lowing of Stiff's cattle, sounds lost in the darkness, wailing from some remote and invisible post.

A part of me wanted to pierce the boundaries of the yellow ribbon perimeter and run over to Cody and comfort him, but, hell, I probably wouldn't have known what to say anyway. Just tell him the same damn lies I was told after my daddy passed: I know how you feel, I know what you are going through, or Everything's going to be alright.

There were no words adequate for comforting a man after the death of his father. It was a wound that would not heal, a wound you just hoped might not hurt as much in the future. But the scar, the evidence that you would spend the rest of your days without him, hell, that scar would always be there as a permanent abrasion, haunting you on silent and especially lonely nights, brewing in mnemonic places, dancing in forgotten memories.

All that was gone for Cody now, piled up beneath a bright blue tarp and riding in the back of an ambulance, the man that loved him more than any man ever would love him. Cody would never hear his voice again, never hear his laugh, or feel his touch. This was death in the most profound and morosely intimate way. Death was real to Cody now, as it was real to me. It was no longer a thought you could avert or some far-off occurrence that only happened to the sick and weak. It was real and palpable and authentic, and the presence of it enveloped the whole damn place.

Seemed almost like death was still there, still walking around us in the night dark shadows, still lurking stealthily beyond the gyrating blinks of blue lights. It wasn't anything me or anybody else could have told him to make him feel better now. His father was dead, his life was never going to be the same, and there were no words to comfort him. Really, there were no words to comfort me because suddenly, I felt so out of place, as if I was at the home of a stranger I had never met.

Then, Wannamaker shows up, pulls right into the damn drive, and parks his car where the ambulance had been. The only emotion I could feel then was anger—how much I hated that son of a bitch, how many lies he had told me, how he had me convinced my father and Cody's father were murderers. I didn't even want to see his face or that damn smirk he seemed to always have.

I walked over to my truck and leaned against the hood, hoping to avoid conversation with him. Luckily, he was walking toward Huck and his wife, his gait deliberate and arrogant. Then, another car pulled into the yard, and a man stepped out. He was wearing a ball cap and a Polo shirt tucked neatly into stiff jeans and carrying some kind of notebook pad that he fitted beneath his right shoulder.

"Wannamaker," he yelled, as he slammed his door. "What in the hell are you doing out here? This is county business. No need for you to be out here."

Chief Wannamaker, whose haughty procession had been interrupted by the man's first words, turned and ambled with more cautious steps back toward the well-dressed man.

"I just thought I would come and see if y'all needed any help," Wannamaker replied, shrugging his shoulders.

Although I could not see him in the darkness, I could imagine him standing there with that egotistical smirk on his face, as if he were some kind of hero or emperor or authoritative figure who deserved our complete acquiescence. Whoever that man was, one thing was for certain, he was not intimidated by Wannamaker. He walked straight to him and told him firmly that he didn't need his help.

Wannamaker patted the man on the shoulder and walked back to his car, acting as if the man's words didn't bother him. He had been shamed and not just in front of strangers but people he had known for most of his life—people whose respect he had been attempting to earn since he had been designated the chief of police in Turkey Creek, South Carolina. I could only imagine how furious he must have been, driving back to the town that would never want him.

The man introduced himself to Huck and his wife, Becky, as Detective Wright. He pulled the notepad from his armpit and a pen from his front pocket.

"Now, as I understand, ma'am, you were a witness to this crime?" the detective asked.

"Yes, sir," Becky answered. "I saw the whole thing."

"Tell me what happened in your own words, then," the detective requested.

About that time, I heard my phone vibrating in the front seat of my truck. Until then, I never had even noticed that I did not have it with me. I picked it up, typed my password, then checked the screen. Two missed calls from Ashley and one new text message from her. I opened my messages.

"Meet me at the rock quarry."

What in the hell was she doing at the rock quarry? I almost left right then, but I did want to at least speak to Cody before driving away. I put in a pinch of Copenhagen and turned my attention back to the detective's interrogation.

"And you say you never saw this girl before?"

"I don't think so," Becky answered. "Face looked familiar, but I can't think of where I might have seen her."

"So she just picked up the gun that was there on the tractor and shot Mr. Jenkins without any provoking words from him?"

"Yes," Becky answered. "Damnedest thing I ever seen. Picked that gun up, aimed it at Stiff, and asked him if he knew her daddy."

She paused for a moment as if she was about to cry again.

"What did Stiff say?" the detective asked, encouraging her to continue the story.

"He asked her for the name of her father," Becky replied, then slumped against the shoulders of her husband.

This time, the detective didn't rush her. He kept writing in his notepad as if he was trying to catch up with her answers or rewriting his own notes. I looked down at my phone and wondered if I should text Ashley back. Instead, I chose to concentrate on the enduring interrogation of Becky Strawhorne.

"She told Stiff her daddy's name, but Stiff said he didn't know of him. And that's when she shot him. Shot him twice in the chest, then stood right over him and said, 'Neither did I, you son of a bitch.' Then, she walked through the damn door and got into the car, as if nothing ever happened."

"What did she say her father's name was?" the detective asked.

"I'm not real sure," she answered. "It was something unusual, like Clifton or Clelan or something."

The detective nodded, looking only at the paper on which he was scribbling his notes. When he looked up, he looked toward Huck.

"Any ideas on who might have done this, Huck?"

"No," Huck replied, shaking his head and stroking the hair of the woman he loved.

I guess, maybe then, the detective realized he would not get any more information from Huck, who was probably already planning an act of revenge against whoever murdered his friend. The detective turned again to Becky.

"Now, back to the gun, Mrs. Strawhorne. You said she picked up the pistol that was on the tractor. So, the pistol was already there? She didn't bring it with her?"

"No, sir," Becky answered, lighting a cigarette to placate her emotions.

"Was it Stiff's gun?" the detective continued.

"No," she responded, looking up at Huck, as if she needed his permission to continue with the detective's interrogation.

"Well, whose was it?" the detective quizzed. "How did the gun get there?"

Huck turned his head and looked my way, then nodded his head at me. I didn't know what the nod of his head implied, but I interpreted it as a sign that I needed to tell the detective where the gun came from—that, as a man, I was supposed to confess the truth and accept whatever the consequences may be.

"I brought it," I shouted across the dark.

The detective slowly turned toward me, approaching cautiously and still holding his notepad. A sudden breeze whistled through the old barn, rustling the summer-dried leaves of the ancient trees that bordered the barn. Time seemed to die, each moment collecting memories from long-ago happenings, each moment gasping for some hint of life and for some reason to warrant another breath.

"What's your name?" the detective asked, as his shadowed silhouette developed in the grim sparsity of light shivering from the barn.

"Luke Stiles," I proclaimed.

"The son of John Stiles?"

"Yes sir," I responded.

I was the son of John Stiles, the legend of Turkey Creek, and the fiancée of the girl who had murdered Stiff Jenkins. That was me. That was who I had become. After twenty years of listening to stories about how my father became a legend, after fifteen years of believing the lies about me having a chance to play in the majors, this is what I had evolved into. A man leaning against the hood of an old truck, gazing into a star-filled sky, preparing for my interrogation, and preparing for the rest of my life.

"He was kind of a legend around here, wasn't he?" the detective questioned.

"That's what I hear."

"Well, I want you to know that I was real sorry to hear about his passing," he fibbed, extending his hand to me.

"Thanks," I answered, shaking his hand.

My breath felt tight in my chest, like a dog testing the range of his chain. Questions were imminent, I knew that, but they were questions I might not want to answer, questions I might not even want to be asked.

Whippoorwills serenaded the dark silence, brewing in the

bowels of the disturbing night. All my yesterdays kept stabbing at my thoughts, all the memories I had made in this barn on this farm. Seemed as if yesterday we were just kids, me and Cody, tossing square hay bales up to the loft of the barn. We burnt together in the hot summer sun, shirtless boys with golden tans and broad shoulders, believing in happiness, believing in dreams, believing in immortality. But no lesson we had ever learned, whether in school or on the baseball field, could have prepared us for an encounter with death. Dying was something that would never happen to us, an abstract thought we just tucked into the farthest recesses of our minds.

"Now, son," the detective continued. "I need you to be completely honest with me here. Why did you bring the gun into the barn?"

"Do you know who Stiff Jenkins is?" I asked him.

"Hell, everybody knew Stiff Jenkins."

"Then, you know what people said about him. I was stupid enough to believe the rumors. Thought I might need it to protect myself."

"So, why did you leave the gun on the tractor?"

"I didn't want to leave it," I admitted. "Me and Huck went to run an errand, and he told me to leave it here. I forgot I had even brought it."

"Alright," the detective sighed, as if he didn't really believe what I was saying.

"So, you don't know anything about the identity of the girl who walked into the barn and shot Stiff with your pistol?"

His eyes were already accusing me, convicting me with calloused stares that augmented in the ominous absence of light. I didn't even want to be there anymore. I no longer cared that Cody was my best friend. His grief no longer bothered me. All I wanted was to get to the rock quarry and see Ashley, find out what the hell was going on, and hold her in my arms.

"No, sir," I answered, staring directly at the detective, who in the passage of only a few moments, had become my greatest enemy.

"Well, seems kind of odd to me," he argued. "Bringing a gun to the place where somebody would use it later to commit a murder."

"Like I said, Mr. Wright, I didn't want to leave the gun. Stiff asked me to leave it. Said I wouldn't need it."

"Wait a minute now," the detective interrupted. "Did Stiff ask you to leave the gun, or did Huck ask you? I think the first time you told me the story, you said Huck asked you to leave it?"

"I don't really remember which one asked me to leave the gun," I wearily replied. "It didn't seem like a moment I was supposed to remember."

"Don't get smart with me, son," the detective barked.

Luckily, Huck had walked up beside me by then. He placed a hand on my shoulder.

"Detective, I am the one who asked him to leave the gun," Huck confessed. "This kid just buried his dad. He's got a lot of shit going on in his head right now. Don't you think that's enough questions for tonight?"

"I guess so," he offered reluctantly. "But don't go skipping town," he warned. "I may have to give you a more intensive interview in the future."

"Yes, sir," I complied.

I returned to my truck and drove away. I didn't even check to see if Cody and his mother were still standing beside the barn. I no longer felt compelled to speak to Cody anymore or anyone else for that matter. I wanted to be gone, to be shed of this town and all its memories. I wanted to be rid of it all—the town, the memories, the what-ifs, and the what-could-have-beens. I was ready to move from the yoke of what used to be into a place where I never was, where there had never been a sport called baseball or a legend like John Stiles—a place unfamiliar and absent of remembered faces, a place where I had never been, a place where I had never existed.

THE QUARRY

I disappeared again. Not literally or physically, like I desired. Just emotionally and, I guess you could say, dreamily, as the lights of my truck did into the visceral darkness of the lampless Caldwell County backroads. No better idea could I have fathomed than eternal obscurity, to be released from all these burdens that had been aggravating me since the day I watched Daddy die. Whereas I once wanted to know why the residents of this perishing town called my daddy the legend, now I only wondered what all would be different if I had never begun my damned investigation.

Stiff would still be alive, that's for damn sure, and Fudge Pickens would probably still be sitting at Floyd's bar drinking beer rather than lying comatose in some hospital bed, not even knowing who in the hell he was. And I sure as hell wouldn't have been driving to the fucking rock quarry in the middle of the night to meet my fiancée, who I was pretty damn sure had just murdered the father of my best friend.

I blamed myself for all these events, every damn one of them. And I had no idea any longer what my future held. I was once twelve years old, the hero of Turkey Creek, a boy destined for imminent glory, the son of a legend, the great Luke Wilson Stiles, brainwashed into believing the grandiose tales fed to him by his coaches and adult peers. I was that at some moment in a not-so-long-ago time. Now, I was just a troubled kid searching for purpose in a world constructed from futility, a kid with no father, a kid with no dreams, a kid with no heart—dying in a hostile world void of purpose and equity.

The turnoff to the rock quarry was about three miles past Stiff's farm. The road itself was about two miles long, the first mile paved, the next half mile gravel, and the last half mile just dirt, clay-hardened or muddy, depending on the weather. Even dry, the road was marked by dips and puddles and deep ruts carved by oversized tires of quarry trucks weighted down with tons of rocks. Many people had busted axles and deflated tires on the last half mile of the road, including myself. Just had to go slow and take it easy, which was difficult sometimes for teenage boys.

But that night, after leaving Stiff's farm, I drove the final half mile very slowly because I wasn't even sure I wanted to see Ashley or anyone else for that matter. I wanted the night to end, wanted it all to be over. I wasn't prepared for any more funerals or hospital visits or small town rumors or broken engagements. Life was becoming too difficult. I wanted to be in someplace fun and exciting, where people still laughed and smiled. I wondered if places like that still existed because that night, maneuvering through the hazards of Rock Quarry Road, I couldn't think of even one reason to be happy, not even one.

I doubted that seeing Ashley would invoke any other emotion except sadness or sorrow. There was a part of me that believed happiness would be eternally absent in my being, that all the moments of joy in my past would be the only encounters with that emotion I would ever have. Still, I continued to move forward to the quarry, clinging to a fragile hope that, someday, life would be better, that, someday, there would be a reason to live again, a reason to dream, a reason to smile.

I saw Ashley as soon as I turned into the quarry. She was sitting in her sedan, smoking a cigarette with the driver's door open.

"When did you start smoking?" I asked, as I parked beside her.

"First one I've had in years," she replied, lifting her eyes to look at me, emotionless and wary.

"What happened?" I asked.

The boulders that confined the quarry looked like monsters in the unfiltered darkness of night, and the quarry itself was just a silent abyss. You couldn't even see the water from standing on one of the boulders. You wouldn't even know it was there. But you could take a rock and chunk it into the hidden vessel of water, and the splash could be heard if you were listening for that particular sound.

When we were teenagers, me and Cody and some other guys we used to hang around would jump off the ancient stones into the water. I remember that feeling of falling, especially on incredibly dark nights when there was no moon. It was almost as if we became weightless, floating in a space where there was no gravity, like astronauts we had seen on television shows. On nights like that, we couldn't even see the water until we were about to splash. Even though that span of time was likely only a second or maybe even less, it felt like moments, like you were in a dream and falling. Just as you were plummeting toward certain death, you plunged into a life-saving body of water.

I took hold of Ashley's hand, and we walked to the nearest boulder. I brushed off some leaves and dirt to make her a seat, then cupped a pinch of Copenhagen into my mouth. The wind was still, and the night air breathed hot on us. I placed my arm around her and drew her tightly against my side, kissing her on the forehead.

"So, are you going to tell me what happened?" I asked again.

"I killed Stiff Jenkins," she confessed, beginning to sob again. "I wasn't even planning to do it. I only went over there because Katie texted me and told me how mad you looked when you left the house. I wanted to talk to you before you did something stupid. That's all I wanted, just to talk to you."

She wiped her face with a tissue she had crumpled up in her hand.

"Then, I'm the one that did something stupid."

Her breaths were heavy and steeled, and I wondered how long she had been here, sitting in her car, waiting for me, scared and befuddled.

"Tried to call you a couple of times, but you didn't answer," she added.

"I didn't take my phone with me into the barn," I admitted, suddenly realizing my simple act of forgetfulness may have led to this whole damn sequence of acts.

Ashley pulled away from me a bit and began nodding, like she was plumb out of tears, like all of her sorrow and grief and regret had been twisted into the singular emotion of hopelessness.

"When I saw your truck at Stiff's farm, I stopped and walked into the barn, not really knowing what I might see. Right away, I could tell you were not there. The only people I could see were Stiff and Mrs. Strawhorne."

She paused for a moment, then lit another cigarette to calm her nerves.

"I didn't know if they had killed you or not," she continued, inhaling the smoke of her recently lit cigarette. "I didn't know what to say or even what to do. I picked up the gun and shot him. He fell to the ground, and I put two more bullets in him to make sure he was dead."

She took another draw from her cigarette, then leaned against a depression in the boulder. "Now, I don't know what to do. I don't want to spend the rest of my fucking life in jail. I mean, I wanted to be your wife, and I wanted to have children one day. I wanted to be sitting on the porch with you, growing old together and watching our grandchildren playing in the front yard. I imagined all this stuff in my head. Now, it is just gone, disappeared from my fucking brain somehow. Can't even get those dreams back."

She pressed her cigarette into the surface of the boulder, then flipped the butt into the invisible crater of water. Madness hung heavily in the still summer air, decimating whatever scintilla of hope I may have wanted to find. Mosquitoes hovered around me, buzzing and biting at my flesh, but it didn't even matter anymore. Nothing did. It seemed as if I was paralyzed in despondency and unable to defend myself against the badgering congregations of mosquitoes and whatever else was flying around in the dead night. I leaned forward and spit a plume of tobacco juice onto the boulder.

"Stiff didn't kill your daddy," I finally revealed. "He didn't kill anybody. Neither did my old man."

"What?" she cried. "What about all those newspaper clippings you showed me? What about all that stuff Katie told me about how mad you were when you left the house and how you wanted to kill Stiff yourself?"

"That was my intent when I left the house," I confessed. "But I was wrong. I was wrong about everything. Huck proved that to me tonight."

"Oh, shit," she cried, standing and waving her hands. "Are you telling me I killed an innocent man? That makes what I've done even worse."

I stood and tried to hold her, but she pushed me away.

"Stay away from me, Luke," she screamed. "Just stay the hell away from me. I'm a murderer now. A fucking murderer."

I reached for her again. This time, she didn't resist but fell into my arms crying—guttural cries that labored inside of her.

"What are we going to do now?" she sobbed. "I fucked everything up, baby. I'm so sorry. I fucked everything up. My life, your life, Cody's life, Katie's life, my parent's life. What am I going to do?"

"I don't know yet," I said. "We'll think of something."

"Luke," she whispered, pushing away from me again. "You didn't have anything to do with this. You need to stay away from me."

"No," I countered, pulling her toward me. "You killed Stiff because of misinformation I gave to you, all because I wanted to find out why they called my daddy the legend of Turkey Creek. None of this shit would have happened if I had just buried Daddy and not worried about what happened in the past. I became obsessed with it, I guess. Never thought all this would happen."

"Did you find out who did kill my daddy?" she asked softly.

"I think so," I answered. "From what Huck showed me tonight, I have a pretty good idea."

"What did he show you?"

"Well, I went to Stiff's tonight with the intention of killing him. Huck and his wife were there, so, I guess I got too nervous or something. Huck noticed the pistol I was carrying and took it off me, and set it atop the hood of that tractor. Stiff asked Huck to take me for a ride and wouldn't let me take my pistol. I got into his truck, and he drove me to this gated dirt road. We jumped the gate, started walking the dirt road, and, somehow, ended up in the backyard of Chief Wannamaker's home. I followed Huck into the barn, and he showed me, clear as day, the marks on that truck. Then, he told me Wannamaker was the one who run over Fudge. He suspected Wannamaker was responsible for all those crimes and that he was trying to frame Stiff because he was jealous of him. He wanted everybody to respect him as they did Stiff."

"So you think Chief Wannamaker killed my dad?"

"Yeah, I do," I responded. "I believe he killed your dad and several other people."

"Damn, Luke," Ashley cried. "What are we going to do now?"

"We'll think of something," I assured her. "We'll think of something."

THE LAST DANCE

Dawn came on us fast the next morning. Vapors from the invisible pit of water ascended ominously from their nocturnal rest, spread through the forests, and feasted on whatever shadows lingered from the previous night. Ashley and I had spent the night in her car with the seats reclined and the windows down. Not that we slept much that night. I dozed off a few times but never slept for long. Every time I did wake, Ashley was also awake and staring into the darkness.

Her eyes were empty; her soul was lost. I tried talking to her a few times, but the only response I got was maybe a nod of the head or a shoulder shrug. She didn't know what to do next, and neither did I. As much guilt as she felt for pulling the trigger on the gun that killed Stiff, I felt just as much, maybe even more, for being the one that placed her in that position, for telling her that my father and Stiff were the ones responsible for the death of her father.

When I awoke at dawn, she was finally sleeping. She looked so innocent lying there. I could never imagine her being a murderer or someone who would spend the rest of her life in a penitentiary filled with crackheads and rapists and killers. She didn't deserve that fate. After all, the crime she committed was instigated by my misinterpretation of events and her love for me. I guess she thought if Stiff was alive, she and I would never be happy and would never be able to marry. I didn't know what she was thinking when she pulled that trigger. She sure as hell wasn't thinking about her future or our future, for that matter.

Now, one of us, maybe both of us, would be spending the rest of our life staring at the walls of a prison cell. Who was going to believe I didn't leave that gun for her once they figured out who she was? I didn't stand a chance in hell of getting out of this shit. I thought about Katie, I thought about Carter, and I wondered if I would ever see them again. I even thought about Momma and all the good times we had shared together before Daddy began having his strokes. Then times when we were still a family and able to laugh and smile and play kickball in the backyard. I always thought that Ashley and I would have that kind of life, that we would have children one day and play kickball with them in the backyard, sit on the porch in the evening, and drink coffee. None of that would be possible now. When she pulled that trigger, she didn't just kill Stiff Jenkins, she killed us and every dream we ever had, every hope that remained in our fucked-up lives. Everything was gone, emaciated by one regrettable moment.

I pulled my cell phone from the back pocket of my jeans. There were three missed calls from Katie. I opened my door quietly and breathed in the morning air, then pressed the button to return Katie's call as I walked farther away from the car.

"Where in the hell are you?" she answered on the first ring, not thinking about a proper salutation, I suppose.

"I'm at the rock quarry," I answered.

"What in the hell happened last night?" she asked. "You leave out of here last night with a gun. Then, about two o'clock in the morning, that dickhead Wannamaker shows up, banging on the door, telling me that Stiff Jenkins is dead, that somebody shot him, wanting to know when the last time I saw you."

Her voice had changed from anger to anxiety to plain sorrow by the end of her rant. Nothing would have satisfied me more than to give her a consoling embrace. But there was no way I was going to be able to hug her, probably never would be able to hug her again. That was what made the sadness so profound and surreal, the thought of never seeing her again, the thought of never seeing Carter. I was supposed to be there for them. I was supposed to protect them from all the shit that was going to happen to them in this fucked-up world. Now, I never would.

"I didn't kill Stiff," I answered politely, attempting to conceal my much more visceral apprehension.

"Do you know who did?"

"Yeah," I answered hesitantly. "It was Ashley."

"Jesus, Luke," she replied with disgust. "Why in the hell did she shoot him?"

"Because of what I told her," I confessed, "Because of what I made her believe."

"What in the hell are you talking about, Luke?"

"I told her about those newspaper clippings you found."

"Why in the hell would that make her want to shoot Stiff?"

"Because one of those men, Cleve Astings, was her daddy. She wasn't even a year old when they recovered his body from the lake," I replied. "Don't even remember him."

There was a pause in the conversation, and I could tell that Katie was crying, struggling to embrace the gravity of what had happened.

"Well, what are you going to do now?" she asked, still sobbing, her words breaking into pieces as she spoke, tumbling into the unfathomable chasms that would eternally separate us.

I remember riding bikes with her down Red Barn Road when we were just kids. We would ride down to the duck pond that butted up against the power lines, sometimes try to catch a frog or a turtle, sometimes just to talk. It was like our secret little hideaway, a place where we could attempt to discern the mysteries and enigmas of small-town adolescence. Somebody bought the property not too long ago, drained the duck ponds, and sold off the land in two-acre parcels. Nothing but trailers down there now, trailers and memories and kids that would never even know the duck pond had been there. Kind of like our family, I suppose. Nobody remembered us as we once were, nobody remembered the family we had once been. They just remembered us as we were now—a family fractured by divorce and disease and death, shredded into fragile slithers of small-town gossip.

"I don't know, Katie," I finally admitted.

"Where's Ashley?"

"Sleeping in her car."

"Is there anything I can do?" she asked in desperation.

"I can't think of anything you could do," I responded, the sadness now present in my own words. "Do you remember when we used to ride our bikes down to the duck pond?"

"Yeah," she confirmed. "I remember that."

"Those were good days," I said.

"Yeah," she revealed. "I miss those days."

"Me too," I confessed. "Life seemed so perfect back then."

"I can't lose you, Luke," she said, struggling for words. "I need you; Carter needs you."

"I know," I responded. "I'll think of something."

"Luke," she cried. "Promise me that you'll call later."

"I promise."

I hung up the phone and walked back to the car.

Ashley was awake by then. She was leaning against the passenger door, staring at the circles of mist that surrounded the quarry—still lost, it seemed, in a suddenly unfamiliar world.

"I was just talking to Katie," I said, approaching the car. "She had been trying to call all night."

"Did you tell her what happened?"

"Didn't have to," I answered. "She already knew."

I put a pinch of tobacco behind my lips and proceeded around the front of the car, walking slowly until I was standing beside Ashley.

"Do you know how people always tell you, when something bad happens in their lives, that they feel like they are in a dream?" she asked.

I didn't respond; I just nodded in agreement and spit tobacco juice onto the ground.

"I guess that's because it's true," she continued. "Feels like none of this ever happened."

"But it did," I affirmed.

"I don't know if I can live with this, Luke," she admitted. "Killing an innocent man. I can't get him out of my head. I keep seeing it in my dreams, happening over and over again."

She walked away from me and back to the boulders. The breezes of night began to wane, and I could feel the heat of summer sizzling in the dispersing mists. Reluctantly, I followed her to the boulder, then sat between a creviced gap, maybe five yards away from where my fiancée stood. Shadows were dying in the ascent of the sun, burying themselves beneath a brush of brambles and burrs and pine straw piles.

We had made love here before, in this very place, panting and sweating in our adolescent passion. We had no worries or concerns in our juvenile minds, just fervor and lust and a mutual belief that love could triumph over every sorrow or encumbrance we may ever have. So much for those days. Everything was different now, and every memory from our past, whether kind or malignant, was interred in perpetual obscurity, woven into fragile cords that could easily be released. I scratched along the sides of the ancient boulder with a pointed stone, feeling the sunlight beginning to burn the back of my neck.

"I've been thinking about where we could go, Ash," I said. "I think I know of a place where we could stay and be safe."

"Where would that be?"

"There's a woman that lives in Georgia, in a small town right across the river. Daddy used to date her some years back. I think she would let us stay with her for a while until we figure out what to do next."

"That's just it, Luke," she sobbed. "We're never going to be able to figure out what to do next. I murdered Stiff Jenkins. They will always be looking for me."

"I know, baby, but we can't stay here."

"No matter where we go, no matter what we do, I will always be wanted."

"What do you want me to do?"

"There's nothing you can do," she replied. "I thought about it all night. Even though in some ways, it sounds so fucking romantic, you and I on the run together, outlaws, like fucking Bonnie and Clyde, it's not realistic. And, to tell you the truth, no matter if we are together or not, I will always carry the guilt of killing an innocent man."

"Look, Ash, I feel as guilty as you do. How do you think that gun got in the barn? I brought it there. I brought it over there intending to kill Stiff myself. Until I went for a ride with Huck, I wanted Stiff dead just as much as you did. Only difference is you had an opportunity to pull the trigger, and I didn't."

"I didn't know that," she confessed.

She turned and walked toward me, settling beside me in the

gaping crevice. She wrapped her arms around me and kissed me softly.

"Do you remember the night we made love out here?" I asked.

"Yeah, but it wasn't on this boulder," she answered. "It was on that boulder over there," she said, pointing to the boulder to the left of us.

"How do you remember which boulder it was?"

"Because," she began. "Don't you remember what we did before we made love that night."

"No," I shyly admitted.

"See that big flat place on the boulder," she reminded me, still pointing. "We danced there that night. Was the only flat place we could find. And you were so sweet. You pulled your truck up against the back of this boulder so we could listen to the radio."

"Damn," I replied. "You've got a good memory."

"I even remember the song we danced to."

"No way," I said.

"Yes, I do," she said, smiling. "It was *Nights in White Satin*. Remember, we had to look it up on YouTube because neither one of us had ever heard it before. Don't even know what radio station we were listening to. Just the first slow song we heard, I reckon."

"I remember now."

"Will you dance with me now?" she asked, rising from her seat. "The rest of our lives are going to be fucked up, Luke. I just want to hold you again and remember the way it feels to hold someone you love."

"Don't feel like a time to dance."

"It does to me," she prodded.

So I did. I danced with my fiancée on the flattened surface of that ancient boulder beside the rock quarry. I even found *Nights in White Satin* on YouTube. We danced as the summer sun filtered through the pine forests. We danced like nothing ever happened, as if we were just two people in love, a pair of teenagers with dreams as big as the sky. I can't remember how long that song lasted, but I wish it would have lasted forever because right after the dance was over, she jumped into the water. I never saw her again.

Two hours later, Katie came to the quarry and sat beside me. My clothes were drenched and cold.

"What happened?" she asked.

"She jumped in," I answered. "I tried to find her, but it was too damn dark."

"You're shivering," she said, wrapping her arms around me. "Let's get you home, okay?"

I nodded, stood, and walked to Katie's car. She was right. I just needed to go home.

Jeff and his wife, Sherry, live in the small town of Pelzer, South Carolina. Jeff is a graduate of Lander University. He and his wife are both active members of PJ Parkinson's Charities and The Shepherd's Hands Ministry in Matoaka, West Virginia. You can follow Jeff at https://www.facebook.com/jeff.wiles.1257.

Made in the USA
Columbia, SC
13 January 2025

51747055R00146